# A STRANGER IN THE EARTH

# A STRANGER
# IN THE EARTH

### ✳✳✳

*Marcel Theroux*

Phoenix House
LONDON

The quotation on page oo is taken from *The Loves of the Plants*,
the second volume of *The Botanical Garden* by Charles Darwin

First published in Great Britain in 1997 by
Phoenix House,
The Orion Publishing Group
Orion House, 5 Upper St Martin's Lane
London WC2H 9EA

A CIP catalogue record for this book is available
from the British Library

ISBN   1 86159075 X (cased)
        1 86159 176 8 (trade paperback)

Typeset at The Spartan Press Ltd,
Lymington, Hants

This book proof printed by
Antony Rowe Ltd, Chippenham, Wiltshire

The village of Great Much has been going downhill since the Black Death, so when his grandfather dies, twenty-two-year-old Horace Littlefair decides to turn his back on the place and start a new life in London.

Underprepared and overdressed, Horace arrives to begin a career in local papers but instead is plunged into a turbulent world of drugs, Scrabble, and political intrigue.

Threatened by disaster, and aided by several unlikely friendships, Horace struggles to adapt, falls in love and uncovers the sinister motives behind Barnaby Colefax's campaign to save the urban fox.

*To procure a crowned elephant with a perforated trunk and an elongated face, much gold, many jewels, is easy; but for mothers to bear children who prosper by their own virtue, is of all things in this earth surrounded by the deep waters the most difficult.*

TAMIL PROVERB

*Because of the mountain of Zion, which is desolate, foxes walk upon it.*

LAMENTATIONS 5:18

# PART ONE

# CHAPTER ONE

IT HAD BEEN raining all night, and the lanes were still alive with the ticking and dripping of water. Damp rose up from the ground and impregnated the morning air with the tang of garlic mustard. It was January.

Horace Littlefair closed the door of the cottage and stepped out into the wet lane. He was carrying a huge duffel bag over one shoulder and his thick leather soles snapped on the slick road as he walked.

The high banks on either side of him wound down a slope into the heart of Great Much, passing a church on the left. There, among the tomstones – some faded to illegibility by four centuries of West Country weather – was a fresh one, its inscription crisply cut into the glittering black marble. It said, 'Joseph Raymond Littlefair 1910–1996', and below it in italic letters as the old man had specified: 'I am a stranger in the earth; hide not thy commandments from me.'

His grandson did not pause to enter the churchyard: he was hurrying to catch the bus. The heavy bag bounced on his shoulder and the leather soles snapped faster on the road, which was generally known as the B2407. Its older name of Keening Lane commemorated the only remarkable episode in the village's long history. Six hundred years earlier, the people of neighbouring Otherbury had brought cartloads of their plague dead along this road to be interred at the church at Great Much. Otherbury's own consecrated ground was crammed with bubonic corpses and they needed somewhere to put the overspill. Armed with improvised rustic weapons and ancestral broadswords, the people of Great Much confronted the procession just at the point where the bus-shelter now stands at the entrance to the village. 'Not in our graveyard,' they told the mourners from Otherbury as they turned them away. Future generations of villagers would quote them approvingly over pints of the soapy local bitter in the Trollop Arms. The skeletons of Otherbury's plague dead lie under six feet of grazing land on a tree-less hillside five miles from the churchyard.

This prompt action diverted the epidemic: the plague of the fourteenth century spared Great Much, though it decimated Otherbury. Local historians still debate whether this caused the subsequent change in the fortunes of the two towns. Some say the deaths in Otherbury forced the farmers there to consolidate their land-holdings into larger, more efficient farms. Others argue that the shortage of able young men to work the fields pushed up the price of labour in Otherbury and tempted away the more ambitious sons of Great Much. Fatalists maintain that the changes would have taken place, plague or no plague. But what is beyond question is that in Otherbury, pestilence was succeeded over time by prosperity. A monthly cattle market was followed by mills, factories, and eventually a railway station.

A few miles up the road, Great Much stagnated. Its young people left the village. The technological innovations of subsequent centuries skirted it just as the plague had. Finally, towards the end of the twentieth, it got a bus-shelter, paid for by subscription, where the village's few teenagers drank cider, flirted with unwanted pregnancy and caught the bus into Otherbury, where the descendants of the mouldering bones on the hill had a night-club called Hula's and looked down on the people from Great Much as yokels.

Horace's bus had not yet arrived. He had to return the keys of the cottage to Mr Tither, who was the proprietor of Great Much's single store.

The jangling above the door summoned Mr Tither from the curtained-off sitting room that doubled as his warehouse. It was said in the village that among the dusty boxes were cases of dried egg and tins of an unpronounceable South African fish that dated from the Second World War. Horace had, more than once, bought a packet of soup or a tin of Spam emblazoned with a special offer for a cookbook in pre-decimal money, or a competition with a closing date that had come and gone in the early 1970s. But as Mr Tither's was the only shop in the village, and as most of the villagers had been weaned on his dusty boxes of Angel Delight and chicken noodle soup, and more especially because he took a flexible attitude towards licensing hours, most people were willing to overlook the antiquity of his dried goods.

Mr Tither pottered through the bead curtain in his white coat, his smooth round face as dusty and pink as one of his marshmallows. Horace handed him the key and said goodbye. Mr Tither leaned against the cash register. 'Don't expect we'll be seeing you back here soon.'

'You never know,' said Horace.

5

'Well, it's always a pity when one of our youngsters leaves the village.'

'Not so young any more, Mr Tither. I'll be twenty-three next November.' Horace shuffled his feet on the floor of the shop: he was eager to get going.

'I went up to London many, many years ago,' said the old man, who had fallen into a reverie. 'I'll never forget it. A man said to me, "Do you want a room in Soho?" I said "What for?" He said, "You know what for, Sonny Jim." I said, "No, I don't. Nor do I want to, neither."' Mr Tither shook his head, but whether in outrage, or in the forlorn contemplation of a missed opportunity, it was impossible to say.

'I'd better be off, then,' said Horace.

Mr Tither scratched his chin and dust came off his whiskers. 'How are you getting to the town?' he said.

'Bus. One'll be along soon,' said Horace.

'Nay,' said Mr Tither, preserving an archaic form of the negative still used in Great Much. 'I won't hear of it. I can drive you in. They won't miss me for half an hour.'

'In the Red Revenge?'

'Not the Red Revenge. They've gave me another.' Desmond Tither was not only the village's sole shopkeeper, he was also its postmaster. A red van was one of the perquisites of the job.

Mr Tither flipped over his open sign and the two men walked around to the back of the shop. The Red Revenge has been hoisted on to concrete blocks and Mr Tither's chickens were pecking and scratching around its flaky vinyl upholstery. Its successor sat beside it, as scarlet and gleaming as the teenage bride of a senile billionaire.

Horace slung his bag in the back while Mr Tither started the new van saying, 'First time I drove this, I didn't even know the engine was on, it's that quiet.' Then his knobbly old hands steered it on to the wet and narrow lanes between Great Much and Otherbury. Some way ahead of them, Horace could see the bus he had now missed disappearing into the distance.

'What about this job, then?' said Mr Tither.

6

'They're taking me on as a trainee,' said Horace.

'Newspaper, is it?'

'That's right. Granddad's brother-in-law owns it.'

'I'll have to keep a look-out for your name. Money good?'

'Not bad,' said Horace. The figure was close to eight thousand pounds a year, but he didn't like to brag.

'You'll want to put some away,' said Mr Tither. 'But it won't go as far as you think in London.'

Horace remained silent in the hope that Mr Tither would do the same. Never a speedy driver, Mr Tither had the habit of easing his foot off the accelerator whenever he began speaking. The van was now travelling at a fast walking pace and had acquired a train of other vehicles that followed it slowly through the winding green lanes.

'They will follow so close!' said Mr Tither. 'Very dangerous. Townies, most probably – can't wait to get where they're going. Worse yet, they want to put a load of holiday cottages over yonder.' He jabbed a stubby finger towards a field. 'You know what I tell 'em?'

'What?' said Horace, without much hope of being surprised by the answer.

'Not in our graveyard!' Mr Tither chuckled and slapped the steering wheel, sending out a blast from the horn that took him by surprise.

Horace looked at his watch uncomfortably. If he missed the morning train, he wouldn't be in London until early evening. But to his relief, Mr Tither appeared to sense his impatience. Having reached the brow of a hill, the van was now moving rapidly down the series of long straight slopes into Otherbury, as silent as a glider and outpacing the queue of cars behind it.

'Beautifully quiet, this engine,' said Horace.

Mr Tither was muttering to himself. 'I don't understand it. The steering's locked.'

'The steering's locked?'

'Yes, locked up good and tight, I'd say. I don't understand it. I always switched off the Red Revenge.'

'Why?' said Horace, trying to suppress the note of alarm in his voice.

'Save petrol. No point letting the engine run when you're going downhill. Brakes aren't working neither.'

The van coasted to the bottom of the dip and rose up the other side, slowing as it did so. Without any sign of panic, Mr Tither restarted the engine, resumed his place at the head of the queue of cars and made his way into Otherbury with defiant slowness. 'Learned that in National Service,' he said proudly. 'Must have saved the Post Office a fortune.' Then, a few moments later, he said, 'I dare say Mrs Barmbrake will miss you.'

Horace turned to look at him, but the old man's eyes were inscrutably fixed on the road ahead.

The level crossing outside Otherbury closed moments before they reached it. Horace and Mr Tither waited in the red van while the London-bound train sped past them. Five minutes later, they arrived at the empty station.

'If we hadn't been stopped at the bloody crossing, we'd have made it,' said Mr Tither, without a trace of irony.

'I'll get the next one,' said Horace, who knew from experience that old men rarely admitted to their mistakes.

'I'll take you back to the village and bring you here in time for the next,' said Mr Tither.

Horace looked at the old man. He had a sudden vision of himself making the journey back to Great Much, then setting off again with Mr Tither in the red van, missing the train to London that evening, and continuing to miss it for the rest of his life. 'I wouldn't dream of it. I've put you to too much trouble already, Mr Tither. Besides, there's one or two errands I can do now I'm here.'

'Well, I'll say goodbye, then,' said Mr Tither. 'You look after yourself in London. They're a sharp and unfriendly lot by all accounts. Ever so many darkies. They don't have our clean ways.'

'My grandfather was a Londoner,' said Horace, ignoring Mr Tither's last remarks.

8

'That's what I mean,' said Mr Tither, with a wink. Then, having retarded Horace's new life by six hours with a generous gesture, he tooted his horn and set off towards Great Much in third gear.

Horace bought a map of London at a bookshop, wrote a letter to Betty Barmbrake and posted it, then mooched around the Museum of Otherbury, whose exhibits celebrated the history of the entire area but made no mention of Great Much – perhaps as retaliation for that ancient snub.

At two o'clock, Horace returned to the ticket office. Two railway tracks had served Otherbury station at the height of its Victorian prosperity, but one had been pulled up and weeds had reclaimed the hollows where the sleepers had lain. Horace felt inside his jacket pocket and pulled out two pieces of paper. One was a letter that had gone soft with rereading. It was typewritten and headed with the crest of the *South London Bugle* (motto: *in veritate vince*). Twin columns along each margin listed the affiliated newspapers: the *Tooting Sentinel*, the *Lambeth and Brixton Advertiser*, the *Wandsworth Post*, the *Mitcham Gazette*, and the Boothby Press, publishers and distributors of local history books. The first two words of the letter were handwritten:

*Dear Horace,*
*It is with great sadness that I write to communicate my grief at the passing of your beloved grandfather, and my brother-in-law, Joseph. Regrettably, I am unable to attend the funeral but you know that both Cilla and myself extend our deepest condolences. I have been a purveyor of words for close to half a century but on occasions such as these I still find them inadequate to console or comfort.*
*The loss is heavy. It must be some consolation that it was not entirely unexpected. Joseph lived a rich and full life, to which you in no small part contributed.*
*This sad event will, however, allow you to take up the opportunity about which we have corresponded. I cannot promise you lucrative employment, but an honest day's*

*pay for an honest day's work – in this case, £7,500 p.a., taxed at source. I shall be returning from my annual holiday on the tenth of the month.*

Then, in a big flourish of ink, 'With deepest sympathies, Derwent Boothby'.

The train squeaked to a stop and Horace got in. He stowed his duffel bag in an overhead rack and settled himself by the window. The rain had started falling again, obscuring the view of the fields. Horace closed his eyes and listened to the rhythm of the train on the rails, rocking like a typewriter sliding back on its carriage, tapping out a new chapter over the sleepers as it swept towards London. Then he fell asleep.

The train pulled into Waterloo a few minutes before five o'clock in the evening. At the next platform, another train was filling up. Two flows of people met at the ticket barrier in an eddy of confusion and bad temper, but the current that was rushing towards the departing train proved stronger. The stream of homeward-bound commuters blocked the way forward.

Horace stood to one side as they spilled towards their train. One or two gave him a sidelong glance. There was something in his appearance that caught their attention. It was not his height, which was average, nor his face, which was pleasant enough but not striking. It was not the straight brown hair that flopped into his eyes. It was his clothing.

Horace was dressed from hat to shoes in clothes that had belonged to his late grandfather. In keeping with the political beliefs of his youth, Joseph Littlefair had favoured a functional and unostentatious wardrobe, much of it bought in the late 1950s from a gentlemen's outfitters in Beaminster. The shoes were solid brown brogues, much-repaired and now attached to a thick new leather sole. Worsted socks connected these to Joseph's (now Horace's) walking breeches. Horace wore a generously cut three-quarter-length tweed jacket, while a flat cap jutted out over his head.

Unaware that anyone was giving him a second look, Horace was busy unfolding the map he had bought in Otherbury. It was Ordnance Survey 176, which shows West London on a scale of one to fifty thousand.

Late passengers were still running to catch the train when the guard whistled it out of the station. A woman with frizzy hair had her hand on the door of a carriage and swore loudly as it pulled away, out of her grasp. Horace folded up his map, gave his ticket to the inspector, and passed through the barrier into the vastness of an unfamiliar city.

The new leather soles of his brogues smacked the hard white floor of Waterloo station. He drew a breath and looked around at his dirty and vivid new surroundings. The concourse was thronged with people. Food smells mixed in the air. Waiting passengers munched pastries, which shed crumbs on their smart coats and ties. They stared up at the departure tables, which announced each delayed or cancelled train with the quiet clapping of its rolling, lettered shutters. The board burst into a soft round of applause as two or three were cancelled at once.

Two pigeons flew overhead, up into the false sky of the glass roof, straddled with steel beams. Horace watched as their flight path took them past a huge plastic dog that was bursting playfully out of one of the advertising hoardings. The birds followed the curve of the building out of sight towards the international terminal. Horace went after them. A pale man with dreadlocks and a ring in his nose eyed him from behind a stack of mirrored waistcoats.

A man with a mobile phone clamped to his ear was pacing up and down near the queue of people waiting to use the pay-phones. His voice waxed and waned as he paced. 'Here's what I want you to do for me,' he was saying. 'Just put it in a fax and send it to my office. The answer will be no, but I promise I'll see that he gets it.'

It was Horace's turn to use the phone.

'I can't do more than that.'

He put in his ten pence and inadvertently punched a button

specifying that further instructions would appear in French, *'Décrochez,'* said the display. *'Composez votre numéro s.v.p.'*

'Then, of course, there's the question of the fee,' the man with the mobile phone was saying.

Horace began to call the London home of his great-uncle, Derwent, unaware that he was at that moment swaying from side to side in a stopped chair-lift over the French alps.

'The thing I want to know, Bob,' Derwent Boothby was saying, 'is this: I have a dream about driving a train into a tunnel, all well and good. No doubt you'll tell me it's a dream about sex.'

Mr Garbedian made a half-hearted attempt to disagree.

'Hang on a second,' said Mr Boothby. 'But say I have a dream about sex – and I have had them – is that really a dream about trains? Do you follow me?'

Mr Garbedian stared forlornly at the line of chair-lifts that had come to a stop ahead of them. He supposed one of them contained his wife and Mrs Boothby. He looked down, past Boothby's orange ski-boots to the fat black branches of the pine trees. The snow was so fresh and thick it squeaked underfoot, but the light was fading and this would be the last descent of the day.

'The fact is, and no disrespect to you and your wife's profession, it's the rich that get counselling. The rest of us just get up earlier,' Boothby continued. 'I didn't get where I am by moaning on about how hard life is. I know *you* know what I mean. These holidays aren't cheap.'

'Shut up, you boring arse,' said Mr Garbedian, but only in his heart. His cheeks were aching, and rime had started to form on his moustache. Boothby's face was glowing as he puffed out his frozen opinions. It was as if the metal bars of the chair-lift were drawing heat from Mr Garbedian and conducting it into the body of Mr Boothby.

In fact, Mr Garbedian merely nodded. In his imagination, he was already sitting in a steaming bath in his hotel room, drinking a glass of duty-free gin. You had to agree with one thing, he thought, Derwent Boothby had to be congratulated. You had to agree with it, because if you didn't congratulate him, he had the tendency to get the job done himself and at considerable length. Within a few minutes of meeting them, Boothby had begun to acquaint the Garbedians with his life-history, and with every opportunity he returned to this autobiography to amplify it.

The son of a bicycle repairman, he had risen through the echelons of local newspapers: delivering them, then delivering messages for them, reporting for them, editing them, and now, at sixty-three, owning them. And yet, for all his boasting, it was clear that Boothby's was not a media empire, nor even a media republic. It was a tiny fiefdom that covered several South London boroughs and included some publishing interests in local history books. And sooner or later – and it was looking like sooner these days – Boothby would take his tiny fiefdom and surrender it to one of the imperial powers that controlled most of the newspapers and magazines and television stations in the country. He would give it all up, like a plucky but defeated Celtic leader, dumping a cartload of rusty swords at the feet of a Roman proconsul in return for a seat on the board and an executive salary.

Suddenly, the chair-lift lurched forward, groaning and clanking metal like a manacled ghost. The dimming light had made it a world of monochrome. The snow-covered spectre of Cilla Boothby greeted the two men as they ski'd off the lift.

'Cilla had a fall,' said Juanita Garbedian, who was helping Mrs Boothby to dust the snow off her salopettes. Mr Boothby snowploughed to his wife's side.

'It's the same thing every time,' said Mrs Boothby, apologetically. 'I get into a tizzy and get off too late.' Her husband bent down to fasten the clasp of her ski-boot.

'Maybe see you at the bottom,' said the Garbedians, fleeing down the mountainside.

'If not, we'll catch you at dinner.' Mr Boothby's voice pursued them through the falling snow.

Six hundred miles to the north-west, Horace Littlefair was also listening to his great-uncle's voice. 'Hello,' said Mr Boothby. 'You have reached the home of Derwent and Cilla Boothby. I am afraid that neither of us is able to come to the telephone at this moment in time. Please speak slowly after the long signal and we will return your call as soon as possible.'

Horace hung up. It was half past four. He decided they were probably at work, or shopping, or out in the garden where they couldn't hear the phone. Perhaps, if he had had the services of Mr Garbedian or his wife, he might have uncovered the unconscious sense of urgency that had made him, after two decades in Great Much, arrive in London one day early.

Horace checked in his duffel bag at the left-luggage counter and walked down the ringing metal steps that led to Waterloo Road. His breath preceded him in frosty clouds. Apart from a man standing beside his broken-down car, the pavement was empty. Horace brought a history of London from a remainder bookshop on the corner of Lower Marsh and carried it away in a bright yellow plastic bag.

The street market was over, the stalls had been chained up: dirty skeletons of plywood and rusty metal. But the shops were still open. Half-way up the street, jazz music was playing out of one of them. Long silk dresses were hanging in the window, which shone with a strong yellow light. Horace stood in front of it and his eyes fell on a pile of boxes to one side of the display. They had been heaped into a crude pyramid, at the apex of which stood a single shoe.

And what a shoe! It was a walking boot made of brown leather, with strange leather brackets supporting each side of the instep. The texture of the tongue suggested it was both breathable and waterproof, while the uppers were topped with a peculiar rubber seal. The price was fifteen pounds; it was clearly a bargain.

Horace entered the shop with a sense of predestination. The musty smell of old clothes rose up from the interior. Racks of jackets hung at one side. On the other, glass cases held ashtrays, bric-à-brac, crumbling copies of *Picture Post*, ancient tins of talcum powder and pots of pomade. A bank of Bakelite radios stood along one of the shelves. Another glass case at the far end of the store was filled with more valuable items – cuff-links, watches, silver-backed brushes and cigarette holders. The cash register sat on this last case. It was, as far as Horace could tell, identical to Mr Tither's. Behind it, a woman was bent over an exercise book.

When she looked up, Horace indicated the shoes he wanted. The shop assistant, a plump, dark-haired girl in her early twenties, spoke with an accent that he assumed was Cockney. 'We have only size nine. We had nine and half but I think this is gone. I will check. One moment.'

The shoes were fetched and fitted. The lacing of the strange side panels posed a problem and had to be improvised; but the promise of future experimentation intrigued Horace. He was determined to buy them, ignoring a warning voice in his head that told him that the rubber hinge at the top could never be broken in.

Before he left the shop, the woman said, 'Excuse me. Can you tell which is correct? You can help because you are English.' She turned the exercise book towards him. ' "He keeps his milk in a cup, pot, jug, barrel." Which?'

'Let me see. Jug. In a jug.'

'What is *jug*?'

Horace tipped his fist and made a pouring sound in his throat. 'Jug.'

'Ah, yes.'

'You're learning English?'

'Obviously. I am from Poland. Have you been there?'

'No.'

'I am from Krakow. It is a very beautiful city. You are from London?'

'No. I'm from Dorset.'

'Dorset? This I don't know. Have you been to Ireland? I would like to go there, but not to Dublin, only to the countryside.'

She looked past Horace as she spoke, as though she was reading the sentences off a blackboard. He liked her brightness. She was full of words and when she spoke they seemed to pour out of her.

'But your family is from London?' she said.

'Sort of. I'm an orphan.'

'*Orphan*. Yes, like the boy in the story whose parents were eaten by wolfs?'

'Wolves,' said Horace. 'I don't think I know the story you mean. It was a bit less dramatic in my case. I didn't know my dad. No one did. Well, obviously my mother did, but she was killed by falling masonry.'

'Sad!'

'Do you think so?'

'Yes, of course.'

'Yes, I suppose it is.' Horace was fiddling absently with a novelty lighter in the shape of a car. A space under the boot held the cigarettes. By depressing the steering wheel, a flame could be made to appear from the bonnet, but since neither the flint nor the fuel had been replaced, the hood ornament just flipped up, revealing a bedraggled wick. Horace pumped the wheel and the bonnet opened repeatedly.

'And where are you living?' said the sales assistant.

'When am I leaving?'

'No, *living*.'

'I'm staying with my great-uncle Derwent. I should probably go and ring him again, now you mention it. Where do you live?'

'Finsbury Park.' She made it sound like one word.

'Is it expensive?'

'It is fifty pounds a week. It is cheaper because of my landlord. She is Polish.'

'That's handy. My name is Horace, by the way.'

'I am Jana. Nice to meet you.' Jana smiled. As Horace shook her hand, he noticed her eyes were blue and gold like a peacock's tail.

'I'd better go,' he said.

'You will come back, I hope.'

'Yes, I will.'

By eleven o'clock that evening, Horace had almost finished his history of London. Most of the time had been spent sitting under the fluorescent lights of Lone Star Burgers, and punctuated by fruitless phone-calls to Boothby. He tried ringing the newsdesk of the *South London Bugle*, but a grumpy-voiced man simply said that Boothby wasn't expected it and wouldn't elaborate.

Horace checked out his duffel bag from the left-luggage stand and counted his money. After buying the shoes, he'd been left with thirty-five pounds and assorted change. His duffel bag contained a cheque made out to himself from the Beaminster bank account he had closed the previous day.

He stood in the queue of swaying, red-eyed men to buy a hamburger and then sat down to read more of his book. At midnight, the departure board finally gave up the ghost. With a soft death-rattle, the letters spun into oblivion and stared blankly out. The idea of spending the whole night at the station was growing steadily less appealing. There was an alternative: he could spend the last of his money taking a taxi to Tooting, find a cheap hotel or bed-and-breakfast, then, after a good night's sleep, present himself at the offices of the *South London Bugle*.

As he waited for a cab at the rank, Horace unfurled Ordnance Survey Map 176. Tooting was clearly marked off to the south-west, but the roads and commons between Waterloo and his destination were an indecipherable labyrinth of capillaries and vesicles; it could have been a diagram of the veins in a leaf, or a wino's nose. None of the roads was named.

A taxi pulled up. Horace was still struggling with the map. The driver leaned over and pulled down the off-side window. He peered out. He had a pony tattooed on his forearm.

'I'm trying to find a hotel in Tooting,' said Horace. 'Do you know any?'

The taxi driver appeared to think for a moment and then nodded. Horace slid the duffel bag inside first and sat with the map open on his knee. The taxi chugged away from the rank and into the dark, wet streets.

'First time in London?' The driver's eyes lighted on him from the rear-view mirror.

'How did you know?'

'Just a guess.'

'I'm up from Dorset,' said Horace. And then he added, to relieve the silence, 'Hardy country.'

'Oh, yes.' There was little traffic about and the taxi moved steadily along the empty roads. The driver's voice took on a more friendly tone. 'Of course, you know that after midnight I have to charge twice what it shows on the meter?'

'I didn't actually.'

'Thing is, it's a supplementary charge for driving at night: the insurance premiums are astronomical. If we didn't do it, all the cabbies would want to drive during the day and you'd never be able to get a taxi after eleven.'

Horace looked at the red numbers. 'Double the whole thing?'

'Oh, no. Just the numbers on the left. The number on the right is the charge for your baggage: that's the same, night or day.'

Horace was too preoccupied with the ascending numbers to be aware of the city outside the cab. He willed the taxi to outrun the digits on the meter. At each increment, he doubled the total and subtracted it from the money in his pocket. When the figures reached ten pounds, he asked if it was much further. The driver slid open the partition.

'A little way yet. Thing is, because of this Jubilee line extension there are roadworks round the way I wanted to take you, so I've had to come round a slightly longer way. It shouldn't be too much longer.' He was about to close the partition, but paused and added, 'Of course, if you know a quicker way, I'll take it.'

'I'm afraid I don't,' said Horace.

At fifteen pounds, Horace slid resignedly down the seat. 'Are we close?'

'Not far now, squire.'

At seventeen pounds he asked the driver to drop him off. He was too proud to ask for a favour and decided to walk the rest of the way. He handed over all the money he had.

'Right enough. That's Trinity Road over there. You want to follow that straight down. It'll take you to the Upper Tooting Road. It's about five minutes' walk. And a word to the wise. Be a bit careful round here. You want to watch out for those minicabs. They don't have to do the Knowledge, they don't know London, half of them don't even have licences. They'll rob you blind.'

The cab chugged off into the chilly night air. Horace was left with his duffel bag and his useless map, standing on the north side of Wandsworth Common. He crossed the road and walked onto the grass. Away from the lighted paths he was enveloped by darkness. He felt safe and invisible. In the distance he could hear the triple bark of a dog fox calling to its vixen. It crossed his mind to sleep here on the ground, but the grass was wet. There was a hard wooden bench under a horse-chestnut tree where two paths bisected the common. Friendless and penniless, his heart tightening in despair, Horace Littlefair lay down on the bench and tried to sleep.

# CHAPTER TWO

EACH MORNING AT seven o'clock Sheila Doolaly unlocked the offices of the *South London Bugle* and its affiliated companies. She would switch on the neon lights, which thrummed in an intermediate state between on and off before blinking into life. She would gather the letters, bring in the milk and the huge raft of newspapers, empty the rubbish and vacuum the carpet tiles. Her routine had hardly varied since she had first got the job forty years earlier as an apple-cheeked eighteen-year-old girl fresh from County Cork. In those days, the newspaper's offices had occupied a single floor above a shop on Trinity

Road. But the *South London Bugle* had outgrown its original premises and was now housed in a converted cinema on Upper Tooting Road, which she was paid four pounds an hour to keep clean.

On this particular morning, however, Mrs Doolaly had not yet begun to remove the keys from her handbag when she saw a young man sitting asleep on the steps of the building with his head propped against a large duffel bag. She cleared her throat and he woke up with a start. Horace asked, 'What time is it?'

'It's five past seven.'

'Is Mr Boothby here yet?'

'No, dear. He's not due in till this afternoon. Is it him you're after?'

'I'm Horace Littlefair. I'm supposed to be starting work here.'

'You'd better come in. It's bitter.'

Inside, Mrs Doolaly made some tea while Horace explained that he hadn't been able to contact Mr Boothby the previous evening. He didn't tell her about his night on Wandsworth Common and his early-morning walk to the offices of the newspaper. In a rare moment of anger, he had crumpled up Ordnance Survey Map 176 and abandoned it in the bin by the underpass on Trinity Road. Mrs Doolaly explained in turn that Mr Boothby had been enjoying a skiing holiday in Haute Savoie with his wife Cilla.

Gradually, the employees of the paper began to trickle in. Horace and Sheila were sitting by the coffee-vending machine to one side of the newsroom. The bulk of the weekly papers had been put to bed the previous day, so there was less activity than usual in the building. One wall was taken up with a large map of south London. In front of it was a circular table with several phones. It was at this that a pasty-faced man with bags under his eyes was smoking while he filleted the day's papers for useful items. This was Mr Pratt, the news editor.

The whole room had an air of neglect. It was too big for Mrs Doolaly to manage on her own and, despite her best efforts, it had the resigned shabbiness of a place that is in constant use and never properly cleaned. Dirt was the climate of the newsroom, changeable but constantly present, carving its name on every object in it, individuating them over time with personalised whorls of grime and coffee rings.

Seated at a typewriter opposite Horace was the newspaper's star reporter: the white-haired Harvard Machine. He was wearing a pair of half-glasses and clacking the keys in short bursts. The *South London Bugle* did not use computers. Years of experience in newspapers had made it clear to Derwent Boothby that computer technology was a passing fad like 3-D movies and bubble cars.

Harvard paused, casting around for a phrase, his lips moving inaudibly. His eyes met Horace's. 'Can you think of another word for France?' he asked, in a soft Scottish accent. Horace shook his head.

After washing in the men's toilets, Horace changed into baggy trousers and an old tank top. He left the office and opened an account at the Bank of Karnataka, two doors up the road, where his new bank manager advanced him some money. Then he ate breakfast and came back to one of the empty desks in the newsroom to read back issues of the papers.

The *South London Bugle* itself appeared twice a week, but the press published additional weekly titles which had their own logos and lead stories targeted at their area's readers: 'Gas Main Fury in Tooting High Street', 'Bigamist was Known to Balham Council', 'Second Mummified Pensioner: Wandsworth's Double Shame'. But only the outside pages of each of these were different. The centre sections contained the same sad tales of fatal and non-fatal violence (nose bitings, muggings, pub scuffles), gardening competitions, football reports, school plays, profiles of local characters, fawning restaurant reviews, openings of supermarkets and fêtes, open days and galas. If any of these events were attended by celebrities then the article would be accompanied by a photograph, and, as likely as not, Derwent Boothby would be in it.

Boothby returned from his holiday just after lunchtime. Mrs

Doolaly had told him that Horace had arrived. He squeezed his great nephew's fingers in a tight handshake.

'Mr Littlefair, I presume?' Only the lower half of Boothby's face was suntanned, because he had worn his large skiing goggles unfailingly. His cheeks and forehead were pale, and the darkened skin below them looked like the stubble of a felon on a wanted poster.

'Hello, Uncle Derwent.'

'I trust you had a pleasant journey.'

As he had with Mrs Doolaly, Horace avoided mentioning the telephone calls from Waterloo, being bilked by the taxi driver, and the night on Wandsworth Common. This was the first time he had met his great-uncle and by nature he was not inclined to begin with reproaches.

'Let me show you something of your new place of employment.' Boothby had an orotund way of expressing himself, and tended to do it in a way that suggested irony, as though he was amused at having woken up to find himself rich and speaking in polysyllables. He insisted on introducing Horace to everyone in the building. Horace felt that the other employees looked at him with a mixture of curiosity and resentment: some wet-behind-the-ears relative of the owner who was going to be foisted on them as a colleague.

At the end of the day, Boothby drove Horace home in his Jaguar, talking all the way about the skiing holiday. 'Ever been skiing, Horace?'

'Never been out of the country, Uncle Derwent.'

'Pity.' Boothby was an expert driver: his was always the first car to race away from one set of traffic lights and pull up sharply at the next. 'Travel broadens the mind. We met a couple of headshrinkers from Dorking.'

'That *is* strange.'

'Thingumabobs. Psycho – you know, therapists. Didn't half talk a load of rubbish.'

The Boothbys lived in a large detached house with a circular drive just outside Croydon. In the centre of the drive, a

Sagittarian weathervane pointed his arrow at the dreary grey sky to the west.

Before supper, Horace helped Cilla move the garden ornaments out of the conservatory, where they had spent the holiday, and back on to the lawn. While they were doing it, she explained that vandals had abducted Grumpy, Happy and Sleepy the previous summer. 'I won't let Derwent help me because of his heart trouble,' Cilla puffed as the two of them manoeuvred a limbless representation of Modesty out into the garden. 'The aggravating thing about it is that they don't make the large size of dwarf any more. I bought those with the insurance, but it's not the same, is it?' She indicated a set of card-playing elves that had come from the same pottery in France. Horace positioned them around the bubbling green swimming pool. 'I do love my little people,' said Cilla.

Derwent Boothby avoided saturated fats for medical reasons and meat for moral ones. Cilla had prepared a casserole of aduki beans and a green salad. Derwent smacked his lips as he drank red wine he'd brought up from the cellar. 'You don't miss it,' he said.

'Miss it?' said Horace.

'Meat,' said Derwent. 'Even with a good red wine, you don't miss it.'

Horace rotated the bottle to look at the label, which was in French.

'That's our house red,' said Derwent. 'It's just your basic *vin de pays*. Do you drink much wine?'

'Not really,' said Horace. The aduki beans were small and dense. 'This is delicious,' he said.

Cilla smiled.

'Eating meat,' said Derwent, 'there's just no need. Look at me. I'm not exactly wasting away.'

'I miss sausages,' said Cilla, confidentially. 'There's plenty more, by the way. Now, Horace, have you thought about where you're going to live?'

Horace looked from one face to the other and put down his

knife and fork. 'I was planning to start looking around tomorrow. My bank manager, Mr Subramaniam, said he knew of a few people in the area looking to let.'

'Well, there's no rush. You can stay here as long as you like,' said Cilla. 'Derwent doesn't go into the office much any more, but the trains are very good, and there are the buses.'

'That's very kind of you,' Horace said, but instinctively he didn't want to be marooned on their hospitality. He pictured himself carting the gnomes in and out every night, and sitting at the table listening to Derwent go on about headhunters and vegetarianism. But he filled his mouth with a forkful of aduki beans and kept his thoughts to himself.

After supper Cilla went up to bed, saying she was tired from the trip. Horace and Derwent sat in his big oak-panelled study. Boothby explained how he had bought the room at auction – it was the original billiard room of the SS *Eumenides*, a cruise liner from the golden age of sea travel. 'You don't see craftsmanship like that any more,' said Boothby, stroking the wood. 'That's more quality than you need.' He took an object off one of the shelves and passed it to Horace. 'Any idea what that is?'

Horace examined it. It was like a brown gourd. Boothby's face was twitching with suppressed laughter. 'No, none at all.'

'It's a penis sheath.' Boothby burst out laughing. 'Can you imagine? Oh dear.' He wiped his eyes. 'We got it in Port Moresby last year on the way back from Australia. Cilla's mad on primitive cultures.' He put the penis sheath back on the shelf next to a 'Thank You for Not Smoking' sign.

Another shelf was filled with tiny carved figures: netsuke from Japan. 'Cilla's,' said Derwent. 'That's my favourite. Look at the carving on that. You wonder how they did it. That's the Japanese for you.' He passed the little carving to Horace. The piece of bone had been carved in the shape of two tiny animals, chasing each other nose to tail so the carving formed a ring. 'Dog-eat-dog world, eh, Horace?' said Derwent.

Horace looked at the carving closely. The bone had yellowed with age. 'These are foxes,' he said. 'Look at that one's brush.'

He turned it over in his hand. The anonymous carver had painstakingly rendered the grain of the fur, the catchlights in the animals' eyes, the whiskers pressed back against the muzzle, the bared teeth. 'It's lovely. What's it for?'

'They're toggles. You hang things from them. There's no pockets in a kimono, right. So you tie whatever it is on to this, your bus pass and car keys and what-not, and slip it through your belt. This bit catches on the top. I'm not telling you how much I paid for those, but it was a lot. Still, Cilla loves them.'

Horace passed the carving back to him. The two of them sat drinking tumblers of whisky for a while and staring at the gas log fire until Boothby broke the silence. ' "If you can keep your head while all about you are losing theirs, di dum di dum," ' Boothby muttered and drummed his fingers on the armchair. ' "And – which is more – you'll be a Man, my son!" '

'Poem, Uncle Derwent?' said Horace.

'Kipling's "If". Best poem ever written.' Boothby stared glassily at the fire and took a slug of his drink. 'You can have the rest of your poetry as long as you leave me that,' he said, as though Horace had been threatening to expropriate him of his library. 'I've more or less based my life on that poem. Didn't you read it at school?'

'I didn't go to school,' said Horace.

'Really?'

'I studied at home. Granddad liked to say he could teach me in six weeks what it would take them six years to teach me at school. He said the only things I'd be better off learning there were smoking and vandalism.'

'Well, you need qualifications now to get on.'

'I've got A levels.'

'That's good. Of course, I didn't even have *them*,' Boothby said, and proceeded to talk Horace through the first ten years of his career in newspapers.

That night, Horace lay awake in one of Boothby's spare bedrooms. Despite having slept badly the previous night, he didn't feel tired. He got up and put on his dressing gown and went downstairs. The moon was shining through the skylight above the staircase. Horace wandered into the library and turned on one of the desk lamps. He padded quietly around the room, thinking. He was remembering how he had caught the bus into Otherbury to take his exams in a hall at the secondary school. His examination number put him in the last row of desks, out of alphametical order and away from the other students, who brought in cartons of sugary drinks, and had rubber mascots on their pens, and formulae inked under their watchstraps.

Horace stopped in front of the shelf of netsuke. The tiny army of wood and ivory figurines were all somehow more real in the half-light. Boothby was right, they were ingenious: fancy going to all that trouble to make a toggle.

The other students in the exam room had neither been hostile to him, nor friendly. He would sit quietly, reading a book in the break between papers, while the boys played football between the desks with a furry pencil case and the girls giggled in the corners. After the exams had ended, he took the bus home to Great Much, and walked back to the quiet cottage, which smelt of paper and soap and old age.

Horace heard rain at the french windows and felt a momentary thrill. Now he was in London. Now he was beginning his new life. He picked up the carving of the two foxes and held it. The ivory felt cool and heavy like a billiard ball. You hung things on a thread from the ring and then slipped the netsuke through your belt. He passed the tiny shape through the cord of his dressing gown – back and forth. It would stay up because of the weight of whatever was on the end of it. The Japanese wore wide belts with their kimonos. As he pushed the carving gently against his hip, it snapped cleanly in half like a piece of shortbread.

'Oh, shit,' said Horace, holding a tiny ivory fox in each hand. They fitted back together perfectly, but as soon as he tried to put the carving on the shelf they slipped apart. His face felt very hot. So this was his new life. He thought of waking the Boothbys up immediately and confessing everything. Could he ever find another one? Could he afford it if he did?

Horace took a deep breath. It had probably been broken before. It was bone. Bones heal. Bone can be glued. Glue the bone.

He could take it away to glue it – but that would make him a thief. Concealment was the best policy – but where? Not in a drawer, not on a shelf. Somewhere no one would look.

Horace opened a small cedarwood box sitting on a shelf in front of the complete works of Sir Walter Scott. It held a backgammon set – no good, who knew how often it was used? He could stuff the pieces into a vase full of coloured marbles higher up, but they might be seen.

On a lower shelf, he found a humidor filled with fat Cuban cigars. He took them all out and put the pieces of the carving on the bottom. Then he covered them up with the cigars. He would bring some glue and fix it as soon as he could. He was safe for the time being, he reasoned. The Boothbys were vehement non-smokers. He had plenty of time.

Whatever Boothby said ('You'll be a natural, it's in the blood'), Horace's first day at work was a deep disappointment. His odd clothes were a source of amusement to the other employees. Horace was naturally unselfconscious, but each time he looked up he seemed to catch sight of a group of people looking his way and tittering. Unknown to him, they had nicknamed him One-man after a nursery rhyme that went: 'One man went to mow, went to mow a meadow.' It was also the title of a programme of televised sheep-dog trials. Wherever he went in the newsroom, he overheard people humming the tune.

After lunch, things got worse. Horace was asked to write an account of a fire that had destroyed part of a house in the area. He began his report with this sentence: 'The residents of Dorlcote Road were sleeping soundly in their beds on the night of the 10th January 1996.'

A sub-editor gave the copy to Mr Pratt. They chuckled among themselves before calling Horace over. Mr Pratt's eyes glittered inside their baggy brown pods. 'Horace, it may be news to you that the good people of Dorlcote Road are getting a decent night's kip, but all anyone else cares about is the fact that somebody's house has burned down. It's not our policy to cover every street in South London where someone is sleeping.'

'I thought it would be best to begin at the beginning.'

'Look, if you want to write a work of fiction, you can begin wherever the fuck you like. But when you're writing a news story, you begin with the fucking facts, right? And the facts here are that somebody's house has burned down. Do you understand?' Then he added, 'Do you understand?'

Horace went back to his desk. He was too flustered to begin writing. 'Don't worry about the Pratt,' said Harvard Machine, who was sitting at the next desk. 'He's a little bit underfunded in the tact and charm department.'

Horace went to get a cup of tea. His hand was shaking as he poured in the milk. Of course you began with the facts. Everyone knew that. 'A fire swept through Dorlcote Road.' You put all the important facts at the beginning, then less important facts, and finally all the facts that no one cared about in the slightest.

With a little help from Mrs Doolaly, Horace rewrote the piece and gave it back to the sub-editor. While he was waiting for Mr Pratt to look at it, Horace practised rewriting stories he knew well in this new style. 'Cinderella is living happily ever after following a wedding that observers described as a "fairytale marriage."' 'The King of Denmark was killed yesterday along with his nephew and heir in a tragic bloodbath that took the lives of at least two other people.'

When Mr Pratt received the corrected version of Horace's report on the fire he waved it at him. 'Much better, Horace mate.'

Horace was taken off news for the rest of the day and sent to work compiling photographs for the local history books.

The newspaper's stills archive held photographs of London going back a hundred years and more. The archivist showed

Horace how to sift and collate them, and then caption them for inclusion in books that would be sold through the newspapers and local libraries. Some were dramatic pictures: bewhiskered firemen pulling nightgowned women out of blackened tenements; air-raid wardens marshalling people through the rubble; an escaped circus lion padding curiously through a deserted street market. But the ones that held Horace's attention were the street scenes: the shadows on the houses sharpened by the bright sun of a late Victorian summer; children stopping play to stare in revealing bemusement at the photographer; the wide and oddly car-less streets.

There was so much space! The dog-eared prints seemed to give out an echo of hoofs and distant laughter. There was a faint smell of horses, warm cotton, the sun on the dusty pavement. Horace looked at the pictures and realised he was homesick. It was not Great Much he missed, though that was all he could remember. It was something else; a time before it, a time of which he had no recollection. Looking through the old photographs in their dusty boxes, he sensed that this was something that reflected his own sense of loss. The irrecoverable past stared out at him: the children who were dead, or grandparents, great-grandparents, themselves; and in the distance, those who had been too busy to wait for the slow click of the shutter, rendered translucent, blurry, fleeting, ghosts.

At the end of the day, Horace bought some glue from a newsagent on the way to Tooting Bec station, then he went down the escalator into the roaring guts of the city. A grey mouse vanished into the dirt under the tracks as a train approached. Horace examined the map of sprawling tubes. It was like a digestive system, funnelling him back home to the Boothbys'. Then he saw Waterloo on the map, and decided to go and see Jana.

There was someone else in the shop when Horace got there. As he opened the door, he could hear an accented voice whispering, 'I will come for you on Saturday.'

Jana hissed, 'Go away!'

The man pushed past Horace without looking at him and slammed the door.

'Friend of yours?' said Horace.

'He would like. Oh, Morris, this man, he is crazy. He wants me to marry him. He is from Iran. Every day he is coming. Today he brings with him five thousand pounds and he says he wants to share his life with me. I say, do you think a woman is a thing that you can buy with money? He thinks if he shows me he has money I will love him. Many Arab man are like this. I tell him no, but every day still he comes.'

'He wants to marry you?'

'He *says*. I don't know what he is thinking. The other day I was sitting in Hyde Park – in Poland it's normal to be alone – and a man he was about sixty-five came and started talking about the weather, like all English. He was being very polite, then he said, "Excuse me, but I have never kissed Polish girl." And I said, "And you never will!" and I got up and went away. I couldn't believe it.' She laughed.

'Sixty-five?'

'It was unbelievable. But the Arab men they are the worst.' She closed the exercise book she had on the counter.

She was besieged by men, Horace thought, and now he was pestering her because she was the only person he knew in London. But he asked her if she wanted to do something after work and she suggested the pub. 'Pubs I like. We don't have pubs in Poland. We have kind of bars that are underground.'

'It sounds interesting,' said Horace. The two of them walked across Hungerford footbridge to the Embankment.

'This is the prettiest place I know in London,' said Jana. Looking east, the river curved out of sight to the right. The grey dome of St Paul's was visible to the left. A train passed behind them.

'This is the first place I've been to that looks like London,' Horace shouted over the noise. 'The city's not at all what I expected.'

'Me also. What is the work that you are doing here?' They started walking again.

'I'm journalist. I mean, I'm *a* journalist.' Horace was beginning to find her speech patterns infectious. Beneath them, the Thames moved slowly against its concrete restraints. 'I mean, I'm *trying* to be a journalist.'

'You are lucky. I would like to be journalist but I cannot write. I start writing and all words are coming and coming but I cannot say what I want. Always I write too much.'

'Well, I think I hate my job,' said Horace. 'At least, I don't know if I can do it.'

'I too hate my job. All day long, it is so boring, I am waiting and no one is coming in.'

'You could always get a different one.'

'But it is difficult. I have only tourist visa. I had student, but this is gone.'

'Visa?'

'To work you must have visa. But for work visa, you must go to Home Office. And if they say no, you must leave.'

'I see. And what about a tourist visa?'

'Tourist visa I have. You can go to Amsterdam, get tourist visa, and return for six months.'

'I wonder if I need a visa?' said Horace.

'No. You are English. You don't need visa to work in your own country.'

'Oh, I see.'

'I can work for example in shop or as au pair, but this is all. Because if they ask to see student visa, I have none.'

They sat at a sticky table in a dark pub just off the Embankment. Horace bought Jana a soft drink and carried it to the table. 'I had a thought,' he said. 'I saw some jobs you could do in the *Bugle*. Look.' He took the paper out of his jacket pocket and flattened out an advertisement for an au pair in the *Help Wanted* section. 'It doesn't look too bad.'

Jana studied the ad, then thanked him and put it in her pocket. 'You are not wearing your shoes today.'

'Those ones? No, they need to be broken in.'

'*Broken in*? What is this?'

They chatted for an hour or so. Horace told her about his grandfather, who had been a communist and had met Stalin. Jana wrinkled up her nose. 'I do not like Josef Stalin.'

'No. But, then, who does nowadays?' said Horace.

Horace had to leave at ten o'clock to get back to Victoria. They stood outside the pub for a couple of moments to get their bearings and Horace took her hand. She let him hold it as they walked to the station. Her fingers were warm and slightly damp.

He waited with her on the platform for her train and kissed her on the lips as it pulled it. She closed her eyes. 'Oh, Morris,' she said, and he didn't have the heart to correct her. She disappeared onto the train and Horace went to catch his own.

By the time he got back to the Boothbys' house, his great-aunt and uncle had gone to bed. They'd left him a tray of food in the kitchen. He wolfed down two sandwiches and went into the library with his tube of glue. The room was bare. The books and ornaments had all been packed away in tea-chests, which were stacked in the middle of the room under a dust-sheet. The broken carving was embedded somewhere inside the layers of possessions like a fossil. He knew he would never find it.

Horace lay in bed thinking about the troughs and peaks of his day. He thought about Pratt's anger and Harvard's equanimity. He thought about the children in the old photographs. He thought about the broken carving. He thought about standing on the bridge with Jana and the brown river moving under them, and the wind and the lights making tiny scales on the water.

# CHAPTER THREE

MR SUBRAMANIAM, HORACE'S account manager at the Bank of Karnataka, put him in touch with a friend who was letting a flat above a newsagent on Glenburne Road. The owner, a Ugandan Tamil called Mr Narayan, charged seventy-five pounds a week rent.

The 'flat' was really a largish bedroom that had been subdivided to contain all the amenities of a home: a kitchen, a shower, a bed, a desk, and a toilet. But it had taken some ingenuity to incorporate them all. Varnished wooden planks had been laid across the fitted carpet to give the impression that the floorboards were fashionably bare; but the planks had not been nailed down and they rocked when Horace crossed the room to get to the tiny fridge-less cubby-hole of a kitchen. From inside the kitchen, two makeshift wooden steps led up into the shower cubicle. If he had wished, Horace could have reached out of the shower to stir his baked beans with one hand while lathering his hair with the other. Finally, the toilet had been placed next to the shower unit in a tiny space that was separated from the kitchen with a fibreboard partition. Anyone wanting to use the toilet had first to step into the shower cubicle to reach it. The arrangements struck Horace as entirely satisfactory.

The electricity and the gas, which heated the shower, were metered from two boxes on the landing. The electricity took fifty-pence pieces, but the gas meter only accepted the larger ten-pence pieces, which were no longer legal tender. Horace had to keep buying the old coins from Mr Narayan, but since he himself only had three or four of them, this meant opening up the meter constantly to retrieve the coins so Horace could re-buy them. Eventually they hit upon a compromise. Horace would pay Mr Narayan a couple of pounds and one of his sons would crouch on the floor, passing the worthless old money through the mechanism over and over again until it whirred like a sewing machine.

Mr Narayan had been kicked out of Uganda in the early 1970s along with the rest of the country's Asians. There, he had been a university lecturer and his wife had owned small businesses around the capital. Now he was in Tooting, muffled in a scarf as he stood in the shop to sell cigarettes and lottery tickets. Mrs Narayan had not survived being transplanted. On the days when he left the running of the shop to Madhu, the eldest of his three children, Mr Narayan sat in the front room above it, watching television, or listening to cricket on the radio, or just thinking.

After a while, he and Horace got into the habit of playing Scrabble together when Horace returned from work.

'Are you a university man?' asked Mr Narayan, during one of their games.

'No,' said Horace. 'How about you?'

Mr Narayan wagged his head and shuffled his tiles. 'I took my master's degree at Madras Christian College.' And then he closed his eyes and recited:

> 'Thy baths shall be the juice of July-flowers,
> Spirit of roses and of violets,
> The milk of unicorns, and panthers' breath
> Gathered in bags and mixed with Cretan wines.'

'Poem, Mr Narayan?'

'Ben Jonson, the bricklaying playwright.'

From then on, Mr Narayan's literary allusions became part of the game. A seven-letter, triple-word score jumped out of the bag and into his hands fully formed 'like Minerva from the head of Zeus'. After Horace made a series of dismally low scores with high-value letters and then turned in his tiles, Mr Narayan crowed, 'You have made your Procrustean bed, and now you must lie on it!'

Mr Narayan was naturally better at the game than Horace, but his gamesmanship made him almost invincible. He invented words, disputed obscure ones, and – Horace was sure – arranged interruptions to the game on the rare occasions he looked likely to lose. During these games, he would shuffle into the hall and have a brief, whispered conversation with his daughter Lakshmi, or one of his sons, while Horace was trying to consolidate his victory. Mr Narayan would return to the room and, moments later, Lakshmi would pop her head round the door. 'Father, Madhu says he needs you urgently downstairs.' With a great show of irritation, Mr Narayan would disappear and the game would be adjourned. When Horace returned, the board would have been cleared away, and the meticulously formed words broken up and put back in the old sock where they were kept.

The day after he moved in to Glenburne Road, Horace went to

see Jana in her shop. She hadn't called him at work and it had been over a week since he'd kissed her at Embankment station. Sometimes he worried that she had weakened at the thought of the five thousand pounds her Iranian suitor had been offering. Perhaps she had been waylaid by another forward Englishman.

Each day that passed had added another nuance to the memory of their last meeting. He replayed their kiss in every key he could think of. Her 'oh' could be admonitory, passionate, regretful, urgent, patronising, encouraging, or wistful. He heard it in all these tones and others. And then there was the 'Morris' to worry about. Was it an error, the name of a rival, or a word in Polish?

He had his cap in his hands as he paused at the threshold of the little shop on Lower Marsh. In the instant she looked up he was startled by the change that had come over her. The long brown hair was gone; she was taller; her face had lost its roundness and gained some stubble.

'Oh,' said Horace.

'Can I help you?' said the middle-aged man.

'I was looking for Jana.'

'You mean Joanna?'

'The girl that works here.'

'Friend of hers, are you?' The man's glance flickered over Horace's clothes.

'Yes. Can you tell me where she is.'

'I'm afraid she's not working here any more.'

'Where's she working now?'

'She's not working.' The man smiled the rueful smile of someone with bad news. 'She's been deported.'

'Deported?' Repeating the word made it sound meaningless, and Horace had a mental image, for some reason, of Jana being put into a suitcase.

'Yeah, it was over a week ago now.'

'How?'

The man drew a long breath. His suspicion had given way to sympathy. 'I'm sorry, you wouldn't have heard. She went for a job as an au pair – at least I think that's what it was. She said the hours here weren't giving her enough time to study.' He shrugged. 'I don't know, probably true. Business like this, we have to stay open long hours or we wouldn't get the custom. Well, as it turned out, it was the Home Office that had placed the ad for the job she was after. I've never heard of them doing it, but there you go. Poor old Joanna shows up along with a couple of Brazilians. They saw they didn't have no visas and . . .' He whistled through his teeth to convey the velocity of Joanna's exit. 'She rang me from Heathrow in tears. Didn't even give her time to pick up her clothes. Back to Gdansk, or wherever she was from.'

'Krakow,' said Horace, sorrowfully.

'Why the hangdog look?' said Mr Narayan when Horace got home. Horace explained but Mr Narayan was unsympathetic. 'You're only a young man,' he said. 'There are plenty more fish where she came from.'

The next day at work Harvard Machine took Horace to one side. 'I've noticed you looking a bit down-in-the-mouth today, Horace. I know Pratt is giving you a rough ride but that's just his way. You have to give as good as you get.'

'It's not that. It's a personal thing.'

'I see. I'm sorry. If you want to talk about it, you know, a problem shared is a problem . . . well, shared.' Harvard patted him on the shoulder. He listened as Horace explained. 'It was a Home Office ad? Are you sure?'

'That's what the bloke in the shop said.'

'Right.'

'I feel confused about the whole thing.' Horace sighed and looked forlorn. 'I didn't know her very well, but I miss her. It's strange. And it was such a shock. She was the first person I met in London and we seemed to get on so well. I feel like it's my fault.' Horace had almost grown accustomed to the feeling of anxiety that had pressed against his ribs since his arrival – as though, rather than breaking the Boothby's carving, he had swallowed it whole.

'What I'm going to tell you probably doesn't seem like much consolation at the moment,' said Harvard. 'You're understandably upset about losing your girlfriend. Fair enough. But just remember this: you're a journalist. You possess the gift of turning all kinds of human misery to your advantage.'

'What, even my own?'

'Anyone's.'

'I don't think I follow you.'

'Let me explain.'

'Home Office Sting – Illegal Workers Deported' was the lead story in the next issue of the *Bugle*. Horace and Harvard had a joint byline. The story got picked up by the nationl papers the following day. One printed the *Bugle* story verbatim, but merged the names of the two reporters into one: Harvard Littlefair.

Horace was the object of admiring whispers when he came into work. 'Nice work, One-man,' said one of his colleagues, Romford, a sports reporter. Romford explained that they had nicknamed him 'One-man', because he was a one-man investigative news team. Horace supposed he ought to feel flattered but instead he just felt sad about losing Jana. He had a sudden memory of her in the pub on the Embankment, brushing the hair out of her face and saying in her melodious voice, 'For example, do you know the poems of Szymborska?'

As Horace was making a cup of tea for himself and Mrs Doolaly, Pratt called him into his office.

'Horace. Take a seat. Got something I want you to do. Nice work on the deportation story, by the way. You're obviously getting the hang of things. Right, what this is. Feature piece, right up your street – dropped-intro kind of thing. We do an occasional series called "South London Centenarians" – bit of a mouthful, I know, but we can't call it "Crumblies Look Back". This old dear's a friend of your uncle Derwent. She's a hundred next Tuesday. I don't know if she's fully *compos mentis*, but she's bound to have one or two tales to tell. Here's the address.

Better give her a ring first. Check her diary's not too full. Ha ha. Little joke. All right?'

Horace waited for further instructions. There were none. But as he was going out of the door Pratt called him back. 'Get a couple of old photos off her if you can. It always adds to the piece. Her playing tennis aged seventeen sort of thing. Makes a good contrast with her now.'

Horace drove one of the *Bugle*'s four Minis to the old woman's house. It looked like a simple journey on the map but the traffic imposed its own pace on him, and when he wasn't simply stationary, he was travelling too fast to read the road signs. It took him an hour and a half to find it. Outside the house, he double-checked the address and rang the bell. He waited for a while, then pressed it again and peeked through the flap in the door.

Agnes Kettle was making her way up the hallway with stiff and halting movements like the second hand of an ancient clock. She had grown insubstantial with age, and her twiggy fingers struggled with the brass latch. She opened the door and gazed at Horace through thick smeary glasses. 'What a beautiful check suit!' she said in her raspy alto. 'Let me take your coat. My, that's a beauty too.'

Horace had brought his brown overcoat with a short built-in cloak at the shoulders. A little brass lion held the flaps of the cloak together. The old lady stroked the fabric. 'Thank you,' said Horace. 'The cloak does give added warmth.'

They sat together in the front room of her house eating Club biscuits and drinking tea. Horace spent three hours listening to her reminisce. Mrs Kettle had been born in Siam, where her father, a judge, had devised the penal code for the king.

'Thai was my first language, you know. I learned it from my nurse,' she said. 'But we came back here when I was ten. You see, when the king died, the Imperial office cabled my father to tell him he would be the British Empire's representative at the funeral. "Full ceremonial dress must be worn," the cable said.

Oh, he cabled back, asking if he could attend in tropical kit instead – you know, pith helmet, light clothing. But the fools at the Imperial Office weren't having any of it. Of course, you see, they knew better. We were only in Siam, what did we know? So the poor man had to wear a horse-hair wig and great long robes, and march round and round the catafalque all day long with the sun beating down on him. That was the custom, you see. He knew it would kill him, and it did. More tea?'

'It killed him?' Horace held out his cup. 'Thank you.'

'Sunstroke. It was tragic, really. When we got back to London, the FO told my mother they wanted to give him a posthumous peerage. My mother refused it. They weren't offering a single penny in compensation. She was a widow, trying to bring up her children on his pension. She said, "I'm not having shop assistants putting up prices for me because I'm Lady Kettle." She told them what they could do with their title.'

They sat quietly for a while listening to the hiss of the gas fire. The old lady stirred her tea and the spoon tinkled in the cup, then she rapped it three times on the rim and laid it on the saucer.

'I don't suppose you have any photos?' said Horace. 'Of you as a child, or anything really. Playing tennis?'

'Playing tennis? Oh, no, I never really went in for that sort of thing. I wasn't the sporty type. My sister was, though, poor thing.' She thought for a moment. 'I have lots of photographs, though, somewhere – but where are the bally things?' She said *photographs* with a short *a; photograffs*, making them sound quaintly old-fashioned, like piano rolls or detachable collars, and her outmoded slang reminded Horace of his grandfather's: *bally, top-hole, first-class.* 'Now, where did I put those albums?'

She got to her feet creakily to search for them, and after a time unearthed a stack. Horace picked one out and opened it at random. He saw Agnes in early middle age, dressed in a nurse's uniform, the starched folds of her cap framing her head. She had never been pretty, but she had been more solid, more fleshly, than the papery presence beside him with her slow walk and her odd angles of bone.

'Can I borrow this one for the article?' he asked.

'Of course you can. I haven't looked at these for years. Which one is it? Oh, yes, that was taken just after the war.'

The picture set off a chain of reminiscences, the war, the bombing of the Café de Paris, Anderson shelters, but Agnes was tired and lost the thread of her thoughts more often. Horace turned the page of the album. 'My sister,' she said. 'She went to teach in Doncaster. Never got married. I think she had girlfriends, but I don't know if she was what you'd call a *lesbian*.'

Horace pointed at another photo on the same page. 'And who's that?'

The old woman looked at him in surprise, as though he was teasing her. She tried to answer, but her false teeth came unfixed and yawned alarmingly, muffling her voice. She mumbled them back on to her gums and repeated herself. 'Why, that's *you*.'

Horace felt uneasy and stared at the picture. It was a group photograph. The man was older than him, and there was little resemblance. He didn't want to confront the old woman with her mistake because he thought it might frighten her. But her confusion upset him. There was more than a hint of insanity about it.

'Of course,' he said, improvising to spare the old lady's feelings. 'Can I borrow this one too?'

The sub-editor dropped all references to Justice Kettle's death in Siam and spiced up the description of the bombing of the Café de Paris with his own impressions, gleaned from a film about the war in Vietnam. Horace barely recognised the finished article as his. Inaccuracies and exaggerations had crept into the piece during the rewriting. Mr Pratt called Horace in for a chat and he entered the office fearfully.

'Nice work on the Blitz heroine. That wartime-spirit cobblers is magic – official.' Mr Pratt realigned the blotting pad in the middle of his desk. 'I've just been talking to Mrs Doolaly – or listening, rather. She's been bending my ear about your talents as a gardener. You should have told me you had green fingers.'

For the past few days, Mrs Doolaly had been pressing her home-baking on Horace, who would accept it politely and listen to stories of her extended family, her hopes of leaving London for Ramsgate, and the mixed fortunes of her garden. She had caught in him an echo of her younger self, new and unschooled in the ways of the city.

'Well, I'm no expert.' Horace felt uneasy. He was guiltily aware that the section of the article on Agnes Kettle which had been singled out for special praise had in fact been concocted by the subeditor. 'My grandfather was a keen gardener. I couldn't help picking up a little. She said her herbaceous borders were looking a bit tatty.'

'The reason I mention it is that Mr Boothby, your uncle – '

'Great-uncle, actually.'

'Whatever. He's keen to get more gardening stuff in the paper, particularly now that spring's on the way. What would you say to a sort of ongoing nature stroke gardening column?'

'I'm not sure.'

'It doesn't have to be a huge amount of extra work. Mix it up a bit. You'd have the odd observation, tips about what people should be planting, replies to reader's questions.'

'The thing is – '

Pratt cut him off before he could raise any objections. 'I think it would be very useful for you to develop a specialisation. Journalism is an extremely competitive business. I get letters from Oxbridge graduates begging to be taken on here. Only the very best of them can cut the mustard as general news reporters.'

Horace looked out at the dirt and apathy of the newsroom.

'You don't have shorthand. You don't understand libel law.' Pratt crumpled up a piece of paper and lobbed it over Horace's head into the wastepaper basket. 'I'm afraid you're not going to be a lot of use to anyone unless you develop a niche.'

'What kind of an itch?' said Horace, puzzled.

'The specific niche is not as important as your general attitude.' Pratt had the ability to make anything he said sound vaguely threatening. He looked straight at Horace and said: 'You need to be hungry.'

'I can be hungry,' said Horace. 'I can be very hungry.'

'I'm glad to hear it,' said Pratt. 'I probably don't need to remind you that gardening's the nation's number-one pastime. With your previous knowledge, you're well qualified to write about it.' Pratt paused. 'How about this, then? You do the column, and at the same time I'll let you shadow Harvard one or two days a week and pick up some of the basic journalistic skills you're short of.'

What choice did he have? 'I'll give it a go.'

'Good man.' Pratt leaped out of his chair to get the attention of Harvard Machine whose white head was sailing past the door of his office.

Horace didn't have the first idea how to begin. A nature stroke gardening column? What was it? It seemed humiliating even to ask. In his heart, he felt sure that Pratt knew he didn't know. These tasks were designed to catch him out. Pratt was asking him to turn straw into gold, but Horace didn't understand the haphazard alchemy that seemed to govern his new world. How could he succeed?

His anxieties multiplied. He was failing in his job. The broken carving preyed on his conscience. He missed Jana.

Horace went to the public library on his way home. Every available chair, every available surface was in use. People were coughing and sniffling and rustling newspapers. It was like a doctor's waiting room.

A respectably dressed middle-aged man was occupying an armchair by the section of books on gardening. Horace was browsing through the shelves when he became aware of a smell so strong it made his eyes water. He took a couple of steps back to clear his head and then tried to approach the books again. He was rebuffed by the stink. It was like trying to penetrate the atmosphere of a malodorous little planet. The source of the smell was absorbed in a book on Roman coins. In the end, Horace held his breath, scooped up a sample of books and re-entered the airspace of the library. The librarian gave him a sympathetic smile as she stamped his books.

Mr Narayan caught Horace's eye as he walked past the shop and waved. He was leafing through the local press. It had become more of a habit since he had befriended Horace, who was a young man with prospects, he had decided. What's more, he thought, he dressed like a real Englishman.

Horace went upstairs and pored over the books at his wobbly desk with the clarity of mind that only comes with a crisis. He had chosen indiscriminately, but there was enough material for his purposes. He rewrote gobbets out of one of the books on gardening and made suggestions for small projects to under-take at that time of year in what he took to be a jaunty style. 'Just because the garden is looking brown and bare, it doesn't mean you can sit back and be idle. This is the time to make long-term decisions about trellis-work and pruning back shrubs.' He added a paragraph containing his advice to Mrs Doolaly and topped the whole thing off with some florid observations about the state of the plane trees on Tooting Common. It was, he reflected, complete cobblers, but having written it, he felt the unearthly resignation of a man who had just penned his suicide note.

He left the piece on his desk and went to find Mr Narayan for a game of Scrabble. Mr Narayan controlled most of the game, then, in almost the last round Horace scored a famous victory with 'quartzes' on a triple-word score, picking up an additional fifty points for using up all his tiles.

Pratt was delighted with the column. 'There's a lot of mileage in this. Marketing's the key. I've asked someone upstairs to see if we can get one of the garden centres to sponsor us. Now, shut the door a second. I've got an idea for something else. I think you should include a quiz.'

'A quiz?'

'That's right. I've been trying to get one in for ages. All the tabs do it.'

'The tabs?'

'The tabloids.' He looked up at Horace and added, with a slight snort, 'As in "keep taking them".'

Horace looked blank. Fifty per cent of everything Mr Pratt said was incomprehensible to him.

'Never mind.' Mr Pratt held a felt-tip pen between this thumb and tar-stained forefinger. 'It works something like this. Here's your column. Here's all that stuff about gardens. Down here we have a multiple-choice quiz question and a phone number.' He sketched in crude blocks on his blotter. 'Readers ring up and record their answers. We use an 0898 number so we make money off the calls. It costs them about fifty pence a minute. Whoever wins gets a seed catalogue, or a book on hedgerows or something. All you have to do is think up questions. Easy ones.'

'I think I can manage that.'

There was one other thing. 'Turnover's high here. We like the columns to be written under a pseudonym. Except for Colefax's, obviously. Happy Shopper and Madame Zoroaster are both being done by one of the other trainees at the moment, simply because it would look fucking silly if she had two identical bylines, right? So I thought we'd make you the Rambler.' He patted Horace on the back as he left the office. 'Nice work, Horace. Lots of good ideas there.'

# CHAPTER FOUR

AGNES KETTLE PADDED slowly around her kitchen in a house-coat making herself a cup of tea. She could never sleep past five nowadays. Thankfully her eyes seemed to be holding up – touch wood – so she could still read, but nothing too heavy: large, slushy romances that the mobile library brought round once a fortnight. Her marble ankles protruded from the furry cuff of the slippers that she always wore round the house. That was one of the consolations of old age. You could let your hair down a bit. Not that there was much left of that, she would reflect with regret, remembering how stubbornly its once-tight curls had resisted efforts to brush them into submission and fix them with pins under a nurse's cap.

Talking to the young man from the paper (what was his name?) had stirred up the dregs of old memories. They drifted around in suspension: tea-leaves that told of her past. She had dreamed of Siam for the first time in years, sepia dreams that she couldn't for the most part disconnect from her old photographs, but with every now and then a flash of colour like startled plumage: white sheets dripping in the sunlight; the salt-dried plums the Chinese servant gave her – mouth-puckering tartness, and then a spiciness like her father's pipe-tobacco in its leather pouch.

The front door buzzed. A face loomed through its frosted glass. 'Hello. You must be . . . you're on my list somewhere, hang about. Here we are, Agnes Kettle. How d'you do? Trevor Diamond, Fox Outreach.'

'You've come about the garden.'

Long residence in London couldn't quite conceal the remnants of his Yorkshire accent. 'I've just parked next door. Is it all right for me to block their drive for the time being? I can move it. It's just that I've got one or two bits and pieces in the back that I might need.'

'I'm sure that would be quite all right,' said Agnes. 'Can I make you a cup of tea? Or coffee?'

'You know what. I'll be honest with you. I could *murder* a cup of tea. I haven't stopped since five this morning. It's been one thing after another.' Trevor masked his awkwardness with a bluff manner that could be unsettling. But Agnes's capacity for finding fault with people had waned over the years like her other faculties. It was a necessary corollary of ageing. It made it easier to make do with a diminishing circle of friends, unreliable relatives and professional carers. The only people Agnes permitted herself to dislike were her ex-husband's late second wife and her own next-door neighbour, whose driveway she had just given Trevor permission to block.

She followed Trevor out to the garden. It was short, maybe

48

twenty-five feet, and its rickety rear fence backed onto a ragged expanse of common land. Trevor was scrutinising the perimeter of her garden intensely enough to make her feel self-conscious about the state it was in.

'I don't go in for gardening much any more, but I do like it to look neat – though you wouldn't think it. It's the rubbish that's such a dreadful nuisance – all over the place – and my new plants spoiled.'

'Little buggers will do that, given half a chance,' murmured Trevor. 'Probably caching bones in the flower-bed.' His interest in the garden made him almost oblivious to Mrs Kettle. He hopped over the fence at the end and stalked around the common for ten minutes, poking into shrubbery. Agnes went back to the kitchen to make him a cup of tea.

'I've got good news and bad news, Mrs Kettle,' he said, when he came back. 'Which do you want to hear first?'

'Bad news? Oh dear. I suppose I'd better hear that.' For someone who had lived through the best part of a turbulent century, the prospect of bad news threw up alarming precedents.

'The bad news,' Trevor continued, not noticing her worried expression, 'is that some foxes – I don't know how many – have decided that your garden is the local takeaway. The good news is that their earth's not on your land so, as far as I'm concerned, it's a simple deterrent job. That should do the trick for the time being, but we might have to have another go round in March, April, after the cubs are born, in case the vixen has an eye on your place for an adventure playground.' He slapped his palms together. 'Right, I'll just get the things I need out of the car.'

Agnes watched from the window as Trevor filled a large weed-sprayer from the outside tap. He hung the large plastic reservoir on his back like an aqualung and started to circumnavigate the garden extremely slowly, squirting the little wand on the fence, around the rubbish bins, at the garden gate and around the plants. He was thirtyish, with cropped rufous hair and aviator glasses and he limped slightly as he made his way around the shrubbery. He was wearing a fleece-lined denim jacket over a T-shirt, jeans and trainers. Every so often he would break off and return to the outside sill of the kitchen window with his wand and aqualung, and sip his tea with a look of deep concentration.

It took about forty minutes for him to spray the perimeter of the garden and the approach to the rear fence. He rubbed his hands as he came into the kitchen. 'Right, that should do the trick. Give me a shout if they come back and start chucking rubbish about. But that should do it for the time being.'

'How much do I owe you?' Agnes didn't have much idea what had just taken place in her garden but was sure she had to pay for it.

'There's no actual charge for a deterrent job as such. Obviously, if you could make a contribution towards the cost of the materials, that would be greatly appreciated. Fox Outreach relies solely on voluntary donations and sponsorship.'

'Would, say, twenty pounds be enough?' Agnes's shaky hand fumbled through her purse.

'For twenty pounds, you become a sponsor and are entitled to receive our newsletter.' Trevor took a sip of tea and looked around the room. His eyes fell on the tiled mantelpiece. A piece of paper was propped against the ornaments, it read: 'I am delighted to send you my warm congratulations on your 100th birthday together with my best wishes for an enjoyable celebration. Elizabeth R.'

'It's just a bit of silliness,' said Agnes, with a certain pride. 'It's just a birthday like any other. I don't know what the fuss is about.'

'Happy birthday.' Trevor thought about returning the money but changed his mind. 'Well, in that case you *definitely* get a subscription. That's not a bad innings at all.'

'It's a century, isn't it? But they make such a fuss. They sent a young man from the paper to come and find out my life story. I must have bored him silly, going on. Don't let me do the same to you.'

'Don't worry about me.' Trevor was thinking. 'What was the name of the bloke that interviewed you?'

'His name. Let me see. I cut out the article and put it down somewhere. Could you pass my glasses?' She combed the page with her unsteady finger. 'Here it is. Horace Littlefair. *Littlefair*. Fancy me not remembering that.'

A man on a cookery programme was preparing soup from pigs' trotters. Mr Narayan had the volume turned up loud. If it was loud enough, it would blot out the noise of the shop downstairs. When he wasn't behind the counter, he preferred not to hear the till ringing and the door opening and closing.

He got up to pull the curtains shut against the chilly sky. In the hiss of the drizzle he heard the echo of another downpour: rain drumming on the roof and churning up the dust outside the lecture theatre. 'Let us see how the poet achieves his effects.' Row upon row of black faces stared back at him, or wrote down his words in silence. It was some of these very students that had set fire to his car the year Ashok was born. To be wealthy and resented for it in Uganda, to be poor and resented for it in England: that was the meaning of being foreign. To come here and be called a Paki, as if the whole colonised world had been an undifferentiated, dark-skinned mass.

They had arrived at the refugee camp in Southampton on a day of bright sunshine, his wife and his two tiny children. An Anglican priest had come to tutor his sons. Mr Narayan had assumed he was teaching them to read, but in fact he was teaching them to speak Welsh. They had forgotten it all once they moved to London.

Why Welsh? he had wondered. But he sometimes thought that with all his reading he knew less about England than if he'd known nothing. His books had prepared him for a different place. In his imagination, he had seen a wooden O rising in a dusty suburb of Kampala or Madras; dark-skinned poets, drunk on arrack, brawling in unlit streets; cross-legged

51

philosophers in *lungis* crying *sic probo* over cups of rose milk. London was somewhere altogether different.

His youngest child, Lakshmi, who was sixteen, had crept up behind him. She looped her thin arms over the back of her father's chair and under his chin, bringing her mouth close to his ear. 'Dad, Dad, when I've finished my homework, can I go to the Manhattan?'

'If one of your brothers takes you,' said Mr Narayan gruffly.

'It's only down the road.'

'You know the rules. If Ashok or Madhu can't take you, you have to stay here.'

'What about Horace?'

'Don't bother Horace, he's busy.'

'No, he isn't, he's in his room, reading.'

'I don't think it's really his scene.' He was staring at the television. The presenter was tasting the soup. Lakshmi smiled. *Not really his scene.* The phrase sounded odd in her father's accented English.

'How do you know? You've never been.'

'Ah. You're inviting *me*. That's another matter. I'm warning you my dancing is a little rusty.' Lakshmi had her hand against his adam's apple and jiggled it in annoyance so his voice vibrated.

'Da-a-ad!' She made the three syllables dip and rise. 'Can I go with Horace?'

'You can ask him. If he says no, you stay in.'

The Manhattan took up the second storey of two shop-fronts on the Upper Tooting Road. It was a large function room divided in two by a circular bar that was often rented to wedding parties. The regulars were the teenagers of the area's Asian families. Parents did come along to the Manhattan. They could sit and eat onion bhajis on one side of the bar while the younger customers danced to live and recorded versions of Indian film songs on the other.

In Lakshmi's eyes, the Manhattan's attractions ran a distant second to those of Cosmic Tribe: a vast, purpose-built dance complex up the road in Wandsworth that bussed in customers from central London and closed at six in the morning. But she knew that her father would agree to her going there as readily as he would agree to her posing topless in the *Daily Flag*, and she was philosophical about the luck of Jane Best, a girl at school who was infamous for doing both.

As Lakshmi had guessed, Horace was in his room reading a book on wild flowers and jotting down possible questions for Pratt's quiz. Lakshmi rapped on the door and went in.

'All right, Horace. What you up to?' She stood by his desk, a slight figure with tiny hands, her hair lightened and dyed with henna, against her father's wishes.

'Hello. Not much. Bit of reading.' Horace and Lakshmi had established a relationship of amicable incomprehension. She found him irredeemably square; he found her codes of music and fashion impenetrable.

'Right.' Lakshmi tried not to peer too obviously at Horace's possessions, but she couldn't help noticing how bare the room was. There were a few library books on the shelves, a vase of dried flowers, a black and white photograph stuck to the wall above the desk. 'Look, I was going to go down the road to the Manhattan and I thought you might want to come – if you're not doing anything else.'

'Why not? I've not seen much of London's famous nightlife.' Horace began to put on the long brown overcoat that was hanging on the back of the door.

'You won't need that,' said Lakshmi.

'Are you sure? It was freezing earlier.'

'It's warmed up a lot. And it's boiling in the club. Honestly, you won't need it.' Lakshmi badly wanted to go out, but not badly enough to go into the Manhattan with a man dressed in a full length brown overcoat with a built-in cape that had a lion-shaped brass fastener.

'I'll just take this, in case.' Horace took a frayed cardigan with elbow patches out of his cupboard.

Lakshmi decided not to object in case he produced something

53

more monstrous still. As they left the house, her father's voice shouted after them, 'Back by ten, Lakshmi!'

'All right, Dad,' she shouted back, then, under her breath, '*Raas.*'

Horace walked along the outside edge of the pavement and rubbed his arms. 'It's freezing. I'm going back to get my coat.'

'There's no point. Look, it's just there, on the corner.' Lakshmi paused before adding, 'You need some new clothes, man.'

'Why? What's wrong with these?' He looked at her in surprise.

'Well, *you* know. They're just not what people your age should be wearing. Your clothes say a lot about you. They say what group you belong to. They say what music you like, and what clubs you go to.'

'Well, what are your clothes saying?'

'Mine say, "larging it with the junglist massive".'

*Larging it with the junglist massive?* thought Horace, but he said nothing for a moment. Then he said, 'I thought you liked that pop group with the two yobbos.'

'They're not *yobbos.*' Lakshmi's favourite band was fronted by a pair of loud Mancunian brothers. As far as Horace could tell, the group's appeal lay in the threat of imminent fratricide whenever they appeared on stage together. 'They love each other, but they hate each other as well.'

'Why don't they just split up and form separate pop groups?'

'Stop saying "pop groups". Say "band".'

'Pop groups. Pop groups. Pop groups.'

'Horace, honestly, you're worse than my dad.'

Lakshmi steered Horace through the crowd to a quiet corner of the Manhattan. Sitting at the table was a black boy of about Lakshmi's age. Despite the heat of the room, he was wearing a hooded sweatshirt, an anorak over it, and a baseball cap. 'Darrell,' said Lakshmi, 'this is Horace, he's a friend of my father's.'

'All right.' Darrell nodded. 'Horace did you say your name was?'

'Yes.'

54

Darrell shook his hand gravely. 'I might get some food,' he said. 'What's *kheer*?'

'*Kheer*'s nice. *Kheer*'s nice. *Kheer*'s like *payasam*.' Lakshmi was bouncing with excitement.

Darrell made a face. 'I don't want anything spicy.'

'It's not spicy, it's sweet.' Lakshmi was sitting on his lap and holding one side of the menu.

'Go on, then. You choose.'

'I've eaten.'

Horace left them and went to buy a drink at the bar. When he got back, Lakshmi and Darrell were dancing. Darrell's trainers squeaked on the lino as he danced with a look of concentration, still wearing his anorak and avoiding eye-contact with Lakshmi. She watched him with obvious pleasure, twirling her hands in the air above her head. She caught Horace's eye and waved at him. 'Come and dance,' she mouthed over the music.

Horace resisted and pointed at his glass, but Lakshmi came over, grabbed his hand, and pulled him onto the dance-floor.

At first, he tried to follow the rhythm of the glugging drums, but he kept getting distracted by the shrill voice of the female singer. Instead, he copied Lakshmi's movements and then began to invent his own. He started with a stylised imitation of Mr Tither arranging groceries on a stack of shelves. After a spell as Mr Tither, he changed into a toreador, then he picked apples and wrote a letter on a manual typewriter.

A circle of smiling brown faces formed a space around him. They clapped in time to the music as Horace dug in some compost, wiping his brow from the exertion, built a dry-stone wall, and cooked a full English breakfast with mushrooms and a fried slice.

'I'm going outside to get some fresh air,' Lakshmi shouted.

'Your dad wants you home at ten,' Horace shouted back, as Lakshmi and Darrell disappeared. He popped two slices of bread in a toaster and towelled his hair dry. Meanwhile, a group of young Asians had begun to imitate Mr Tither arranging groceries on a stack of shelves.

'What do you think of Horace?' said Lakshmi, in the alley outside the club.

'He's cool,' said Darrell. 'He's doing his own thing.'

'We'd better go back and get him,' said Lakshmi.

'Five minutes,' said Darrell, and stroked her hair gently.

At ten to ten, Lakshmi and Horace said goodbye to Darrell. He seemed shorter on the pavement, a compact figure in his anorak and sweatshirt. Horace, whose shirt was damp from the dancing, touched the anorak approvingly. 'That looks serviceable.'

Darrell edged away slightly. 'Tommy Hilfiger,' he said. 'Three hundred and fifty quid.'

'See you,' said Lakshmi.

'Yeah, see you,' said Darrell. He looked at Horace. 'Safe,' he said, then left them.

'So Darrell's your boyfriend,' said Horace, as they walked back.

'What makes you say that?'

'I may be a yokel, but I'm not a total ignoramus.'

They walked on in silence a little way. Then Lakshmi said, 'it would be better if you didn't mention it to my dad. He'll jump to conclusions. Do you mind?'

'I won't lie if he asks me, but I won't volunteer it.' The formula satisfied Horace's sense of divided obligations.

'Dad cheats at Scrabble,' said Lakshmi, as though this would cement their conspiracy.

'I thought so.'

Lakshmi hummed to herself and then said, 'Do you have a girlfriend?'

'I used to, but she got deported.'

'Maybe she'll come back to find you.'

'Maybe.'

'Wasn't there someone at home, where you come from?'

'There was someone. Not exactly a girlfriend.' Horace thought about the rough red hands of Betty Barmbrake.

'There was a call for you, Horace,' said Harvard Machine,

peering over his half-glasses. 'Said he was a friend of that oxygen thief you profiled. Kettle. She gave him your name, apparently.' He fumbled around on his desk. 'Here you are.'

Horace examined the message uneasily. It occurred to him that it might be from a relative of the old woman, upset about the inaccuracies in the article. 'Trevor Diamond,' the message said, and gave his number.

The phone was answered almost instantly. A voice said, 'Fox Outreach.'

'Can I speak to Trevor Diamond please?'

'Speaking.'

'This is Horace Littlefair from the *South London Bugle*.'

'Ah, yes. I've just been visiting a friend of yours called Agnes Kettle. Nice old lady, just turned a hundred. She said you'd been on to her.'

'Right.' Horace wasn't sure if he was hearing a tone of reproach or heavy sarcasm.

'She had a bit of a problem that I helped her with. She thought you might – '

'Mr Diamond, I think you should know that that article was heavily edited before it appeared. In many ways, the first draft was a better reflection of her original remarks.'

'She thought you or someone on your paper might be interested in the work I do caring for the urban fox.'

'The urban fox?' Relieved, Horace felt a rush of goodwill towards his caller.

Horace and Trevor crouched behind a dustbin on a patch of waste-ground in Southwark. Less than thirty feet away, two foxes were mating noisily. The crystal shaft of Canary Wharf twinkled in the distance behind them. The shrill cries of the female rose up into the night air. It was two o'clock in the morning.

'Do you think we could switch on the torch for a better look?' said Horace. Only the vaguest outline of the animals was visible in the darkness.

'Put it this way, if you was about to jump your missus and I popped out of the cupboard waving a torch, you wouldn't be best pleased,' said Trevor. A bead of freezing moisture hung on the end of his nose. 'It's not like sex with humans. There's none of those bits and pieces.' Trevor gestured with both hands as though adjusting the knobs on an old-fashioned crystal set.

There was a sudden movement, a snarl, the flash of bared teeth. The dog fox trotted off down the road and was briefly visible. 'He's got a barbed penis,' said Trevor. 'It's usually over in seconds but sometimes it'll get stuck. First thing the vixen does when it's over is give the bloke a good hard bite.'

A nail-clipping of moon slipped out of the clouds. A printing plant faced onto the tussocky open land – waste-ground in London, anywhere else a field. In the weeks he had spent in the city, Horace had never travelled this far east. He had driven through the mangy streets, lit with their orange lamps, thinking: This is the real London. Just over the river lay the Monument, the Tower, the City – the landmarks of the capital. It was all more urban than the south-west London streets he had begun to think of as home. Less grass and fewer commons broke up the great swathes of stone and concrete. All that cold stone and the cold slow river running through it: it made flesh seem raw and vulnerable.

Trevor drove them back through the deserted streets, past the kebab shops and the minicab companies. The headquarters of Fox Outreach was a desk in the sitting room of Trevor's one-bedroom council flat. The mantelpiece above the gas fire was crowded with photographs: Trevor in surgical gloves feeding a new-born fox cub from a syringe; Trevor receiving an award from the Mayor of Southwark; a fox, its eyes bright from a flash gun, frozen in some dark garden over a mess of dog-food.

'Fancy a cup of tea?' Trevor asked.

'If it's not too much trouble.'

Trevor had to step over a sleeping Labrador to get to the cooker. The flat was filled with animals and furniture. The deep-pile carpet and the doggy smell of the Labrador made

58

Horace feel for a moment as though he was trapped in the coat of an enormous animal. He sat down with his cup of tea still too hot to drink and tried to negotiate the awkward roll of the springy sofa. He settled back in the seat and dislodged a complaining cat. A little tea slopped over the edge of his mug and onto his trousers. A squeaking in the corner of the room drew his attention to a hamster scampering round in a wheel.

'What is it about foxes that you find so interesting?' Horace asked, noticing that his tweed trousers were hairy with cat fur.

'Everyone asks me that. Foxes are very misunderstood animals. They're persecuted. What I want to say to people is that foxes won't harm your pets. They've got as much right to be here as you or me.'

Horace was trying to concentrate on Trevor's face. His blue eyes were wide and intense behind the large lenses of his aviator glasses. Each time Horace looked away, his glance discovered more animals, eking out an existence in the hairy coat of Trevor's sitting room. For all his years in the countryside, Horace had never been in such proximity to so many species of animal. It was faintly oppressive, as though the whole room was a terrarium, and he and Trevor the largest things in it. There was a cage of mice, several more dogs and cats, something reptilian stirring under a heat-lamp by the television set, a blue-green tank of shimmering fish.

'People have got nothing to fear from the urban fox,' Trevor was saying. Horace tried to repress a shudder as the Labrador made its way over to the sofa and licked his hand. Trevor slid a cassette into his video recorder. 'This'll tell you a bit more about the work I do. One of the local TV stations did it. It's a little bit out of date in places.' The saliva on Horace's hand was going cold.

The first shot showed a fox on its hind legs, stretching to reach inside a Southwark Council dustbin. *'Who said Docklands has no nightlife?'* asked the voiceover. *'This is Simba, one of London's urban foxes. She owes her life to this man: Trevor Diamond.'* Trevor was shown sitting at the wheel of his car, peering into the gloom, presumably at Simba. He'd been hairier then, wearing a scraggy beard and a longer, curlier hairstyle.

'I have to keep it short,' said Trevor, self-consciously. 'It grows straight out at the sides.' He mimed an astronaut's helmet around his head. 'I look like a white Michael Jackson.'

On-screen, Trevor was tapping away at his computer. The green letters of the display glowed in his glasses. *'There are almost thirty foxes in Trevor's database – just a fraction of the thousands that live in London . . .'*

'That's probably a bit high.' Trevor was amending the commentary as it went along.

*'Trevor can tell all of them apart by sight.'* Bearded Trevor was limping down the path to his car. His voice could be heard in the background, *'Ever since an accident at work four years ago, I've devoted myself to caring for the urban fox . . .'*

'Colour television fell on me leg. Buggered up me cruciate ligaments.'

*'Trevor gets by on charitable donations and the money he earns relocating unwanted earths . . .'* Trevor was shaking out tins of dog-food onto a patch of grass.

'That's where we were tonight.'

*'I just want to say to people, foxes are deeply misunderstood creatures. You've got nothing to fear from the urban fox. They won't harm your pets. They've got as much right to be here as you or me.'* The narrator appeared on-screen, clutching a microphone. *'It's now just after three in the morning . . .'* she began.

Trevor halted the tape. 'It gets boring after this,' he said.

# CHAPTER FIVE

DERWENT BOOTHBY KEPT his wine in a climate-controlled vault beneath his home, and the keys to it in a drawer of his desk. The first opened the locked door at the top of the steps, the second the metal gate at their foot. The third unlocked a hatch in the cellar that sealed off the old coal chute, which had been cleaned and fitted with a set of rollers to ensure that the cases of wine enjoyed a safe and stately descent from the driveway to the cellar floor.

The paraphernalia of the cellar always provoked a thrill in Boothby as he descended the steps, clinked the key in the lock of the gate and stepped into the cool but not cold, moist but not wet cellar air. The wines were pigeon-holed around the walls by region, appellation and year. Deep in their tiled slots, the glass bottles gave off a dull gleam. The humidifier hummed. Mr Boothby patrolled the bins, looking for what he wanted. He was carrying a wire basket with hoops to secure each bottle of wine. Amontillado – slot – Château Grillet – slot, slot.

He looks like a bloody milkman, thought Barnaby Colefax MP, who had followed his host to the foot of the cellar steps. Like a milkman, delivering pintas before sunrise on a damp winter morning. He'll start whistling in a minute.

'This should do us for the time being,' said Boothby.

Upstairs, he worked off the lead capsule reverently and gave the cork a quick sniff. 'This one is a little bit special. The concentration of the fruit is just phenomenal.' Boothby swilled it around his mouth. 'Apricots, hawthorn, honey. And, yet, it's a dry wine. Incredible, don't you think?'

'I've always found the Rhône Viogniers rather overrated,' said Colefax drily. 'I know a lot of people *do* rave about them.' He couldn't resist teasing Boothby a tiny bit. His posturing was too absurd. Taste in wine was no longer an index of anything. Any pedant with the patience to wade through the colour supplements and the money to buy the videos could pose as a wine buff. He assumed that Boothby would now confess his dream of owning a vineyard. He imagined Cilla and Derwent up to their knees in a tub of must and grapeskins. Oenophiles, stamp collectors, trainspotters: there wasn't much to choose between them. Except stamp collectors and trainspotters never expected you to share their enthusiasm.

Taste in furniture on the other hand was something else. Boothby had an unerring eye for the worst reproductions. 'That Bulgarian stuff from Tesco's is *rather* good, you know,' said Colefax.

'Now I know you're pulling my leg, Barnaby.'

'No, really. It's ever so good.'

Cilla Boothby was regaling Patricia Colefax with her

husband's medical history. Mrs Colefax was whippet-thin and shared with her husband the aerodynamic face of the English upper classes. 'You show such a lot of patience. It's no surprise he's achieved all he has,' said Mrs Colefax, stealing a glance at her watch.

'It's kind of you to say so, Pat, but he was rich before he met me.' The wine and the compliments had made Mrs Boothby glow.

'Really.' *Pat*. Mrs Colefax winced imperceptibly at the contraction of her name.

'Who's for a little more wine?' said Boothby. 'Top-up, love?'

'Just a wee spot if it's going spare. Thanking you,' said his wife. She turned back to Mrs Colefax. 'You must know all about making sacrifices. Your husband's chosen such a demanding career. It can't have been easy for you either.'

Patricia Colefax looked at her earnest, pudgy face and decided it didn't conceal a malicious intention. 'At times, of course, it's absolute hell. But there's a great camaraderie among the wives. And the children are getting to the age when they can almost be relied upon.'

'That must be wonderful,' said Cilla, glancing at her husband, her glow dispersing a little.

'Now tell me, have you bought any more of those wonderful *objets d'art* for your garden?'

'Oh, Pat, I didn't tell you. When we had the workmen in to replace the french windows one of my little netsuke went missing.'

'What rotten luck. Do you think it was stolen?'

'I don't know what to think, Pat. I really don't.'

'I've had a good run in papers,' Mr Boothby was saying. 'There's no doubt about that, but I can't see myself doing it much longer. I often wonder if there isn't more I could do in the field of politics.' He twirled the wine in his glass. 'I expect that sounds far-fetched to you,' he said, hoping it didn't.

'We've always thought of you as one of our staunch allies,' said Colefax, savouring his wine. The old twit *did* keep a good cellar. 'Our interests have always been best served by having a friend at the helm of an important newspaper group. Each person should do the thing he knows best. And no one knows local newspapers better than you, Derwent.'

'I know I shouldn't be trying to take on more responsibilities at my time of life. I'm too old for politics.'

'I wouldn't say that. Look at Reagan, seventy-odd when he was elected.'

'Yes.' Boothby nodded. 'Reagan.'

'It's too early to rule anything out. On the other hand, these are difficult times for us, Derwent, as I don't need to remind you. We're counting on the help of able, well-connected men like yourself. Of course, there's no doubt that our relationship transcends the grubby realities of politics and what have you. But I've got to be honest with you: I don't think I'd be in the position I'm in without the support of your papers. The pundits love to say that gentrification delivered this constituency into our hands. You and I know that's rubbish. I worked for it, and I worked to hold on to it. I'd say that "Cold Facts from Colefax" has certainly played its part in that.'

'The column's gone down very well with our readers.'

'Sorry to butt in, love.' Cilla put her hand on her husband's shoulder and addressed herself to the politician. 'Are you absolutely certain you won't stay for dinner?'

'We'd love to, but it's the boys' half-term and we promised this would only be a quick drink.'

'Pity,' said Derwent. 'You should have brought them along. Cilla loves kids.'

'They're at that awkward age when they stand round looking scruffy and a bit grumpy all the time. Seb's been pestering us to buy him an electric guitar,' said Patricia Colefax.

'I can't understand it,' said her husband. 'Wasn't there a time when boys his age dreamed of representing their country in the Olympics?'

'At least we were spared the penis sheath this time,' said Patricia Colefax, as their car swept up Trinity Road.

64

'Boothby was dropping heavy hints about going into politics.'

'Really?'

'It's absurd.'

'He's just not the type.'

'What was it Eisenhower said?' Colefax put on a nasal whine in imitation of what he took to be an American accent. 'He may be an asshole, but he's our asshole.'

'Is that what he said? I wouldn't call him an *arsehole*, exactly. Maybe a buffoon.' She looked out of the window. 'You've got your little soap-box in his awful paper.'

The wheels of the car crunched onto the driveway. Patricia Colefax got out. 'I told Hugh that I'd go over one or two things with him at the office,' said her husband. 'I shouldn't be long.'

The car rolled back off the drive as Patricia Colefax went into the house. It was just after eight thirty in the evening. Instead of turning towards central London, Colefax retraced his route back onto Trinity Road and headed south, past Tooting Bec station and on to Streatham.

Colefax smiled. '*Thanking you.*' How could you explain that to someone like Boothby? There were more complexities of tone than Mandarin. Striving too hard for the upper register, that's what gave the game away. It was thoroughgoing, bred-in-the-bone stuff. You could concoct a bogus version of it, but its patina was so false. It gave itself away like reproduction furniture. You could *buy* fine wines, but you would just make too much fuss about them. After all, it was just *wine*. You could buy netsuke, and penis sheaths, and the billiard-room of the SS *Eumenides*, but you couldn't buy taste, and you certainly couldn't buy class.

Colefax turned into a residental street and slowed his car to a crawl. A black woman in a sheath dress teetered over to his open window. She put one hand on the jamb behind his head, the other on the sill, and leaned over towards him, as though introducing her cleavage. 'Looking for business?' she asked, peering into the car. She could smell Colefax's aftershave and the expensive upholstery of the interior. Colefax nodded. 'You know the routine. Ten for a handjob, twenty for anything else. I don't do anal. Nothing without a condom.'

'I want you to suck my cock,' said Colefax. The hooker got in. 'I hope you don't kiss your mother with that mouth.'

She showed him where to pull up: far enough from the street lights so they would be concealed, near enough to her pimp, he supposed, so she wouldn't feel unsafe. He switched off the ignition and the lights. The fascia was glowing, the stereo was still playing quietly.

'Don't you want to get in the back?' she asked him. He shook his head.

The hooker slid her seat back to give herself more space, but she still had to twist awkwardly over the gear shift to dip her face into the pool of darkness underneath the steering column. She stuck her chewing gum on the dashboard and unbuckled his belt. Colefax leaned his head back on the rest as she slipped a condom, and then her mouth, over him. He closed his eyes but opened them again almost immediately.

The rapping on the glass startled the hooker who looked up to see Colefax's frozen face. The police officer was jabbing with his finger to indicate that Colefax should wind down the window.

'From the ancient lands of the Gillingas tribe in Ealing,' wrote Horace, 'to where the Berecingas held sway at the eastern end of the District Line, the Rambler's London holds many secrets. This is one. Trevor Diamond, founder of Fox Outreach, crouches behind a dustbin . . .'

'I take it that's the last we'll be seeing of our friend Colefax,' said Harvard. Horace looked puzzled. 'Have you not heard the cold facts on Colefax? He was found in a car with a tart who was brushing her teeth with his todger. You've not met him, I take it, otherwise you'd be taking more pleasure from his downfall. How about this: "dry man in spectacles once ruled the Holy Roman Empire"?'

'Otto,' said Horace, without looking up. He had begun to receive the first dribbles of correspondence from the Rambler's

66

readers. Some contained usable queries, but an equal number were just disconnected and sad. They should have a column of their own, thought Horace: the ramblers. 'I don't think I know the fellow you're talking about. Does he work here?'

'No, no, laddie. He's a friend of Boothby's. You should know him. He's your MP.' Harvard caught sight of the news editor making his way across the room. 'Pratt. I'd like to volunteer my services for the Colefax story.'

'We're not touching it . . .'

'For fuck's sake, why on earth not?'

'Instructions from Boothby. Nothing I can do about it.'

'For crying out loud . . .'

'I've got something else for you.'

'You've got something bigger, I suppose?'

Pratt soldiered on in a weary voice. 'I've got something *else* for you. Murder in Surbiton. There's a presser at two. I'd like you to go down to the scene now and see if you can pick up some colour. Witnesses, relatives, background. Horace, you can go along too, if you want.' He retreated to his glass cubicle to read the papers.

'I don't believe it. This a huge story right on our doorstep, and we're not touching it because of *Boothby*? No disrespect to your uncle, but that's just ludicrous.'

'Great-uncle,' said Horace.

It was after eleven when Harvard and Horace arrived in Surbiton. The man had been killed in a parking lot just off the high street. A camera man and sound man were already by the cordon, hurrying to get pictures of the crime scene before it was cleared up. A hessian mat covered with blood lay on the tarmac and beside it a man's shoe. There was blood on the bodywork of the two nearest cars. Horace hung back as Harvard accosted a policeman he knew.

'Detective Inspector Crabbe?'

'Guilty as charged.'

'Can you give me an idea of what happened?'

'We'll have a full briefing at two. I'm afraid we can't release the name yet because we're still trying to contact the next of kin.' Horace couldn't take his eyes off Crabbe's moustache, which was bristly and orange like the kind of caterpillar children keep in jam-jars and feed lettuce.

Harvard could feel the camera crew hovering behind him. 'Put it away, boys,' he said. 'You'll have to wait until two.' As Crabbe wandered away, absently stroking his moustache, Harvard caught up with him. 'My deadline's passed, officer. This isn't going to get in the paper for forty-eight hours.'

'It's Harvard, isn't it?'

'That's right. *South London Bugle*, for my sins.'

'What can I tell you? The bloke's name was Till, Derek Till. He was thirty-six. Just moved into the area. Staying at the YMCA up the road. Nasty business – we think it must have been two men. Injuries were very severe – basically he'd been stamped to death. His face had come away from his skull.'

'Employed? Unemployed?'

'He was an electrician, but we're pretty sure he was on the fiddle. That's obviously off the record.'

'Was it a robbery?'

'That's the best guess. We know he left the pub after eleven and went to take twenty quid out the cashpoint.'

'Twenty pounds?' said Horace.

Crabbe plucked at the orange caterpillar and nodded.

'Is it worth us staying for the presser now?' said Harvard.

'We should have a photo of him by then, if you want one.'

'We'll hang about in that case. You're not in a hurry to get back, are you, Horace?'

'Not me.'

'Let's go and see where he was living.'

The two men wandered over to the YMCA building. 'It looks like he was a newcomer to the city,' said Harvard. 'Probably drinking by himself. He staggers out of the pub and heads off to the cashpoint to get out twenty pounds for a kebab. Between the cashpoint and wherever he was going, he ends up getting kicked to death. It's not one of our uplifting stories.'

'Awful,' said Horace, shaking his head. 'Awful.'

The YMCA was spruce and anodyne. The woman at the reception desk was putting flowers in a vase. 'I wondered if you knew anything about Derek Till?' said Horace.

'Is he a guest here? I'll check his room number for you.'

'Never mind,' said Harvard, butting in. He said to Horace, 'I'll buy you a coffee.'

'What was that about?' said Horace, when they were sitting down in the café.

'What's the point? What's she going to say when you tell her he's dead? "Murdered? Oh, how awful. What paper did you say? He was a quiet bloke, hadn't been here long. Not many friends, really, no."' Harvard sighed. 'Maybe when I was your age, I would have pushed it.'

Horace stirred his tea. What about the killers? he wondered. Did they mean to kill him? Could you kick someone to death by accident? Had he fought back, instinctively, or because he was drunk, provoking their fury? Some token resistance had enraged them: 'Think you're hard, cunt?'; the two of them jumping on his face until his skull cracked.

'Is your job always this depressing around here?' said Horace.

Crabbe rehearsed the details of the murder for the other journalists in a tiny briefing room inside the police station. They'd all been given colour photocopies of Till's picture: pallid, smirking, lank blond hair.

'The victim was taken to the hospital shortly after midnight,' Crabbe was saying. 'Regrettably, the medical personnel were unable to revive him.' One of the younger journalists sniggered.

Horace looked at Harvard for an explanation, but Harvard shrugged. 'She's laughing now,' he whispered to Horace. 'Then she'll go back to the newsroom and call it a tragedy.' But on reflection, he decided she probably wouldn't. To qualify as a tragedy it needed more pathos: children burning to death with their mother, that sort of thing. The silly smirk in the photo fitted no kind of tragedy Harvard knew. Who knew the genre of Till's death?

'We do know he'd recently ended a relationship. He'd split up with his partner and moved down here,' said Crabbe.

'When you say "partner",' Harvard asked, 'is that male or female?' The other hacks turned and looked at him.

'I mean his wife,' said Crabbe.

The television reporters clustered around Crabbe for one-to-one interviews after the press conference ended. Harvard recognised one of the print journalists on the edge of the throng. 'Still chasing ambulances?' he said to her. 'I thought they'd have given you a column by now.' They kissed formally on both cheeks.

'Hello, Harvard. Look, I'm just about to file. Are you rushing straight off?'

'I'm in no hurry.'

'Five minutes. I'll buy you a drink.'

'That'll be two drinks.' Harvard pointed at Horace, who was still sitting on one of the plastic chairs and reading the press release.

'What's he wearing?' said Jocasta.

'Horace has a style of his own,' said Harvard. 'You go and do your stuff. We'll wait.'

Jocasta sat in the corner of the room with her shorthand pad and mobile phone. She was wearing a long beige raincoat that seemed a little too loose for her. She chewed a lock of her hair as she dictated her notes to the copy-taker. She spoke in a low voice. Harvard could only hear her when she signed off and tossed back her hair. 'Right, that drink.' She was in her late twenties, early thirties – just like her salary, thought Harvard – and still pretty, in that public-school way, with her overgrown bob and masculine confidence.

'I've just emerged from hibernation,' Jocasta said, taking a sip of her pint. 'Two weeks of night shifts. I look terrible. Too much coffee, too many cigarettes.'

She did look older, Harvard thought. 'This is Horace, by the way. Horace, Jocasta.' Jocasta glanced at him and nodded. Harvard went on: 'Are you enjoying yourself, though?'

'Not really. I always dreamed of working on a national. Now I've got it, I wonder if I can really go on doing this for the rest of my life.' She looked across at Harvard, remembered how old he was and added, 'There's nothing *wrong* with it. I just wonder if it's *me*.'

'Well, you're not missing anything at the *Bugle*. Nothing's changed.'

'No new blood? You're not tutoring any hungry young protégés?'

'Just Horace here.' Harvard winked.

Horace was lost in his own thoughts. He had slipped the photo of Till out of his pocket and was toying with it.

Jocasta lit a cigarette. 'Tell me everything you know about Colefax. I want every last detail.'

'You know as much as we do. He got nicked for soliciting.'

'But in Streatham! I thought they had escort agencies for people like him.'

'It's a bit baffling, I agree. Maybe he was just after a quick handjob.'

'Blowjob's what I heard.'

'That's what I heard too. I'd always suspected his sexual tastes were more deviant.'

'Why?'

'Just a hunch. I had him down as a ligature and amyl-nitrate man.'

'Please.'

'Boothby's forbidden us to touch it at any rate.'

'Can he do that?'

'Not really. But you know Pratt.' Harvard suddenly looked tired.

'He is a miserable git.'

Horace was still staring at the photo. He finally spoke. 'Horrible story, this. The stamping.'

Jocasta shrugged and drank her beer. Harvard didn't like to see that in her: the hack's machismo – suffering is ordinary.

'I liked your question about the partner,' she said. 'Very lateral.'

'Look at his face, smirking away,' said Harvard. 'He doesn't know he's going to leave his teeth in a parking lot in Surbiton. Poor sod. You wonder what it means.'

'Oh, Harvard.' Jocasta made a face. It wasn't her squeamishness. It was her sense of the boundaries of the job. 'You won't find the meaning of life in Surbiton, I'm afraid.'

Lakshmi was planted in front of the television set watching an Australian soap opera. As she heard the door opening behind her, she managed simultaneously to switch it off and bury her nose in a chemistry textbook. She looked up from it with an air of distraction, then saw who it was. 'Oh, all right, Horace.' She turned the set back on and let the book drop into her lap.

Horace had been composing questions for the Rambler's quiz challenge. Few readers had bothered entering the last one. Pratt had said the questions were too difficult. Now he wanted the wording of the questions to include the answer. 'Can I try something out on you?' said Horace.

'Go on, then.'

Horace read out his question. 'The urban fox (*vulpes vulpes*) is a common sight in many of London's gardens. What is its Latin name? Is it: (a) Mr Wolf, (b) Reynard the Rox, (c) *Vulpes vulpes*?'

'Do you think I'm an idiot?' Lakshmi was indignant. 'I know what a Latin name is. Don't take me for a fool.'

'I think that's the reaction I needed,' said Horace. 'Thanks.'

Lakshmi had relaxed her guard and hadn't noticed her father's footsteps in the hallway. 'Lakshmi, you are watching television.' His tone was accusing.

'No,' said Lakshmi. 'Horace was. I just came down to ask him a question. Thanks, Horace. Later.' Lakshmi smiled at her father and went up to her room carrying her textbook.

Horace was staggered by the fluency of her lie. To contradict her would be cruel, but to acquiesce in the untruth, he sensed, would make him her ally. In the end, he said nothing.

'It is time for our grudge match.' Mr Narayan had begun to set up the Scrabble board in front of the television set. He wanted revenge for the humiliation of *quartzes*. The soap opera ended. The news was on.

Horace reached into the sock and plucked out a handful of tiles like broken dentures and began to rack them up. Television was still a novelty to him and he found aspects of it curiously baffling, news in particular. The reporters looked as though they'd been abducted from respectable jobs and forced to participate in the making of the newscast. He could only guess what threats, what cajoling it took to make them appear, with their glum, pasty faces, in the dark and foul weather, outside banks and offices, blinded by painfully strong light.

As for the newsreader, Brent Deal, who was renowned for his barking hostility to interviewees, Horace always got an impression of the man's boredom, as though this fuelled the celebrated aggression of his interview technique: the truculence of a caged animal that will snap at any hand – friend or enemy – that comes too close to its bars.

'Do you allow "re",' asked Mr Narayan.

'What do you mean?'

'With a verb – *redo, revisit*.'

'Of course,' Horace said absently. He was trying to follow an item about the death of some members of a suicide cult. Several of them had tied themselves to breeze blocks and jumped off a car ferry in the Black Sea. Two of the cultists, who were based in Odessa, had come from Woking. A spokesman for the Orthodox church was explaining that such behaviour could only come about through fundamentally misunderstanding religious doctrine. A woman who described herself as a deprogrammer was suggesting that such misunderstandings in themselves shed light on the human need for religious beliefs.

Horace looked at the board. 'Rewoo?'

'Aha,' said Mr Narayan. 'You have already given your permission.'

'Rewoo?'

'She refused to marry me so I tried to *rewoo* her.' Mr Narayan smiled.

Brent Deal moved on to summarise the day's other news while Horace tinkered with his tiles. High winds in America had grounded passenger aircraft for the second day running and destroyed the orange crop in Florida. A tiny explosive device had been sent to the offices of London Zoo.

'Now more on tonight's top story,' said Brent Deal. 'The London MP who insists he won't resign after being charged with kerb-crawling.'

Mr Narayan looked up from the board.

'I owe it to the voters who elected me . . .' Barnaby Colefax was saying. 'There is not one shred of truth to these allegations. I reject any suggestion of impropriety.' He was standing at the front door of his house. His wife stood tearfully next to him, holding his hand. 'That's all I have to say for now. I ask you for the sake of my wife and two small boys to respect my family's privacy. Thank you.' Colefax disappeared into his home.

The Select Committee met in an oak-panelled room that overlooked the Thames. Colefax sat at the back in the chair nearest the window. There was, he thought, a paradox inherent in the price of riverside property. The choicest buildings on the north side of the Thames invariably overlooked ghastly modern eyesores, lighter quays, or frozen storage depots. To get a decent view you had to be on the other side. He glanced around at his colleagues. They were all listening to the witness.

'No doubt harmonisation requires some concessions in this area. I'm not contradicting you there. But on the whole, we feel that the proposed changes go too far.'

Colefax slipped out to go to the lavatory. It had been a bad forty-eight hours. The most terrifying thing hadn't been the press, baying outside his front door for him to come out and make a statement – though that had been bad enough. Undoubtedly the worst thing had been Patricia, picking him up at the police station, her mouth so tight and bloodless it looked as though it had been closed from the inside with a vice. She had driven him back in total silence. That was the other indignity – when breathalysed he had been over the limit: Boothby and his sodding fine wines.

If he had been a sober nobody it would have been so much easier: the summons would have plopped discreetly onto the doormat with the morning's letters, a guilty plea entered, the fine paid, the offence forgotten. But someone at the police station had recognised him and tipped off the press – probably for a handsome fee. Public servants were being bought and sold like share options, thought Colefax with disgust.

It was too bad to be ruined for a moment of carelessness. Well, it was too bad to be ruined for a second moment of carelessness. Colefax had come through his first moment of carelessness unscathed.

Colefax's previous indiscretion had been with a young researcher called Hilda. One evening he found himself deep kissing her in his office after she had gone in to ask his advice about further steps to a career in political consultancy. He had a vivid recollection of lying on his desk with his underpants around his ankles, collapsing like a windsock, and feeling foolish and old.

It had occurred to him then that sex was only the physical embodiment of something more abstract and far more satisfying. You could really only have sex with one person and then only for a relatively short period of time. But you could have politics with thousands of people, most of them unknown to you, for year after year after year. *That* was erotic.

He had slept with Hilda twice after that, until he realised, with a shock, that she was in love with him. The fear that she would press extravagant demands on him, or need intimacy (the one thing that could be evaded in a relationship with the electorate *en masse*) precipitated just the crisis he had hoped to avoid. He panicked, backed off, made her hysterical, and she sent two of his notes to a friend at a national paper.

Colefax insisted it had been nothing more than infatuation on both sides and had gone no further than a couple of passionate kisses. It was a ludicrous and implausible assertion, and everyone believed it. By accepting money for her story, Hilda was considered to have sacrificed her credibility. And with the unlikely claim that he had merely kissed and cuddled her, Colefax retained his.

So there was no telling what you could get away with. Colefax took heart from that. From the moment the policeman's gloved hand had tapped the window of his car, his mind had begun to work. The expensively acquired maxims of a public-school education began to sound in his ears: heads down, bully and shove. 'I was passing this way and she flagged me down, officer. I thought she was in some kind of distress.'

The policeman had not tried to conceal his scepticism. 'If I had a penny for every time I heard that, my friend, I'd have taken early retirement by now.'

'I can quite see how this must look to you,' Colefax had said. But when soothing failed, he tried braying. 'Do you think that the only explanation for a white man being in a car with a black woman is that she's a prostitute? Is that what you think?'

Unflappably, the policeman had answered, 'I've got bad news for you. This *is* a designated red-light district. This woman *is* a prostitute.'

'That's not true. That's simply not true. Is it?' Colefax appealed to the hooker, who answered him only with a look of contempt. He had continued protesting his innocence, the volume of his indignation all the greater because he knew it was groundless. But he had listened carefully when she gave her name: Raylena James.

'Raylena James,' he said out loud, as he flushed the lavatory. He looked in the mirror. At least his face gave no indication of the depth of his anxiety. That was encouraging. What he needed now was a small miracle: a double six on the dice of fate. He walked back to the committee room. The doctor was still waffling on, but now he found the tedium consoling. No one gave him a look as he resumed his seat.

'In the rest of Europe, the chief vector of rabies transmission is the fox. The animals form a kind of wild reservoir for the virus, which occasionally overflows into the population of domestic animals.'

Colefax's attention wandered again. He had in front of him a letter of commiseration from Boothby, assuring him of Boothby's confidence in his innocence, promising that his services to the newspaper would continue to be welcomed in the future.

The doctor was not a bad-looking woman, Colefax thought, eyeing her again. Nice bosom. There was a word you didn't hear any more, but *breasts* didn't really do it justice. It was like a coastal shelf. On the other hand, she did have the affectations he abhorred in professional women: the drab clothes, the humourlessness, the cheerless efficiency.

'There's already firm evidence that the single market has had adverse effects on the health of our livestock. The warble fly is an excellent example . . .'

With his chin cupped in his hand, Colefax glanced at his colleagues. He gently opened the *South London Bugle* and skimmed through his own column, then his eyes settled on a piece that began: 'From the ancient lands of the Gillingas tribe in Ealing, to where the Berecingas held sway at the eastern end of the District Line, the Rambler's London holds many secrets. This is one.'

# PART TWO

# CHAPTER SIX

THREE MONTHS AFTER their first meeting, Horace went to see Trevor again in Deptford. This time, nine or ten cardboard cat crates were lined up between the front door and the entrance to the sitting room. Horace had to slide along the wall to avoid stepping on them. In addition to the doggy smell he remembered from his last visit, there was an unfamiliar sharpness in the air. Trevor had another crate open on the floor in front of the television. He put on a pair of surgical gloves and scooped up a tiny fox cub in one hand. 'These are to stop cross-contamination,' he said.

The cub lay belly-up in the hammock of Trevor's palm. Its fur was a bear-brown, soft and tufty around its oddly bulbous head; its open eyes were slightly glazed and as dark as blueberries; its tiny tail curled between its legs like an apostrophe. Trevor dabbed at a scratch on the animal's side. 'I'd say he's got a seventy/thirty chance. I'm not so concerned about the wound as such. The thing that concerns me is that he's not defecated for a while.' He pronounced it *deefecated*. 'That's the first time I've seen him actually have a tiddle.' He lifted up some of the paper in the box. Urine had soaked right through it. 'My God, that's a tiddle and a half.'

Horace put on surgical gloves and held the cub while Trevor changed the bedding. He sniffed its warm head: it had a spicy tang like brandy-soaked Christmas pudding. He could feel the heat of its body through the plastic gloves. Trevor took the cub back and began to feed it whole sardines from a can. Cradled on its back, the cub munched loudly at the fish, spraying scales and flakes of flesh on its fur.

'Do you think he had brothers and sisters?' asked Horace.

'Most definitely.'

'What do you think happened to them?'

'You can't be sure. It could be one of many things. Because it was a building site, it could have been the vixen transporting them to another earth, a secondary earth. And somehow he's escaped, got separated.' Trevor picked flakes of fish off the cub's fur, then he took a syringe full of milk and squirted it into the animal's mouth. 'You've spilt more than you took then, look.' He chided the animal, which flailed its forepaws, its tail quivering in protest. Trevor cleaned its face with a kitchen towel. 'All right, all right, come on,' he said softly. 'Calm yourself down, calm yourself down. Come on.'

Trevor turned the cub onto its stomach and patted its back. 'To all intents and purposes, I'm the vixen. I'm his mother. I'm the one that feeds him. I'm the one that cleans his shitty mess up. Basically, he's my baby.' He tweaked its nose gently. 'Dear me! Pardon me! Did you hear that? A big bubbly burp then.

Didn't you, kid, eh?' Trevor packed the cub back into the box. 'You just eat and sleep and crap, don't you, son? I'll just put you down and you can go for a nice little sleepy-byes.'

'I've just got the one at the minute, but I've had nine at once – imagine, nine of the buggers.' Trevor had three hours before he needed to be back for the next feeding. He and Horace were walking down Tooley Street.

'See that?' Trevor continued. 'That's where the Jubilee line is going in. There used to be three earths in there. They brought me in to relocate them.'

Horace peered through a gap in the plywood siding; inside was a pocket of wilderness. The plants had run wild. Huge bushes straggled over clumps of masonry. The land was uneven; parts of it fell away precipitously. An Irish workman had uncovered a plague pit here during digging for the new railway. The man had been taken to hospital and placed on an intravenous drip in an isolation ward. Three hundred years on, the bacteria might still be potent. That same dig had found a five-hundred-pound German bomb from the Blitz; a dud that had plunged too deep into the soil of the city to be retrieved. The past was buried three feet deep under the tarmacadam and the highways of the new city.

The two men reached a pub a few hundred yards along from the building site. Horace bought them each a pint of stout.

'I had a run-in with a JCB driver, he was from Gloucester or something like that.' Trevor began mimicking a West Country accent. ' "If oi zee a fox, oi'll run it over with this." I told him, "You'll be breaking the law if you do. That's illegal under the Wildlife Act of 1911." ' Trevor took a sip of his beer. 'Tastes a bit grotty. They must have cleaned the pipes.' He jingled a roll of coins in his hand as he went over to the fruit machines and started playing. Horace stood behind him watching. The machine winked and gurgled as Trevor smacked its buttons, then it spat out coins. He worked it with concentrated atten tion, feeding it money with one hand, burping it constantly with the other.

'Do you know a bloke called Colefax?' said Trevor, as he scooped out tokens from the trough.

Horace said he did.

'I thought you might. He called me up, a few months ago, after that first article you did on Fox Outreach. He said he was keen to come out, meet me, and what have you.' The machine regurgitated a single coin.

'What did he want?'

'He wants Fox Outreach to support him on this wildlife project he's working on.' Trevor's eyes remained fixed on the machine. 'He made what I would call a *substantial* donation. He's going in the newsletter as one of our official patrons.'

'Who are the others?'

'There's just him at the moment.' Having disposed of the last of his coins, Trevor reclaimed his drink from the top of the fruit machine. 'Fancy a game of pool?'

'Colefax was caught in a car with a tart,' said Horace.

'He didn't talk much about that,' said Trevor.

'I'm not surprised, it'll take a bit of explaining.'

Trevor drank his Guinness fast, Horace had to choke his down to keep up. He had never been much of a drinker. Nor was he much of a pool player. After a few shots, Trevor would dominate each game for long stretches, potting ball after ball, while Horace trailed his cue and pint around the pub, looking at the framed photos on the walls.

They dropped the subject of Colefax. Trevor talked constantly, reminiscing about pets and wildlife, excoriating fox hunters, commenting on his own performance at the pool table. But the fourth pint of beer seemed to throw a switch in his head. He became loud and irascible while discussing a report he'd seen on the news that evening. A thirteen-year-old English girl had met and married a Turkish waiter on her first holiday abroad. 'I bet all the Muslims in this country will be saying it's all right to marry a thirteen-year-old girl – a thirteen-year-old child. Child! Horace, you can't say it's all right to marry a thirteen-year-old girl.' He frowned and muttered inaudibly as he lined up his next shot.

To Trevor it seemed that England was a citadel of normal values that the rest of the world was besieging with its crazed and perverted ideas. 'My sister and brother-in-law are going to Turkey. I was supposed to go with them. But I won't now, not after this.' He emptied his pint with a gesture of disdain. 'In Spain, right, there's this village where once a year they throw a goat – a live one, mind – off the church tower.' He looked at Horace incredulously. 'I mean, where's the sport in that? These are supposed to be civilised people.'

'You can say what you like about Colefax,' Trevor added. 'But his heart's in the right place.'

Horace caught the bus home from New Cross Gate. Now that he knew the streets better, he sometimes wondered what route he had taken on his first night in the city. But the streets he knew now bore no relation to the streets he remembered. It was like trying to recapture the pang of bafflement he had faced looking at a printed page before he could read. The mysterious routes of that evening three months before had resolved themselves into the banal patterns of his everyday journeys. Occasionally, his work required him to venture out of familiar areas and the city would open up to him again, revealing vast, unexplored spaces: the *terra incognita* of a new continent.

Since the day of his arrival, he had never regretted coming to London, but there was a curious flatness about his new life. He tried as much as he could to fill it up with work and routine. He would wake up early in his draughty flat-room, dress and go to the Café de Paradise, where he had had breakfast on his first day. He would eat beans on toast, drink a cup of watery coffee, and read two or three newspapers from cover to cover. Mr Pratt had encouraged him to believe that anyone working in newspapers should pay close attention to national and international events. As a result, Horace acquired a working knowledge of two or three Balkan conflicts, learned the names of the chief ethnic groups squabbling in parts of the former Soviet Union, and he mastered the arguments *pro* and *contra* the independence movement in French-speaking Canada. But he never had the opportunity to discuss these subjects with anyone, as no one else seemed to know what on earth he was talking about; certainly not Pratt, and not even Mr Narayan.

Nonetheless, once it had got going, his newspaper reading became obsessional. He found it increasingly difficult to read one that was not pristine, going to the lengths of concealing whole sections of the newspaper in his drawer at work in case anyone should see them on his desk and ask to borrow them. The order in which he read the stories became a matter of great importance: first the front page, then sport on the back page, then the rest. Never having watched a game of football, he was able, from the match reports, to sustain a convincingly well-informed conversation with Harvard, who was an ardent Leicester City supporter. Often he would be struggling through chess reports and obituaries at night, finishing one day's edition just as the presses in Wapping were churning out the next.

Reading the foreign pages of the *Globe*, with their far-off datelines and obscure warlords, he felt as he had in Great Much, remote and invisible, as if real life was going on somewhere else. And for all his concientious interest in the world, and the business of getting up and going to work each day, he was still aware of a hollowness inside him that he couldn't fill up with newsprint.

Trevor had decided not to tell Horace everything about his meeting with Colefax.

On their first meeting, the politician had welcomed him into his tiny office and showed him the clipping of Horace's article.

'Bloke who wrote that's a mate of mine,' said Trevor.

'Really? Well, I found it most interesting. Shall we go and get something to drink?'

As they walked to the bar, Colefax bantered with Trevor about his work. He bought them both a drink and they sat down.

'I don't know if you're aware of this, Trevor,' said Colefax, lowering his voice, 'but your urban foxes do have an impact on a

86

piece of legislation we're looking at at the moment. The present government is thinking of scrapping our anti-rabies laws.' He watched to see how Trevor would react to this information: his eyes were attentive behind the lenses of his dented spectacles. 'Now, as I understand it, under any system there's a small chance of rabies entering the country. If it did, there's a small possibility your foxes would get infected and pass the disease on.'

'There's no way rabies is getting into our country,' said Trevor. *Your foxes*, he was thinking: he liked that. 'We've got the toughest quarantine laws in the world. They've been highly effective for decades.'

'Some people think they're too draconian,' said the politician.

'What I say is if it ain't broke, don't fix it.'

'Precisely, Trevor. You're speaking my language. Now, my feeling is that someone needs to speak out against this bill. But I can't do it on my own. I need help. I won't beat about the bush. I need *your* help. I want Fox Outreach to get involved with me, so I'm making you a small donation.' He slid an envelope across the table. 'Five hundred pounds, in cash.' He lingered on the word *cash* to make a hushing sound. Trevor's adam's apple bobbed up and down twice, but his face remained expressionless.

Colefax leaned back in his chair and took a sip of his beer. When he spoke again, the volume of his voice was louder. 'I think I read in the article that you do deterrent work.'

'That's right.'

'What sort of thing does that involve?'

'It depends on the situation. Usually, we spray a solution around the affected area. Humans can't smell it, but it keeps the foxes away.'

'The reason I ask is that a friend of mind is having trouble with some foxes.' The politician leaned forward again. 'This is separate from the question of my donation. It would be a personal favour to me, Trevor. Please don't go and bruit it about to your friends in the media. A little discretion would be best.'

Colefax paused. 'Her name is Raylena James.' He waited for a flicker of recognition. The name had been all over the papers. There was none.

'Doesn't sound like it'd be a problem.' Trevor licked lager spume off his lip.

'She's not on the phone. But this is the address. Oh, and I'd appreciate it if you'd pass this on to her while you're there.' He handed Trevor another envelope. 'If it works out well, I should be able to find some more projects like this for you.'

Trevor watched Colefax take a sip of his beer. He knew a posh tosser when he saw one. But, he thought, there were posh tossers and there were posh tossers. 'As I've said, Barnaby, the foxes have to come first with me. If we can help each other out into the bargain, so much the better.'

'It's the foxes I'm thinking of, Trevor, believe you me. Believe you me.'

Trevor had been surprised to find that Colefax's friend lived on the sixth floor of a dilapidated mansion block in Streatham. It was just possible that foxes were raiding the dustbins on the higher levels, he thought, but it struck him as unlikely.

'I'm not talking to no press,' said Raylena James, when she answered the door. She was wearing tracksuit bottoms and a sweatshirt. Trevor was struck by her eyes, which were pale orange like a vixen's. Her mouth was red, her skin yellowy-brown in the strong sunlight. Her hair was pulled back tightly over her scalp.

'I'm looking for a Miss Raylena James,' said Trevor.

'I told you, I'm not talking to no press.' In fact, Raylena was entertaining rival bids for her side of the story once the case had been through the magistrates' court.

'I'm not here from the press. What it is is I've been asked by a friend of mine to come and give you this. Name of Barnaby Colefax.' Trevor handed over the envelope that Colefax had given him. Raylena turned away to tear a corner off the package.

Inside was a small wad of cash. Trevor went on, 'Mr Colefax says you've been having a bit of trouble with foxes.'

Raylena looked at him in puzzlement. He didn't appear to want to elaborate. His silence drew her out. 'Foxes? Oh, yeah, right. Foxes.' She kissed her teeth. It must be some obscure code for journalists, she thought.

'This near the common you probably get one or two.'

'Yeah, you do.'

'Where have they been, then?'

'Where have what been?'

'The foxes.'

Raylena looked puzzled again. 'You know, just around.'

'They like to go through people's rubbish, taking out bits and pieces. They'll go for absolutely anything. Omnivores.'

'Yeah, right. They do.'

'I've just never heard of them coming this far up to do it.'

'Well, you know what they're like.'

'I reckon I do, after ten years on the job. Best thing is if I go have a look round. I'll see if I can't deter the little buggers.' Trevor smiled and removed his jacket. Under it, he was wearing a T-shirt that revealed two armfuls of faded blue tattoos. He thought it was most probable that a couple of foxes were coming in from earths on the common, scavenging from the estate's dustbins and caching what they couldn't eat in the flower-beds. 'See you in a bit,' he said, and disappeared down the stairs. They were 1930s flats, built around a central patch of grass with a refuse area on each level and huge cylindrical dustbins on wheels at the foot of the stairwell. It took him over an hour to spray all these and the flower-beds. He came back to Raylena's flat with his wand and aqualung. 'That should do the trick. You can make my job easier by making sure you and your neighbours don't leave any rubbish out.' She watched him curiously from the doorway. 'Now, your friend Mr Colefax is paying me to help you out,' he said. 'But Fox Outreach survives solely on voluntary contributions, so anything you can spare would be very much appreciated. The job requires a lot in the way of raw materials, what with the cubs being born now. There's no obligation, of course.'

'Actually, Mr Colefax should be making a contribution on my behalf,' said Raylena, coolly.

'Is he? Oh, he didn't say anything about that.'

'Well, I've written him a note to remind him. Could you make sure he gets it?' She handed him back the original envelope, resealed with Sellotape.

'Not a problem. As I say, the main thing is to avoid encouraging them. They're persistent buggers.'

She stood on the open walkway watching him descend to his car and drive off the way he'd come.


The day after seeing Trevor and the fox cub Horace went into the empty office.

'In on a weekend, Horace? They must be keeping you busy.' The weekend news editor occupied Pratt's usual position by the round table. He was a genial man called Mr Sneasby and he smoked a pipe. It always surprised Horace how much more pleasant the newsroom seemed when Mr Sneasby was in, placidly smoking his Player's Navy Cut and watching the television.

Horace had heard various rumours about Victor Sneasby. One was that he had been a high-flyer on a national newspaper but had lost his job after a libel case. Someone else said that his wife had run off with a female aerobics instructor. If either of these things was true, they didn't seem to bother Mr Sneasby. True, his hands shook when he cleaned his pipe, and he talked to himself when he thought he was alone in the newsroom, but he was easygoing and Horace liked him.

'Working me into the ground, Mr Sneasby,' said Horace. 'Cup of tea?'

'Better not. Horace. Doesn't mix with my medicine.' Mr Sneasby kept his medicine in a flask in his jacket and diluted it with water from the cooler. 'What's the Pratt got you doing, then?' he asked, with one eye on the television.

'I'm just finishing off my column.'

'Oh, yes.' Mr Sneasby looked at his watch. 'Horace, could you keep an ear on the phones? I want to nip out for five minutes.'

'No problem.'

Horace spent the next hour writing about the tribulations of the orphaned fox cub. He put the finished copy on the sub-editor's desk along with one of Trevor's glossy photos of a cub being hand-fed (not the same one, but what did it matter?). There was still no sign of Mr Sneasby. While he was waiting for him to come back Horace picked a letter at random from the pile in his in-tray. 'Dear Rambler,' it said, in fragile, spidery hand-writing. 'My husband and I have been lucky enough to be visited by the most marvellous family of badgers, who have dug a sett near the bottom of our garden. We are both retired people and we feel privileged to be able to watch these beautiful creatures, particularly now that my husband's health is not what it was. To think that tormenting them is considered a sport!'

It was a strong candidate for the star letter, Horace decided. It exhibited a reasonably cogent train of thought and no obvious psychological disorders – unlike the letter from the man in Esher the previous week who had described in great detail how he had dismembered his neighbour's dog. Horace had forwarded that one to the police.

'Star Letter' had replaced the Rambler's Quiz Challenge. It had become clear that almost the only person who was entering the quizzes was a young boy from Croydon who called up several times each week to leave his answer on the machine under a new name, with a disguised voice, but an identical address. He'd won the competition eight times before Pratt realised what was going on.

Horace was beginning to worry that he would be late for Lakshmi when Mr Sneasby appeared in the newsroom. He gave Horace a hug. 'A monkey on the gee-gees, Horace. This is a red-letter day for me. Thanks for holding the fort. I won't forget it. Here you go.' He stuffed five ten-pound notes into Horace's breast pocket.

'I can't accept this, Mr Sneasby.'

'Nonsense. Big win on the horses. Think of it as an agent's commission.' Mr Sneasby wandered off towards the water cooler, humming to himself.

Lakshmi and Darrell were waiting for Horace by the statue of Edward VII at Tooting High Street. Horace and Darrell shook hands. The three of them went by Tube into the West End.

'Darrell's coming along as a consultant,' said Lakshmi. 'He knows more about men's fashions than I do. Where do you want to start?'

'I don't need much. Probably just a pair of trousers and a sweater,' said Horace.

'That's for starters,' said Lakshmi. She turned to Darrell. 'What do you reckon?'

'It depends what kind of *look*, you're going for. You get me? I mean, *my* look's not necessarily the same as *your* look.'

'I'm just going for the normal look,' said Horace. 'The normal one is fine. You know, that really can be a good look.'

'The normal look?' Darrell looked puzzled.

'Oh, yes.'

'You're bluffing!'

'Gridlock for Men,' said Lakshmi. 'Come on.'

Horace liked almost all the clothes he saw in Gridlock for Men. He hadn't imagined they would be so colourful and so different from his own clothes. 'They're all so lovely,' he said, carrying an armful of crisp clothing over to the changing room.

'Peacock blue, that's a good colour for you, Horace,' said Lakshmi, adding another pair of trousers to the stack.

When Horace emerged from the changing room, Lakshmi and Darrell burst out laughing. 'No, Horace. They're too small,' said Lakshmi.

'If you get trousers like that, man, they've got to be really *bagging* out. Like mine, look.' Darrell opened his jacket to show what he meant. The crotch of his trousers reached almost down to his knees.

'You've got four trousers' worth of material there, Darrell.'

'That's what's *cool*, Horace,' said Lakshmi.

'I didn't say I wanted to be cool. I said I wanted to be normal.'

'You'll never be normal, man.' Darrell was chuckling and covering his teeth with his hand.

Lakshmi slapped his shoulder. 'Shut up, you. Horace, try these ones. Ignore him. He's just taking the piss.'

When Lakshmi had first mentioned the shopping expedition, Horace had worried it would be an imposition. Now he realised it had become a kind of game. Lakshmi, who was so often sullen with her father, was enjoying being in charge for a change, and Horace found that he enjoyed her fussing. It made him think of Trevor clucking over the baby fox.

'Here you go, look.' She held up another pair of trousers.

The three of them prolonged the game. 'What about these?' said Horace, knowing that Lakshmi's reaction would be one of feigned horror.

For his part, Darrell seemed content to let Lakshmi take charge. But Horace noticed her looking at Darrell often, and he wondered if perhaps the whole expedition had been arranged to impress him.

Horace ended up buying more than he anticipated. When he brought the clothes up to the counter, the sales assistant asked him to write out two separate cheques. Horace took out his cheque book and Lakshmi and Darrell fell silent. They seemed like children again.

Lakshmi wanted to go to the Ritz for tea, but they went to a café in the crypt of a church on Piccadilly instead. Horace had tea. Darrell had a soft drink and Lakshmi had a cappuccino, which she stirred but didn't taste. When Darrell went to the toilet, Lakshmi suddenly became serious.

'Listen, Horace,' she said, 'I've got a really big favour to ask. It's my dad's birthday on Monday and I wanted to get him a really nice present to make up for all the arguments we've been having lately. If you don't want to, just say. I'll understand. But I promise I'll pay you back.'

93

'How much do you need?' said Horace.

'I was thinking of a hundred pounds. I know it's a lot, but . . .'

'A hundred pounds?' It was a lot. But Mr Sneasby's gift would cover half of it. And Horace was keen to further the goodwill between Lakshmi and her father: the strife in the house was upsetting. He took out fifty pounds from the pocket of his jacket and added a further fifty from his wallet.

'Thanks, Horace.'

They sat quietly sipping their drinks until Darrell returned from the toilet.

On the Sunday evening, Horace went to play Scrabble with Mr Narayan. Mr Narayan was upset. He'd heard on the radio that a man he knew, a Tamil immigrant like himself, had been shot outside the offices of the newspaper he ran in Southall.

'I don't know what is wrong with this country,' said Mr Narayan. 'The English people are supposed to respect law and order. Here is a man who comes to this country with nothing. He's not even safe on the streets outside his home. You know what is wrong with this place, Horace? Families. There is no respect for families. It is becoming like the USA. Sex is a kind of national sport but families are nothing.'

'It was the Indians who gave us the Kama Sutra,' said Horace, whose reading of erotic literature was as wide as his experience of the act was limited. '*Lingam. Yoni.*'

'That is nothing to do with it. I am talking about parents. Their children are running wild. They are bringing them up to believe that morality is irrelevant. No one is teaching them manners.' He thought of the furious tiny children who ran amok in the shop after school, stealing penny chews and calling him a Paki when he threatened to tell their parents. 'No one is teaching them geography.' He ruminated over his tiles for a moment. 'There, *wrath*. This is a good word for me today.' He put it down on a double word score. 'The question is decency. People in this country are not decent any more. It's a terrible shame.'

94

*Things are going badly in this wicked world*, Horace's grand-father would have said. The old man's disillusionment with politics had eventually soured his view of human beings, Great Britain and the world beyond it. For both him and Mr Narayan, the institution of a national lottery had incarnated the spirit of malignity that was abroad in the land. In fairness, Horace thought, Mr Narayan's position was undermined because he made money from selling the tickets he railed against. And how did his speech on decency square with the copies of *Asian Babes* that lined the top shelf of his shop?

'We are worshipping the wrong god. Everyone wants to get rich quick. We are worshipping Mammon.' The level of indignation on this last outburst increased as Horace laid down his tiles to make *temblor*, clearing his rack for an additional fifty points and forming *la*, *on* and *re* were it abutted *anent*. 'Temblor?'

'It means a tremor.'

'Pass me the dictionary.' There was a hasty rustling as he searched for the entry. ' "Tremblor, chiefly US." *Chiefly US*.'

'Chiefly. That doesn't mean it's American,' Horace countered. Mr Narayan gave him a sceptical glance and he felt obliged to add, 'I let you have "anent".'

'Anent is not an Americanism.' Mr Narayan's eyes were wide with indignation.

'No, but it's pretty obscure.'

The old man felt under siege. He riffled through the dictionary, and stabbed the page with his finger. 'See, it's here. "Anent".' Then he paused. Horace looked at the entry.

'It says "archaic or Scottish",' said Horace.

'Okay, fine. No "anent" – but then also no "temblor".' He began plucking the tiles off the board one by one.

# CHAPTER SEVEN

'YOU ARE AN underworked, overpaid moron,' said Pratt, who was blustering around the office like a tiny hurricane. 'I'll have your fucking job for this.'

Victor Sneasby stood, ashen-faced and trembling, filled with self-reproach. 'I didn't realise, I didn't realise,' he kept repeating, and looked up occasionally as if trawling for a sympathetic glance from the faces at the table. But if no one shared Pratt's sanguinary taste for public humiliation, they weren't keen to side with one of his victims either.

Horace felt nothing but shame. He had natural sympathy

with Victor Sneasby. After all, wasn't it the most human thing of all not to fit in? Didn't Pratt realise that failure was the prerequisite of redemption? Sneasby's incompetence was precisely what proclaimed his humanity.

'Where the fuck's Harvard?' said Pratt. 'He's fucking late.' He waved his hands in the air. 'Is there any chance of getting some real journalists in here?' He looked at each of the downcast faces. 'Horace, you go outside and wait for him. Brief him on the way there.'

Horace was glad to have an excuse to leave the office. Outside, it was another overcast London Monday with a blank white sky that seemed to bleach the colour out of the city below it. He waited on the steps of the building. He was wearing a pair of new trousers, his walking boots, and a canary yellow tracksuit top that rustled when he moved.

'Pratt wants us to leave straight away,' he told Harvard, when he caught sight of him walking towards the offices from the Tube station.

'I want a cup of coffee. What's the rush?'

'Sneasby missed the Southall shooting,' said Horace. 'He must have gone home early, or he was whooping it up after his win on Saturday. Anyway, the point is he didn't raise anyone, so Pratt needs us to go over there now. I think you'd better drive.' He held out the car keys.

'Typical Sneasby,' said Harvard, opening the car door and instinctively dusting the sweet wrappers from the driver's seat. 'The one day he clocks off early, a major story breaks. I bet Pratt's incensed.'

'Incandescent,' said Horace, and through force of habit began calculating the word's Scrabble score.

'It's Pratt's fault. He should never have hired him,' said Harvard. 'Sneasby's ready for the glue factory.'

'Don't say that,' said Horace. 'He's all right. He's got the most boring job in the universe. Anyone would make mistakes in his position. It's a miracle he stays awake.'

'I'm not blaming Sneasby. I've nothing against him as a

human being. I just think he's the wrong person for the job. And we've got him because we won't pay enough to get the right person.'

'Do you want me to map-read?' said Horace.

'I can find Southall with my eyes shut,' said Harvard. 'But it's always a shame to miss the morning meeting. They're so bracingly informative.' He looked at his watch. 'Do we have time to stop off at Mister Egg?'

'I don't think so. Pratt told me to get a move on.'

'Wrong. There's always time to attend to your bodily needs. Pratt's your boss, not your feudal overlord.' Harvard pulled in to a drive-through Mister Egg and ordered a sausage and egg sandwich. 'Did you say Sneasby had a big win on Saturday?'

'He said he won a monkey and he gave me fifty quid.'

'The jammy git.' Harvard drove forward to pick up his food. 'By the looks of things you blew the lot on clothes.'

'What do you think?'

'In all honesty, I'd have to say that jacket was a bit bright for murders.'

The offices of the *Dinakaran* were in an end-of-terrace house just off a main road in Southall. The police were beginning to remove the cordon of blue and white tape as Harvard and Horace arrived. Bunches of flowers were propped around the front door along with pictures of the editor, who had been shot dead as he brought down the building's steel shutters at the end of the previous day. Drips of blood were still visible on the darkened glass of the windows. A young camera man was backing away from the front of the building to frame up a shot of the wreaths. 'Watch your feet,' Horace found himself saying, but it was too late. The man had planted one of his hiking boots in a pool of congealed blood. He didn't notice anything amiss until he turned round to see Horace looking at him in horror. The camera man went to scuff the blood off his shoes on a patch of grass at one side of the building.

Harvard opened the door carefully and went into the

reception area. Horace followed close behind. The room was cheaply wood-panelled and carpeted, and it smelt faintly of incense. A calendar with a picture of Ganesh the elephant god hung above the receptionist's head. Harvard introduced himself to her and asked to speak to the acting editor. The building was hushed with grief and the rustling of Horace's jacket was the only audible sound. Eventually, a young man appeared from one of the doors at the rear of the room. He said the acting editor was busy and introduced himself as the dead man's son. His eyes were bloodshot from crying. 'We've been told by the police not to say anything to the press. I think they're going to give you all the details themselves,' he said, in a hoarse voice. 'I'm sorry.'

'I quite understand.' Harvard had lowered his voice respectfully. 'I was hoping you'd be able to give me some background information about your father. Our readers won't necessarily know who he is.'

'Yes, of course. We've prepared a life history.' He whispered with the receptionist. 'Here's a photo as well.'

The piece of paper covered one side of A4. It explained how Mr Vadarajan had come to London from Sri Lanka, penniless, in the 1960s. He had worked in menial jobs and borrowed money to start the first issue of the paper which he had edited for thirty years. The résumé stressed his love of the Tamil language and literature. In addition to editing the paper, Vadarajan had written poetry, translated Tamil classics into English and campaigned against the Sri Lankan government's treatment of its Tamil citizens. The son wanted to say more. 'It was a professional job. I saw the body. It was a professional job.' He spoke with a kind of quiet anger, shaking his head.

Vadarajan's son took the two journalists on a tour of the building. It had a ramshackle feel. Unpainted plywood doors separated the rooms. Odds and ends of carpet and linoleum covered the floor. At the top of the building, the editor's desk stood empty, while in the basement, the presses were turning out an emergency edition of the paper. Mr Vadarajan's face on

99

its cover, in thick horn-rimmed glasses, moved along the conveyor belts and was bound into stacks by the print workers.

'This is half the normal length. Usually the cover is in colour,' said the son, his grief giving way for a moment to professional pride.

Horace took one from the conveyor belt. Its incomprehensible Tamil script was broken up with adverts in English for local businesses. The last page was entirely in English. It was headed 'Matrimonial'.

'As you know, Mr Vadarajan was the owner and editor of the *Dinakaran*. It was quite a controversial newspaper and took stands on a number of political issues. There has been speculation that Mr Vadarajan was killed because of his political views, but at this time I have no evidence at all to support this.' The police officer was reading haltingly from a press release that had been given to all the reporters. 'Our community liaison officers are pursuing various lines of enquiry. Other theories include a robbery that has gone tragically wrong or, indeed, something more personal to Mr Vadarajan.'

'Isn't that the girl from the stamping story?' Horace whispered.

'Where? Yes, you're right.' Harvard gave her a wave. Jocasta was sitting two rows in front of them. When the press conference ended, she came over to speak to Harvard.

'What line are you going to take?' she wanted to know.

'Well, it must be political, mustn't it? Politics of the subcontinent spilling onto the streets of London, blah, blah, blah,' said Harvard, following her out of the police station. Horace was some way behind them and walking slowly because he was studying the press release.

'You say that,' said Jocasta, 'but the guy from PA said they thought there might be a link with other articles they carried.'

'What sort of thing?' said Harvard.

'Trial reports. Rape trials. Apparently the editor identified the victims.'

'That sounds very unlikely,' said Harvard. 'Where did he get this?'

'He said one of the press officers told him.'

'I don't know,' said Harvard. 'There's a whiff of racism about it.'

'Well, he's going with it. My newsdesk is going to ask questions if I don't at least mention it,' said Jocasta.

Horace caught up with them. 'This might sound like a strange suggestion,' he said, 'but my landlord knew Vadarajan. I think we should get him to write the obit. I'm sure he could say a lot more about him than we could.'

'That's not a bad idea at all,' said Harvard. 'Why don't you give him a ring?'

'I'd lend you my mobile,' said Jocasta, 'but the battery's flat.' Horace went back inside the police station to use the phone. 'The last time I saw him,' she said, 'he looked like he'd just got back from a spot of fly-fishing. Now he looks vaguely trendy.'

'I'm not sure about those new trousers,' said Harvard. 'They're very baggy.'

'I think they're rather *street*,' said Jocasta. 'So – any more gossip about Colefax?'

'Nothing substantial . . . rumours.'

'Let's hear them.'

'Ridiculous stuff. The tart was a transvestite, that sort of rubbish.'

'Can't rule it out.'

'Come on.' Harvard took one of her cigarettes.

Jocasta lit it for him. 'His case is going to be coming up soon,' she said.

'Colefax's? Well, you'll want to get your name down for that.'

'Not a chance. The newsdesk would never let me cover anything that interesting.'

Horace read out the biography over the phone. Mr Narayan kept asking him to slow down, but Horace could tell from his fussing that he was flattered to have been asked to write for the *Bugle*.

'How long should it be?'

'Around four hundred words.'

'Do I have to count every single word?'

'No, of course not. It needs to be about a page long,' said Horace. 'By the way, happy birthday.'

There was a brief silence. 'My birthday is in June, Horace.'

'Really? I must have mixed you up with someone else,' he said, knowing that he hadn't. He hung up the phone and walked back to Harvard and Jocasta looking slightly puzzled.

'Everything all right?' said Harvard.

'Yeah, he says he'll do it.'

Harvard stubbed out his cigarette. 'Good. Jo and I were just saying that we should pay another visit to the *Dinakaran*,' he said.

The three of them went back to the offices of the newspaper. One of Vadarajan's daughters brought them a cup of tea each while they waited to see the acting editor. The drinks had been sweetened with sugar and flavoured with cardamom.

The acting editor was on the phone when they went into his office; he indicated that they should take a seat. Almost as soon as he'd hung up, the phone began to ring again. He ignored it.

'We wanted to ask you whether it was your policy to publish the names of plaintiffs in rape trials,' said Harvard. 'We've heard that this may have happened.'

The editor was almost shaking with anger as he said, 'What we do, we do within the limit of the law. If the law says we cannot print the victim's name, we do not print.'

'Is it possible that you could have printed these names by accident?' asked Jocasta.

'No. I tell you again: we follow the English law. I have answered four, five phone calls. They all ask me the same question. I give them all the same answer. Our paper is not different from yours: we must follow the English law.'

Trevor took the rigid corpse of a frozen mouse out of the deep-freeze and placed it on the carousel of the microwave. As it defrosted, its fur grew darker and damper. The microwave pinged. Trevor took out the soft little body and fed it to the remaining cub. 'There you go, my dove. That'll have to do you until I get back.' He burped the animal and tucked it up on its heat pad.

The relationship between Fox Outreach and Barnaby Colefax was turning out to be mutually beneficial. Trevor had been able to install a brand-new chest freezer in his kitchen and fill it with bags of mice and day-old chicks. His shelves were bulging with jerry-cans of lactol. He had also been able to buy a dark-blue bomber jacket that had 'Fox Outreach' stencilled on the back. He wore it whenever he went to Streatham to spray Raylena's bins and flower-beds, although he soon realised that the deterrent work wasn't the real reason for the visits. Today, he left the jacket hanging on a coat-hook as he walked out of the house. Colefax had urged him to look as inconspicuous as possible.

The traffic was light and he arrived in Streatham slightly early, but Raylena kept him waiting. She was clearly taking her time. Fifteen minutes late, she got into the car and they drove the rest of the way in silence.

The politician was waiting just inside a clump of trees. He spotted the two of them a long way off, moving slowly across the open parkland. Raylena had also tried to dress inconspicuously, but her interpretation of inconspicuous was out of place here in Richmond Park. She was wearing a skirt, a matching red jacket with executive shoulder pads, and celebrity dark glasses. She also carried a brand-new clutch handbag. The heels of her stilettos snagged in the undergrowth and threatened to throw her off balance.

'I think I'll let you two sort this out by yourselves.' Trevor floundered off into the bracken like a family dog until he was out of earshot of Colefax and Raylena.

'I suppose I'd better introduce myself properly, Ms James,' Colefax began, risking a trace of irony.

'I know who you are.'

'Then you'll also know I'm in a bit of a dilemma. I need your help,' Colefax knew he was making a convincingly imploring expression because he could see it reflected in the tinted lenses of her sunglasses, but her lips were pursed in an unyielding *embouchure*. Quite different from their last meeting . . .

'First of all, you already know I can be a generous ally. Let's walk through here.' The previous autumn's fall of leaves had lingered beneath the trees and scrunched under foot. 'The police officer is going to testify against me. They're notoriously credible witnesses. If I were to call you in my defence – and obviously I'll return the favour – what do you think you might be able to say?'

'I'd have to tell them the truth, the whole truth, and nothing but the truth, Mr Colefax, so help me God.'

'That's just it, you see. In my position, the truth isn't going to be an awful lot of use.'

'Well, anything else is going to come expensive.'

'It's not a part of the world I know much about,' said Harvard. The two men were back at the offices of the *Bugle*.

'I only know what I've read in the papers,' said Horace, feeling smugly well informed. 'There's a Tamil minority on the island. Some of them are campaigning for a separate state in the north.'

'Of course, the motive may not have been political at all,' said Harvard.

'It's unlikely, isn't it?'

'I don't know. The rape stuff is very far-fetched. I think they may have just chucked it out at us to waste our time. Perhaps they want to offer us a choice of motives. I reckon the police would be uncomfortable if everyone was sniffing around the same patch.'

Horace nodded.

Harvard had seen him from the beginning as his professional antithesis: watchful and unworldly. He had no qualities that would recommend him as a journalist to someone like Pratt, who admired grit and bluster. But Harvard thought they might make something of him yet.

Harvard had seen hundreds of hard-faced young men and women, fresh from college or journalism school, serving an obligatory six-month stint on the paper as though it were a penal colony; or like young consuls, posted to some fetid African capital, sitting it out in the hope of more glamorous and lucrative assignments later on. Most could barely conceal their eagerness to leave. All quickly grew bored with the grind and the repetition: the death knocks, the door steps, the police calls. 'It's a great training,' they all said. But a training for what?

Each Sunday, Harvard would open the papers to read articles by his former protégés on how heroin was replacing after-dinner mints at commuter-belt dinner parties; how the coming millennium was affecting the behaviour of pets; how modern professional couples were giving up the stresses of the work-place for penurious but fulfilling self-sufficiency – this, by journalists who were immolating themselves with work and caffeine and alcohol and God knew what else.

'As a training? Oh, it's the best.' But he knew that they were wondering what on earth he was doing, the best-trained middle-aged man in local news, stuck in an endless apprenticeship and never graduating to the big money and the fatuous subjects. And he wondered himself.

His evident contentment was almost a sufficient explana-tion. Of course, he could have earned more elsewhere. But Pratt and Boothby respected his presence. He was paid more than anyone else because they saw his old head and his experience as an asset. He represented the kind of newspaper they would have liked to have been running.

During her training on the paper, Jocasta had been the pushiest interrogator, asking why he had stayed so long, why he didn't leave. The reasons he gave were good ones, he thought, but still not the real ones.

'Aren't you ever going to move on?' she had asked. They were at the Taurus Arms. Jocasta drank pints of lager – another mannish attribute he put down to her private education.

'What do you want to do when you leave here?' he said.

'Go to a national. Report for a bit. I don't know. Specialise maybe. Write a column.'

'Right: write a column, do longer pieces. Features?'

'That sort of thing.'

'Don't you ever wonder why the one thing that journalism is supposed to be about – newsgathering – is the least respected part of the profession? All the trainees we get want to be opinion-formers, pundits, celebrity interviewers. But the actual business of going out, knocking on doors, talking to coppers, who does that? The agencies, the local papers. Us. Most of the nationals don't even send on three-quarters of the stories I cover.'

'That's because they're small stories.'

'Partly. But it's also because they'll just take their coverage off the wires for nothing. The money they save doing that will pay for a few pars of a celebrity columnist, or a piece on garden furniture, or hormone replacement therapy.'

Jocasta blew out smoke impatiently and said, 'That's good editing. Gardening's the nation's number one pastime.'

'I wonder where you read that.'

'And as for HRT, if you were a woman, or married, you'd be less flip about it.'

'Fair enough. But who is writing those agency stories? Inexperienced young reporters working for peanuts and jaded old hacks like me. You've seen it: "What are we going to call the daughter, then?" Some of it's pure fiction. It's as though you went to dinner at some fantastic restaurant, paid a fortune for your meal. It's brought to your beautiful table, beautifully served, elaborately presented – but the food itself is just some muck that's been sent from the takeaway. And as for TV – it's where old ideas go to die.'

'I see. So you are, what? Wholesome food in modest surroundings?'

'There are worse things to be. It's your round, by the way.'

Jocasta came back from the bar and settled the over-full pint glasses on the table. 'The thing is,' she said, 'does any of it matter, you know? Really, in the end, does it? I don't think so.'

'Of course it does,' Harvard had said, 'of course it matters.' But it was quite the most disturbing thing he'd ever heard from a trainee, and he had thought about it a lot afterwards.

Horace was different. He seemed to take the order of things for granted. There was no chafing, no unresolved ambitions. He seemed content. He manoeuvred himself to resist the demands of his employers, but unconsciously, like a weather-cock turning its smallest target to the wind. He never questioned Harvard's longevity on the paper, so Harvard didn't have to either.

'This murder,' Harvard was saying, 'it's an amazing story. Something like this comes along every few months. It makes up for all the puff pieces and the routine crap. It's why I do this job.' Horace nodded, and Harvard almost believed it himself.

'You're not growing a beard, are you, Horace?' said Harvard.

Horace had bent down to loosen the lace of his boot. After three months, they still pinched at the ankles, but he'd grown fond of them because they were the only thing that still connected him with Jana. 'Toying with the idea, why?'

'It's been my personal experience that facial hair has very little to recommend it,' said Harvard.

'Well, my grandfather had a beard all his life and it didn't seem to bother him.'

'For left-wingers of his generation, I think it was *de rigueur*.'

'How did you know he was left-wing?' said Horace, straightening up and wiggling his toes inside his shoes to restore the circulation.

'Joseph Littlefair, the communist?'

'That's right.'

'He was a fairly big wheel at one time. *They Call Them Soviets*, and all that. Oh, I've heard of him, all right.' Harvard rolled up the paper in his typewriter to read back what he had written. '*Littlefair*.' He savoured the word. 'If we'd ever had commissars in this country, I suppose Littlefair would have been as good a name as any. *Chairman Littlefair*. It has a certain ring to it.'

'Better than Chairman Machine, anyway.'

'Machine is a good Ukrainian name,' Harvard protested. 'Mashin, it should be, strictly. There are lots of us Ukrainians in Dundee. Harvard is just the way my parents anglicised Arvad. It's also the closest I've come to a university education.' Harvard typed a few words and then seemed to add, inexplicably, 'My mother's side of the family wore Russian jewellery.'

'Jewellery?' said Horace.

'No, *Jewry*.' Harvard looked up from his typewriter. 'What the hell's that noise?'

From the hall outside the newsroom, the sounds of two raised voices grew louder. One a woman's, swooping in protest, the other a man's, incomprehensible, but gruff and furious. Everyone had turned to watch the double doors at the back of the newsroom, which swung open suddenly and banged against the walls. Mrs Doolaly retreated into the room; advancing on her was a short red-faced man with a moustache. He was waving a piece of paper in her face.

'What's this all about?' He slapped the piece of paper with the back of his fingers. 'Twenty-five fucking quid it's cost me. I've got a stack of books I don't want. What are you going to do about it?' Mrs Doolaly's mouth was an O of outraged surprise as he pressed his face close to hers. 'Eh?'

The man stood there in his multicoloured drawstring trousers and scanned the room. His stocky torso was crammed into a cut-off sweatshirt that displayed two arms as meaty as sides of ham. On the front of the sweatshirt was a cartoon of a wild-eyed gorilla with a mallet in each hand pounding a rickety castle of barrels and ladders.

'I'll get the editor,' said Mrs Doolaly, her faint voice only audible because of the silence that had descended. From where Horace sat, he could see a roll of red fat bunch up at the base of the man's head as he swivelled it to look round the room. His hair was shaved all over except for a tiny rat-tail at the back. He looked like a furious, middle-aged child.

'Which one of you is the Rambler?' said the man.

Harvard caught Horace's eye. 'I am Spartacus,' Harvard whispered under his breath.

'What did you say?' said the man, approaching the desk with a muscle-bound waddle. Horace looked over to see Mr Pratt in the glass bunker of his office. Mrs Doolaly was in there with him, gesticulating with both hands. Pratt peered worriedly out at the newsroom.

Horace stood up. 'I'm Horace Littlefair – the Rambler.' He realised, with some relief, that he was almost a foot taller than his irate visitor.

'So you're the genius who thought this up?'

'Do you want to tell me what the matter is?' asked Horace.

'The matter is, I'll tell you what the matter is, that's the fucking matter.' The man waved the piece of paper in Horace's face. 'I've come down to fucking sort this out once and for all.' His eyes were bright windows onto the laboratory of stimulants that was feeding his rage.

'Look,' said Horace, 'would you just calm down?' Then the man's hammy fist caught him on the chin and laid him out among the scuffed carpet tiles.

Mr Narayan sat by the cash register with the brand-new notebook he had taken from the small shelf of stationery items and a biro. The notebook, which was still completely blank, lay on top of a stack of evening papers.

He hadn't known Vadarajan well, but he had seen enough of him to like him: a cheery man with a booming voice and a taste for bad puns. An Anglophile, he made it seem for a moment as though an expatriate with friends could enjoy the best of two cultures and not occupy the sad hinterland between them. His murder seemed to refute all that.

*Vadarajan.* He wrote the name in the curlicued syllables of his own language. The language that Adam spoke: that was how Vadarajan used to describe it. 'It must be, because it has no origin. No one knows where they come from the Dravidian languages.' Malayalam, Telugu, Kannada, Tamil: languages without origin were, Mr Narayan reflected, appropriate for people who had been uprooted.

He hadn't had a chance to start writing until now. But now he had the chance, he had begun to daydream instead. At Mamallapuram they had swum by the submerged temples. He had been proud of his cosmopolitan new bride in her swimsuit. The local women went in wearing their saris and came out with them bedraggled, like wet cats. They had visited relatives in Vellore. Workmen threw up a haze of dust over goggle-eyed carvings of tormented deities. They played carom under the whir of the porch fan. That was the last visit: then Africa, fatherhood, exile, London . . .

He had just begun to write when Madhu came into the shop. He set down the pen. 'Have you seen your sister?'

Madhu said he hadn't. He'd been at the market and was carrying a string bag of leftover vegetables. 'She's probably upstairs already.' There was a conventional front door beside the entrance to the shop, but most visitors to the house, Horace included, stopped at the shop before going up.

'Wait here for a moment.' Mr Narayan went through the back room to reach the stairs. There was no sign of Lakshmi. He went into her bedroom, with its secular shrines to the gods of music and hygiene. It wasn't until he opened the cupboard that he realised clothes and possessions were missing.

Madhu was about to put the exercise book back on the shelf to be sold when he noticed that the first page was marked. Under the incomprehensible squiggle that was the dead man's name,

Mr Narayan had managed three words of his abortive tribute. In black ink on the first line of the first page he had written: 'This terrible loss'.

# CHAPTER EIGHT

'YOU SHOULDN'T HAVE told him to calm down,' said Harvard. 'You should never tell anyone to calm down.' There was no parking available at the magistrates' court so he and Horace had caught the bus to Lavender Hill. It was still before nine and the upper deck was crowded with schoolchildren shrieking and laughing.

'But I *wanted* him to calm down,' said Horace.

'Of course you did. But you have to go about it another way. *Calm down* is guaranteed to inflame the emotions. It's like *Don't worry*, or when a girlfriend says, *Don't get me anything for my birthday*. It's designed to send the opposite message. You should say, "I see you're angry, Mr Towton. How would you like me to help?" Then after he thumps you, you say, "Thank you for caring enough to share that with me."' The bus was locked in the immobile traffic. 'This is going nowhere. Let's walk. How are you feeling, anyway?'

Horace opened and closed his mouth. 'Jaw's a bit stiff when I chew still.'

The driver let them out with a wheeze of the pneumatic doors. It was a day of intermittent sun, and a cold breeze stirred the grit on the pavements of Clapham Junction. The traffic was stationary for the two hundred yards from the foot of Lavender Hill to the courthouse. As they walked up towards it, the reason for the jam became obvious: a large van stood with its emergency lights flashing, blocking the narrow road outside the court. Two men in jeans and windcheaters were unloading equipment from the back – a camera, lights, a huge grey microphone like a Horse Guard's bearskin. Other reporters were already in position by the entrance: television reporters with big hair and trenchcoats; underdressed radio reporters weighed down by their bulky tape recorders; burly snappers wreathed in cameras; spotty agency journalists in bright ties and cheap new suits.

Harvard went over to a dark, stocky man with a protuberant stomach who was chatting on a mobile phone. He motioned a greeting to Harvard as he wound up his conversation and put the phone back in his jacket pocket. 'Harvard, mate. Long time no see. I thought I saw one of your boys here already. Not like you lot to send two reporters where one will do.'

Harvard introduced the man as Terry Took. He was in his early forties and dressed in a smart charcoal suit. 'We're not covering it,' said Harvard. 'We're appearing.'

'In the Colefax case?' There was something voracious in Terry's surprise. His thick dark fingers flexed over the pocket with the mobile phone, like the hand of a gunslinger hovering over his holster.

'No, no. Horace got punched by an irate reader. We're here in case he pleads not guilty. Have you got a list?'

'Oh, yeah, here you go.' He pulled out a scroll of paper from his inside pocket and handed it over to Harvard. 'Must have been quite a story. Investigation?' He nodded at Horace approvingly.

'A telephone quiz. There was a misunderstanding.' Horace looked down the list. Each page listed the morning or afternoon's business in each of the four courts. 'Towton, Common Assault' was in Court Two.

'That doesn't have the overnights,' said Terry. 'Colefax is in Court One. They've got about six different soliciting cases. He's third on the list. But the press gallery is going to be chocka.' There was a sudden commotion on the pavement behind him. 'Excuse me, gents, the pig fuck is about to commence.'

A swarm of photographers and cameramen gathered by the edge of the road as a car pulled up and disgorged Barnaby Colefax.

'This way, Barnaby.'

'Over here, Barnaby.'

The politician made his way through the flash guns and the chirruping autowinders. On the fringes of the rolling maul, cameras were held up over the heads of the crowd and snapped at random. There was a frantic determination among the TV camera men to capture every step of the twenty-yard walk from the car to the door of the building. Horace could just make out Colefax's tanned face between a tangle of arms and heads and cameras. A sound man shepherded a camera man who was walking backwards up the steps at the head of the crowd, fending off photographers with his elbows.

Once Colefax had disappeared, the scrum dispersed, regrouping briefly when one of them yelled, 'Is that the tart?' at a well-dressed black woman who was crossing the road to the public library. While the press pack was diverted, Raylena James was able to enter the building unrecognised just behind Horace and Harvard. Horace held the door for her.

'I'm obliged,' she said, giving him a flash of her newly capped teeth. She was soberly dressed in a black suit with a single string of pearls.

The three lay magistrates sat in front of a blue velvet drape with the lion and the unicorn perched three feet above their heads. Court Two was lit by vertical neon columns; one end was attached to the ceiling, the other sprouted a clutch of spotlights like jets on a rocket. There were six of these. High up, small square windows let in the bluer natural light of mid-morning.

Horace and Harvard sat inside the visitors' box at the rear of the courtroom, separated from it by angled slats of thick glass. Wire-mesh-covered tiny speakers were set into the wall in front of them, but Horace's had been glued up with frayed pink chewing gum. Someone had carved SUPAMAN into the wood veneer beside it. The court itself was a maze of wood-veneer pulpits.

One of the ushers brought Brian Towton into the dock. He was wearing a light grey suit. Its trousers were too long and bunched up over his shiny black shoes like a new school uniform but the boxy double-breasted jacket was an oblong of well-filled cloth. He entered the court with downcast eyes and stood in the witness box looking contritely at his feet. All that Horace could see of his attacker was the thick neck and the tassel of hair on its nape, around which Towton's head had been freshly shorn.

Both the prosecution and the defence lawyers sat to the right of the court in charcoal suits. The prosecutor was a fair-haired young woman. 'The facts in the case are these.' She spoke quietly. Horace sat forward to hear. 'At eleven o'clock in the morning on the thirtieth of April the defendant entered the premises of the *South London Bugle*, a newspaper, situated at 224 Upper Tooting Road. The defendant was shouting, resisted requests to remain in the lobby and demanded to speak to the Rambler, the pen-name of Mr Horace Littlefair, an employee of that paper. When Mr Littlefair made himself known to the defendant, the defendant continued to shout and use profanities. Mr Littlefair asked him to moderate his language, whereupon the defendant struck him in the face, causing him to fall down. The defendant was restrained and the police were called. Mr Littlefair was treated for cuts and abrasions.'

The litany of facts, spoken in monotone, seemed to Horace like the description of a different incident. He remembered lying on the carpet tiles, gazing up at the bottom of his desk, and wondering who had bothered to carve 'Chelsea FC' into it. Harvard and two other journalists hadn't needed to restrain Mr Towton, who didn't struggle but stood there, a stocky and awkward hydrant of spent rage. By the time the police arrived, the pain in Horace's jaw had subsided and he was being consoled in Pratt's office by Mrs Doolaly, who pressed tea and biscuits on the officers as they took statements.

Towton's lawyer stood up to speak. Like the prosecutor, he delivered his lines with the woodenness of a bad actor. 'Sir, my client has pleaded guilty. I have spoken to him, I can tell you he is thoroughly ashamed of what he's done and by pleading guilty he's spared Mr Littlefair the ordeal of testifying. In mitigation of the offence, can I say that my client is a man of limited means. The assault took place after he received a phone bill that showed his son had incurred almost twenty-five pounds in charges from calling a phone quiz run by the *South London Bugle*. I don't mean in any way to diminish the seriousness of the attack . . .'

Horace remembered the quiz questions with a pang of embarrassment.

'. . . I don't know if you are familiar with these telephone lines, but the procedure is that they charge well above the standard rate for a telephone call. Mr Towton was angry that he'd been charged for calls made by his son without his knowledge. He appreciates that what he did was wrong, he knows he overreacted and he is heartily sorry for the injuries he caused Mr Littlefair.' The defence lawyer passed a list of Mr Towton's previous offences to the presiding magistrate.

'Is Mr Towton presently employed?' the magistrate asked.

The defence lawyer conferred with his client. Towton's fat neck bent over the edge of the dock as the lawyer whispered in his ear.

'Yes, he is, sir. He is responsible for security at an establishment in Croydon called Wide Tony's Nite Spot.'

'What is his bail situation?'

'He has unconditional bail, sir. I have spoken to my friend and she agrees that the fact that Mr Towton lives in Croydon with his wife and young son, close to his job, makes it unlikely that he would abscond.' The prosecuting lawyer nodded in agreement.

'The child – that's the son who made these telephone calls to Mr Littlefair?'

'That is correct, sir.'

'Definitely a steroid abuser. You can tell by his shape,' said Harvard, collecting a soft drink as it came thunking out of a vending machine outside the courtroom. 'Roid rage. It could have been a lot nastier. Sure you don't want one?'

'No, thanks. I don't like the bubbles. What happens now?'

'We go back in. The magistrates postpones sentencing, pending reports. Everyone goes home. We might as well stay and see it through to the bitter end.'

In Court One, the public gallery was full. An usher had already ejected two journalists who had failed to find seats in the press gallery and were trying to crouch on the floor. 'No standing in the public box, you'll have to leave the court.'

One of the reporters stared at a small elderly man sitting in the seat nearest the door and drew a twenty-pound note out of the leaves of his shorthand pad. 'Fancy going off to the pub for an hour?' he whispered.

'Hop it. I'm warning you,' said the usher.

Upstairs, reporters were sharing seats in the press gallery, which overlooked the court. They were jammed in like passengers on a rush-hour bus and peered down onto the proceedings.

'As I said,' PC Woolrich was saying, 'after the defendant parked his car, we observed him in conversation with Miss James. Once I was certain a sexual act was taking place, I made myself known to the defendant and asked him to step out of the vehicle.' His voice was loud and slow in the muffled silence of the crowded court.

'You say a sexual act was taking place, Mr Woolrich. What sexual act, specifically?' Colefax's lawyer was tall and angular with a tiny head, like a giraffe. He had brilliantined hair and tiny polished spectacles that glittered like new coins. He looked at least twenty years older than the prosecutor next to him.

'Fellatio.'

'Fellatio. Oral sex?'

'That's right.'

'Very well. Then you saw the defendant's penis in Miss James's mouth?'

'I . . .'

'Didn't you?'

'It was clear what was going on.' There was a hint of annoyance in PC Woolrich's voice.

'With respect, *that* is what I'm trying to establish. It was very dark.' The lawyer turned to face the bench. The three magistrates were looking at him. 'The car had pulled up some distance from the street-light. You, Mr Woolrich, were standing by the window, looking into the driver's side of the car. Now, from where you were standing could you see the defendant's penis?'

'I had good reason – ' Mr Woolrich began.

'You couldn't, could you?'

'Not his penis, no.'

Barnaby Colefax was sitting about twenty feet further back. He could hear paper rustling above him in the press gallery.

'Mr Woolrich,' his lawyer went on, studiously addressing the policeman as though he were a civilian, 'how many people do you charge with soliciting on average – male and female – when you have a street under surveillance in this way?'

'It varies enormously. It depends on the weather, the time of year.'

'On average.'

'Four, five. Sometimes a bit more, sometimes a bit less.'

'Yes. Well, that would be the case with an average, I suppose.' Colefax's lawyer smiled at the magistrates. 'And how many people had you charged that night, before you came across Miss James and Mr Colefax?'

'On that particular evening, none.'

'None, Mr Woolrich?'

'No.'

'None at all? You had not caught a single one. That must be rather disappointing – to go to a great deal of trouble and have nothing whatsoever to show for it.'

'Not really. That happens a lot in police work.'

'You hadn't managed to charge a single person with an offence that evening – despite having this street under surveillance. Suddenly, an expensive car slows down. A young woman gets in – a young black woman. The car drives a little further. Then stops. Highly suspicious, you'd think.'

'Suspicious. Yes.'

'Mr Woolrich, did my client say anything to you when you were charging him?'

'I can't remember. He probably claimed he was innocent. A lot of them do.'

'Did he say, Mr Woolrich, "Do you think" – he was addressing you – "Do you think that the only explanation for a black woman being in a car with a white man is that she's a prostitute?"'

'Yes, I believe he did.'

'Do you believe that's the only explanation for a black woman being in a car with a white man?'

'No, of course not.'

'We'll have to take your word for that, won't we?' The lawyer paused to make a note of something on the papers in front of him. Then he resumed his cross-examination. 'Tell me, Constable

Woolrich, of the many people you have charged with this offence, what proportion have pleaded not guilty? Roughly.'

'Maybe five per cent.'

'So, say one in twenty. And of that number, how many have successfully pleaded not guilty?'

'Half that number, probably. Less.'

'So, let me see, once you've charged someone, the odds of you failing to secure a guilty verdict are roughly one in fifty. Fifty to one on, a bookmaker would say. Those odds are extremely favourable to you, Mr Woolrich, are they not?'

'You think it was roid rage?' whispered Horace, as Towton was led out of the dock for the last time.

'Very likely – as a contributing factor. Your quiz must have pushed him over the edge, though.'

'It wasn't the quiz so much as the phone bill,' said Horace.

'I went to an inquest last year,' Harvard continued, 'young body builder who'd been using steroids and taking E on top of it. He'd gone completely bonkers – he thought he was some kind of superhero. They locked him up but he banged his head against the wall so hard he went into a coma and died.'

'E?'

'As in Ecstasy. I thought you were part of the chemical generation?'

Horace looked puzzled. 'Not as far as I know.'

Harvard looked at him. 'The trouble with you, Horace, is that you've not had your wild years.'

'He started getting violent. He started swearing and stuff, and threatening me. He slapped me around, then he just snatched my purse and pushed me out of the car.' Raylena dabbed at her eye with a handkerchief. 'I didn't know what to do.'

'At that point, did you think of going to the police?' Colefax's lawyer had softened the edge in his voice.

'No.'

'Did it cross your mind?'

'Yeah, right, like they're going to believe a black whore.'
Both the lawyer and the witness glanced at PC Woolrich.

'So, if you didn't trust the police, what did you do after you'd
been beaten and robbed?'

'I just panicked. I ran out in the road. I was just waving my
arms. Then I saw this car.'

'Mr Colefax's car?'

'That's right.'

'So what did you do?'

'I shouted at him to stop. He pulled up and I saw who it was.'

'Who?'

'Him, Mr Colefax. I recognised his picture. I've always
admired him as a politician. I believe in the free market. The
way I look at it, I'm an entrepreneur, right?'

Colefax, who could hear murmurs from the press gallery, sat
with his palms folded together. Her improvisations were
making him uncomfortable.

'Go on.'

'I said, "Please, you've got to help me." I had cuts on my face
and stuff. And he said, "Whatever is the matter?" I told him I'd
been robbed and beaten and he told me to get in the car. But I
could smell alcohol on his breath, you know, and I wasn't sure,
because drinking and driving ain't right.'

There were more murmurs from the press gallery. Colefax
wondered if this was going too far.

'So you got in?'

'I got in and then just as we turned the corner, he started
going, "Ouch, ouch, ouch," like this.' She doubled up, simulat-
ing Colefax's agony. ' "My ulcer, you know, stress brings it
on." He was complaining about this pain in his stomach. And
he said he was going to have to pull over. He just sat there
groaning and I said, "Let's have a look." Right? Because my
sister's an aromatherapist. So I put my ear against his stomach
and I heard this terrible gurgling sound, like a washing
machine or something, you know. Anyway, the next thing I
heard was this rapping sound on the glass, and *he*,' she looked

at PC Woolrich, 'was saying, "Can you get out of the car, please."'

'What was Mr Colefax's reaction?'

'He got very angry, he was saying, just because I'm white and she's black doesn't mean she's a prostitute.'

'Was he doing up his trousers as Mr Woolrich testified?'

'No way, no. He was holding himself like this, where it hurt. His lower stomach area.'

'What did Mr Woolrich say?'

'He said, "She's a hooker, all right." And Mr Colefax was saying, "You're not, are you? Tell him you're not."'

'What did you say?'

'I didn't say nothing.'

'Why not?'

'I knew there was no point.'

The press had cleared a small space for Colefax on the steps of the courthouse. The sky had clouded over and the street was dark, but the politician's face stood out of the throng, picked out in the eerie golden glow of the television lights.

'The first thing I want to do,' said Colefax, 'is apologise. Twice. Firstly, for drinking and driving. There's no excuse for it. I undoubtedly deserved to have my licence revoked. I will be attending meetings of Alcoholics Anonymous. I hope my constituents can find it in their hearts to forgive me.

'Secondly, I want to apologise to a section of my constituents who I feel now that I have somehow let down over the years. I'm speaking of the ethnic minorities who make up such an important part of the life of this borough.

'When my wife and I first moved to this part of London in the early nineteen eighties, there was a lot of talk of police brutality, insensitivity to minorities, and so forth. I, along with a lot of other people, thought that it was just a load of nonsense. Well, I'd grown up to believe in the integrity of the British police force. And I know that, by and large, the vast majority of them are honest people of good character. But making the acquaintance of Miss Raylena James has made me realise that there is a tiny minority within the police force who seem determined to ignore the pleas of the marginalised members of our society – a minority, indeed, who will misconstrue and misrepresent them in the worst possible light.' Raylena stood beside him with her head bowed, wearing her sober clothes and her string of pearls. 'I want to apologise to those people,' Colefax went on. 'And I want to reassure them that, while I'm in Parliament, I will fight to make sure that every citizen, whatever the colour of his or her skin, gets the consideration and assistance it is the police force's duty to provide. We can't afford to be partisan on this issue. Thank you.' Horace, Harvard and Tony watched Colefax swatting the journalists away from him as he got into the car. 'That's all I have to say.'

'I'd say the tart's done quite well out of this whole thing, Tony,' said Harvard.

Raylena was talking earnestly to a couple of print journalists who had stayed away from the main scrum around Colefax's car.

'Too right. Everyone's taking this sort of ballsy, honest-whore line on it. I wouldn't be surprised if she cleans up after this.'

'. . . the consideration and assistance it is the police force's duty to provide,' Colefax was saying. On television, Horace thought, he looked more plausible, younger and handsomer, the cocksure angles of his face flattered by the camera. The clip ended and the bored angry face of Brent Deal returned to the screen.

'MP Barnaby Colefax with some stinging criticism for the Metropolitan Police. In a moment . . .'

The light from the television set was the brightest in the room. Mr Narayan had been sitting in semi-darkness when Horace came in, watching the programme with a look of resignation. An hour earlier he had been watching snooker with the same look and actually preferred the kinetic geometry of the coloured balls. It was reassuringly abstract. Following the patterns released him from his anxieties, if only in a momentary way.

Lakshmi had run away. That was the fact of it. Everyone knew it, but no one could mention it. It simply hung in the air, and the effort of ignoring it invested every routine with an awful labour. Forms were kept to: the deliveries taken each morning; the shelves restocked; meals cooked; dishes washed; television watched. But it all took place with a sense that it was dwarfed by this unspoken meaning.

After the late news, Horace and Mr Narayan played Scrabble. At first, they played quickly, indifferent to the outcome, scoring low points with each word. But since neither wanted to talk, they took longer and longer, gazing at the tiles, pretending to be absorbed in the permutations of the letters.

Horace muttered to himself, pronouncing the words in front of him. With the television off, the room was darker and oppressively quiet. It was his turn. 'Uke. Sky. Tsk. Keys. Keys.' He glanced up at Mr Narayan. His eyes were red. He had been crying. Horace looked down at his tiles. He felt worse because he was sure it was his loan to Lakshmi that had financed her escape; but he hadn't been able to admit this to Mr Narayan.

'I gave the photo to the picture editor.' Breaking the silence seemed to compel him to continue. He didn't want Mr Narayan to feel obliged to answer. 'It'll be going in tomorrow, in all the editions. They tend to get a lot of responses.' The tiles clicked loudly in the silence as he arranged them on the board. Downstairs, the side door banged open and shut and there were muffled thumps on the stairs. 'Ashok and Madhu are back.' Horace could hear the note of false levity in his own voice.

Variations of 'London MP Slams "Racist" Policing' were the headlines in most of the next day's papers. Madhu was unpacking boxes of sweets in silence as Horace took a copy of the *Globe* and left his coins on the counter.

The Café de Paradise had been closed down for refurbishment

so Horace bought a sandwich from the bakery and a plastic cup of coffee, which dribbled down his chin when he tried to drink it through the lid, and spilled and burned his fingers when he didn't.

The new editions of the *South London Bugle* and the other titles were arranged on the coffee table in the corner of the reception area, where the popcorn kiosk had stood in the days when the building was still a cinema. Horace picked one up and opened it. The photo of Lakshmi had come out rather fuzzily. Boothby's printing technology was old and ink came off the page. Employees quipped that it didn't even make good toilet paper.

Harvard was already at his desk. 'Did you hear about Pratt?'

'No, why?'

'Apparently – and this is not in the public domain yet, so keep it to yourself – he's out.'

'What?'

'The phone-quiz fiasco. When Boothby got to hear about it he went bonkers. Allegedly.'

'Really?'

'Well, you can imagine it, can't you? You can insult the reader's intelligence, but messing with their phone bill – that's out of order. It's the kind of concern he shares.'

'What about me? I wrote the questions.'

'No, no. You were wounded in action. You'll be mentioned in dispatches. Also, Boothby may be liable for any injury you suffered. I'd start affecting a limp if I were you.'

'That's good news for us, Pratt going.'

'I doubt it. Human history bears me out. Tyrants are generally succeeded by worse tyrants. And Pratts by bigger Pratts. Anyway, he still has to serve out his notice period. I'm sure Boothby wouldn't pay him a month's wages and get nothing in return.'

'Behind you,' said Horace, quietly. Pratt had arrived and was walking sheepishly across the newsroom with his briefcase.

'It's the dead-ball skills of McAllister that you want to watch.

They'll absorb the attack like a sponge and just hit them on the break,' said Harvard. 'Two words: passing and movement.'

'Morning, Horace, morning, Harvard,' said Pratt gruffly, as he passed them.

'Morning.'

'Morning.'

As soon as he was in his glass cubicle, Harvard continued, 'Have you read the organ today?'

'Glanced at it.'

'You'll enjoy this. Look.' He opened the paper at the centrefold with a flourish as though he was uncovering a salver. 'Da da!'

'Cold facts from Colefax.'

'He's back and he's bad. And think about this: he must have written this before he got off.'

Horace scanned the column. The text was similar to Colefax's speech outside the courthouse. 'They would have pulled it if he hadn't.'

'Oh, definitely. But it shows you how confident he was. The balls of the guy. Unbelievable.'

Derwent Boothby had chosen that morning to make one of his appearances at the office. As the owner entered the room, his employees began sitting up straight, typing and making phone calls. Boothby waved at Horace and came over to his desk. 'Horace, my lad. I was just telling Cilla that we must have you over to dinner soon. I've been very remiss.' Boothby lowered his voice. 'Listen, nasty business about the chap who burst in here.' He gave his nephew an avuncular pat. 'But at least you weren't hurt. That's the important thing. Anyway, keep up the good work. Harvard, it's you I wanted to speak to actually. Can you pop into my office?'

'Me? Now?'

'If you won't be too incommoded.'

'No, no. That's fine. Horace, would you keep an eye on my phone?'

Horace reread Colefax's column. Poor bloke, he thought. The press had given him a rough ride. Just turning up to court to give evidence had left Horace a bit shaken. Imagine being in the dock for something you didn't do, your career on the line. He'd acquitted himself well. You had to admire him.

The phone on Horace's desk rang. 'The Rambler,' said Horace. Unlike the news journalists who drifted from desk to desk, Horace had his own work space and his own phone number, which was printed on his business cards and at the foot of his column. Still, most of his readers preferred to communicate by post. The volume of mail had increased steadily each week since the institution of the star letter. Among the items sent were seed catalogues, blurry snaps of wild animals and pressed flowers. One reader had posted the remains of a giant stag beetle in a shoe box. Its desiccated body had broken up *en route*. The bits rattled around in the box like the parts of a model plane.

'Hello, mate,' said the caller. 'It's Trevor here. Wondering how things are going.'

'Not too bad, you know. Coping.' Horace was cradling the phone with his shoulder, and leafing through the letters.

'Just calling because I've got something I thought you might be interested in.'

'Right.' Horace was wary of Trevor's 'bits and pieces'. They were always clandestine, invariably involved trips to obscure corners of the city, and never came off. 'If it's very newsy I could pass it on to Mr Pratt, the news editor. The fox cubs went down a treat by the way.'

'Did they? Good, good. No, it's nothing like that. It's to do with that bloke I was telling you about, Colefax. He wants to have a meeting with the members of Fox Outreach.'

'So?'

'Well, that's you and me.'

'When are you meeting him?'

'Tonight.'

'Tonight?'

'Curry house on Victoria Street. Seven o'clock. I'll have to call you back with the address because I'm rushed off my feet at the minute.'

'Cubs?'

'Up to my eyeballs in 'em.'

When Harvard came back to his desk he was looking more anxious than Horace had ever seen him.

'What did he want?' he asked.

'He wants me to take over from Pratt,' said Harvard.

'You?'

'Yeah.'

'So why are you looking so worried?'

'I'm worried to find myself taking the offer seriously.'

# CHAPTER NINE

AFTER WORK HORACE went home to iron a fresh shirt. The late-afternoon sun shone through the bedroom window and the light caught the spurts of starch as they crackled onto the hot fabric. He put on a knitted tie and his grandfather's smartest suit, then made his way to the Hanuman Balti House in Victoria Street.

Trevor was already there, the only customer, seated in a little booth divided from the tables around it by fretwork screens. He was half-way through a pint of lager and his mobile phone lay on the tablecloth in front of him. 'He's just called to say he's going to be a bit late,' he said. 'Hold-up at work, apparently. Are you going to do the honours or shall I?'

'I think you'd better. You're the president and founder.' Horace sat down.

'Look at this, eh? Dressed to kill.' Trevor was showing off his tie, which bore a picture of the cartoon character Krazy Kong. He was regrowing the moustache he had had on the video and his hair was slicked down with wet-look gel. It made him look like a comic-book blackshirt. 'I've got the socks to match,' he said, raising a foot onto the tablecloth.

A waiter materialised from the back of the restaurant.

'We're waiting for one other,' said Trevor to the waiter. 'Drink?'

'What are you having?' asked Horace.

'I'm on the beers.'

'I'll have a beer, please.'

'Friends of Mr Colefax?' asked the waiter.

'That's right,' said Trevor.

'Drinks are on the house.'

'Oh, cheers,' said Trevor, and he gave Horace a look that seemed to say: *Welcome to my cornucopia.*

The waiter returned with a bottle of Mongoose lager and a plate of popadums. Trevor spread his hand over the top popadum and pushed down, shattering all of them into tiny slivers. For a while there was just the sound of munching and taped *veena* music playing quietly through the restaurant. Barnaby Colefax arrived about fifteen minutes later.

'Hello, mate,' said Trevor, getting to his feet. Fragments of popadum cascaded from his lap. 'This is Horace Littlefair, he's an associate member of Fox Outreach. Thought I'd bring him along for our chat.'

'Delighted to meet you, Horace.' Colefax extended his large, cool hand.

Horace looked at him shyly, taking in the rower's physique, the coxswain's voice, the immaculately shaved face, the combed-back hair, the too-large nose, the pleased features, and the faint emanation of aftershave.

'I'm afraid I can't stay long,' said Colefax. 'There's a division at nine thirty and I can't persuade any of the other chaps to pair off with me.' The waiter appeared at the table with thick menus bound in gilt and brown plastic like cut-price classics of English literature. 'I can't join you in a beer, either, much as I'd like to. I'm on the wagon. An orange juice, please.' Colefax opened his creaking menu. 'I always say that chicken tikka has become our national dish. I can't get enough of the stuff. Do you fellows know what you want to have? The sooner we order, the better, really.' The politician glanced at his watch.

Barnaby Colefax ordered a chicken tikka masala. Horace, who had no palate for spicy food, ordered chicken and chips. After studying the menu like a crossword puzzle, Trevor chose a non-vegetarian thali and, as he had finished his bottle of Mongoose lager, ordered another.

'You might know Horace better as the Rambler,' said Trevor. The politician made a well-practiced expression of interested incomprehension. 'You know, the thing you read about Fox Outreach.'

'Of course. My wife and I are great fans. We have Derwent Boothby in common, in that case.' Colefax's voice filled the empty restaurant.

'He's my great-uncle.'

'Fine man, fine man.'

'Before we go any further,' said Trevor, with a glance at Horace. 'I'd like to make a quick presentation.' He reached under the table for a flat, gift-wrapped parcel. 'As an associate member of Fox Outreach, I know Horace joins me in this.'

Colefax took off the wrapping to reveal a framed certificate, which Trevor had had laser-printed at a copy-shop. He read it aloud: ' "To Barnaby Colefax MP, sponsor-in-chief of Fox Outreach. In recognition of services to the Urban Fox." I'm touched. Thank you both very much indeed.' Colefax raised his glass of orange juice. 'To the urban fox,' he proposed. The three men clinked glasses.

Trevor went to the toilet. Alone with Colefax, Horace felt

slightly overawed. The politician broke the silence. 'Trevor's been a bit vague about the membership of Fox Outreach. How many of you are there?'

'Well,' said Horace, 'I don't know exactly. Several, several . . .'

'Hundreds?'

'Several hundreds. Oh, yes.'

'And how much has Trevor told you about the work we've been doing together?' The politician looked at Horace intently.

'Only a few bits and pieces. Not much.'

Colefax gave a matey laugh. 'Well, that's no good. We need to bring you up to speed. Tell me what you know about the Quarantine Bill.'

'Nothing, I'm afraid.' Horace was surprised to be caught out on the subject of current affairs. 'I haven't seen anything about it in the papers.'

'Of course you haven't. They're far more interested in covering the really important issues, like the imaginary peccadilloes of innocent men.' Colefax dabbed some mango chutney from his chin.

'Yes, of course,' said Horace, briefly ashamed of his new profession. 'What does this bill involve?'

'That, as they say, is the sixty-four-thousand-dollar question.' Colefax brandished a piece of popadum as though it were a conductor's baton. 'The committee I sit on has been working on a mad piece of legislation supposedly designed to bring some of our laws into line with the rest of the European Union. *Harmonisation* is the ghastly word we use. In a nutshell, it would mean lifting quarantine restrictions on animals coming into this country from the EU.'

Trevor returned from the toilet just in time to hear Colefax's final sentence. As he sat down, he sighed noisily through his teeth and shot Horace a firm look.

'Well, exactly,' the politician went on. 'It's going to be a disaster if it goes ahead. And there are powerful interests who want it to.' Colefax leaned across the booth and said, in a low voice. 'Obviously you're aware of my recent troubles. I'd be a fool to think they're unconnected to my opposition to this bill.'

'You mean . . .?'

Colefax put his finger discreetly over his lips and leaned back as the waiter set down a heated plate-stand with lighted candles in its metal top. By his expression, Colefax indicated that Horace should draw his own conclusions. The chicken tikka masala was placed on top of the stand. Horace's chicken and chips arrived on a plate with a serving of bullety peas. Trevor's thali was a metal platter piled with marinated meat and rice and nine separate stainless steel ramekins of curry.

'*Bon appetit,*' said Colefax, picking up a forkful of his food. 'What it means is that this country's border will be effectively controlled by Brussels.' Trevor sighed again through his rogan josh. In spite of their differences in class, Trevor and Colefax shared an instinctive aversion to all things foreign. *Foreignness,* however, was not a stable concept and had ceased to apply to Indian food, which was by now a naturalised citizen of the United Kingdom.

The three of them ate for a while, then Colefax resumed his speech. 'I don't want to denigrate the Europeans,' he said, 'but this country has been a democracy for hundreds of years. Fifty years ago, our young men, my father among them, were fighting to restore democracy in France, Germany, Italy and the Netherlands. Spain and Portugal were run by fascist autocrats. Now these johnny-come-latelies want to tell *us* how to run a democracy. Frankly, it's insane.

'Let's be completely honest here. You're both sharp enough to realise that there's more to this than just the Quarantine Bill. It's no secret that the European Union is a marriage of convenience between France and Germany with the rest of us along as bridesmaids. The French are terrified that a reunified Germany will soon be goose-stepping along the Champs-Elysées. Germany wants to dominate Europe without being seen to do so – what better way to do that than from inside a Trojan horse called a European Federation?'

Horace had stopped eating. Colefax's explanation made a special kind of sense. It was as though the politician was giving them a glimpse of the truth behind a world of surfaces. Horace felt a shiver go through him. He looked at Trevor to see if he'd felt it too, but he was busy polishing the inside of one of his ramekins with a swatch of nan bread.

Colefax was in full flow and enjoying himself. 'The European Union dominates Europe. And it stands to reason that the most powerful member dominates the Union. Who do you think that might be?' He paused. Horace had no idea. 'The Deutschers. The Jerries. The Huns. Meanwhile, the rest of Europe is pretending it has a choice, like a man being taken for a walk by his dog.'

Colefax reached under the table and picked up his briefcase. He took out a glossy blue book like an instruction manual. The title was the *BMA Guide to Rabies*. 'Take this,' he said. 'You'll find it interesting reading.'

Trevor snorted. 'That is the biggest load of shite any pissed-up doctor could write.'

Colefax smiled. 'Trevor and I have our differences over this but we agree on the main thing . . .'

'If rabies gets into this country,' said Trevor, who was red in the face, 'foxes will be the first to catch it. I sent a fax to that Jacques Delors. I said: "You've got rabies in your rook, you can keep it." I got a fax back saying: "Mr Diamond, thank you for your informative letter." I felt like faxing him back: "Fuck you!" But it's just not worth it.' He shook his head angrily.

'Here's the thing, Horace. Once rabies gets into this country, it'll spread into the fox population.' Colefax spoke slowly; his face was lit from the bottom by the flickering candles of the serving stand. 'We've got the densest concentration of urban foxes in the world, as you know, and they'll act as a sort of reservoir for the virus. We'll never get rid of it. Or, at least, not without rivers of blood. Just think of the implications for domestic animals, pets, strays. They'll all have to be destroyed. We're talking about genocide, decimation, hecatombs. We're talking about a holocaust. And I don't think that's an option that the mass of British people are prepared to tolerate.' He took a sip of orange juice and the ice tinkled in the glass. 'But Brussels doesn't care. They're ready to trample on a thousand years of island traditions. They're not just *ready*. They can't wait.'

'They've gone too far this time,' said Trevor, shaking his finger.

'*Quis custodet ipsos custodes*, Horace?'

'I beg your pardon?'

'It can't be allowed to happen,' Colefax went on. 'With the help of Fox Outreach, I want to be this bill's most visible opponent.' The politician arranged the table napkin in his lap to conceal his tumescence and took a bite of his food.

'How can Fox Outreach help?' Horace asked, as he felt he should.

'The last few months have been hard for me,' said Colefax, who didn't appear to have heard him. 'I won't hide that. I've been vilified and subjected to all sorts of pressure. My sons have been teased at school. Now, I'm not going to moan about it. That's human nature. There's nothing I can do to change *that*. You just have to learn to own it. My job is to rebuild myself and develop a platform from which we can oppose this bill. But that's all going to take time and patience. It's not going to be glamorous work. I'm talking about the odd press conference – maybe a bit of local television, if we're lucky. Real grassroots stuff – the stuff that politics is made of. And I've always said, politics is about people, people first, and people last. Briefly, I need you both in it, because I can't do it by myself. And, after all, all of us have the welfare of the urban fox at heart.'

'Amen,' said Trevor.

The politician ate three more mouthfuls of his food and then pushed away his plate. 'Do either of you fancy dessert?'

'I'm fine,' said Horace.

'I wouldn't say no to a Sambuca and a couple of gulab jamuns,' said Trevor.

'Too sweet for me, I'm afraid, but don't let that stop you.'

The waiter brought Trevor's liqueur and lit it with a match. Horace was mesmerised by the flickering blue flame and decided he wanted one as well. It came in a sherry glass. The liquid was clear and viscous: a single coffee bean crackled in the heat of its burning surface. Although he blew it out before he drank it, Horace still felt he was imbibing liquid fire, and the blue flame seemed to lick at his insides.

Colefax looked at his watch. 'Crikey, is that the time? Look, I have to dash. No, no, don't you hurry. I'll settle up. Stay here as long as you like.' He slipped Trevor an envelope. 'Trevor, this is for Fox Outreach. I'll want you to help me out at the press conference we talked about. It's just a matter of doing the slides. I'll speak to you about it during the week.'

'That might be Horace doing that actually.'

'What?' said Horace.

'I'll explain later,' said Trevor.

Colefax was on his feet and shelling notes off a roll of money. 'Whatever,' he said. 'But it's important that the two of you sort that out between you.' The politician shook Horace's hand. 'It's been a pleasure.' Then he paid the bill and left the restaurant.

'Wow,' said Horace.

'I thought you'd change your mind about him after you'd met him,' said Trevor.

'What's this about a slide show?'

'It's not a slide show, as such. It's a press conference with the odd slide. I'd do it, but I've got to go down to the animal sanctuary in Staines.'

'What will I have to do?'

'Nothing much.' Then Trevor said, 'Right, I don't know about you but I fancy getting pissed tonight.'

The two of them caught the 29 bus to Charing Cross Road and walked to Leicester Square, where the air was sweet with the smell of frying onions. Crowds were passing slowly through a fun-fair on the north side of the square.

They drank four pints of stout each at a pub called the Street Arab. Then Trevor led the way to the Molly Bloom, which had a narrow entrance that descended to a vast underground cavern. Fiddle music was playing loudly enough to be heard at the top of the stairs. The walls of the pub were panelled with church carvings.

Horace struggled through the press of people to get to the bar but when he came back Trevor was already in conversation with a young Irish nurse. 'Siobhan, this is Horace.' Trevor turned away and Horace put his pint on a carved wooden altar. As he drank, he could feel the blue flame from the liqueur flickering in his stomach.

'There's just too many people,' said the man next to him. He fixed Horace with an unblinking green eye. 'There's just too many people.' He was in his forties, and his greasy black hair was indented with the marks of a comb. He told Horace he made carvings.

'What sort of things do you carve?' Horace asked, feeling drunk and voluble.

'I could carve your bollocks,' said the man, lolling his tongue onto his lower lip.

Horace picked up his drink and moved away unsteadily.

The pub emptied onto the streets at eleven. Trevor was determined that the evening wouldn't come to an end. 'It's too early,' he said. The night was mild and crowds were milling around on the pavement still. 'I need another drink. Come on, I know the place.'

Trevor's place was an unmarked door off a Soho side-street. Inside, a big-breasted transvestite charged them ten pounds each to come in. Trevor paid with crisp notes from Colefax's donation to Fox Outreach. They went through to a small, comfortably furnished lounge, which was lit with big candelabra. Horace had the impression that he was inside someone's home, but he was having trouble making sense of his surroundings. The blue flame of the liqueur blazed loudly in his ears. 'How did you find this place?' he shouted.

'I'll tell you the story another time. Get the drinks in.'

Horace looked round at his fellow drinkers. There were about fifteen of them: some perched on stools at the bar, some sat around on sofas. Some were wearing plunging dresses that showed off their cleavage, others wore high-heels and sheer stockings. One was wearing elbow-length satin gloves and drinking from a martini glass. All were unmistakably men.

'They're all men, Trevor.'

'Of course they're all men. It's a transvestite bar.'

Horace went up to the bar and ordered two beers. 'My wife would like you to buy her a drink,' said the barman, a muscular young Filipino with cropped hair and a tight T-shirt. He was indicating one of the three people nearest to him.

'Which one's your wife?' said Horace. The three transvestites laughed.

'Mine's a triple vodka and grapefruit juice, love.'

'I'll just have a double brandy and Coke.'

'Since it's you, darling, mine's a quadruple whisky and soda.'

'That comes to thirty-one pounds fifty,' said the barman. Horace looked dumbly at the handful of coins he had left in his pocket. 'But I'll let you off the one pound fifty.'

'I'll be right back,' said Horace. He found Trevor, installed among cushions like a pasha in a harem and talking to a blue-haired Swedish man called Madeleine.

'I need thirty quid,' Horace told Trevor. 'I just bought a round.' Trevor peeled off the notes without a murmur.

After he'd bought the drinks, Horace flopped into the sofa next to Madeleine and decided he would never get up again. 'Are you okay?' she said. Madeleine was wearing blue lipstick and enormous blue triangles of eye-shadow. Horace nodded, but he was too drunk to sustain a conversation. Cigarette smoke floated through the room like sea fret, and the roar of the voices was like the sound of waves. He closed his eyes and he could feel the floor lurching and the blue flame consuming him.

Horace was woken up by the sound of the phone ringing. He felt as if he was being ripped from the womb into a place of sickness and pain. Needles of light pierced his eyes from the gap between the curtains. His crumpled, smoke-impregnated clothing reproached him from its heap on the floor. He had a vague and disturbing recollection of a kebab that had tasted like slices of smoked suitcase.

It was Trevor. 'Hallo, piss-head,' he said. 'You were in a state last night. I had to pour you into a taxi to get you home.'

A voice Horace barely recognised as his own asked what the time was.

'Just past nine. I wanted to give you the details of that press conference.'

'Can I call you back?' said Horace. 'I'm feeling a bit frail.'

'Not a problem.'

With unsteady fingers, Horace called Harvard and told him he'd been laid low by some kind of gastric flu. Then he fell asleep and had vicious, fragmented dreams. When he woke up again, it was two o'clock in the afternoon. The air in the bedroom was cool and sweet. He could smell grass clippings from the gardens behind the house. Sleep had erased the memory of the kebab; he felt hungry again and now he knew exactly what he wanted to eat. He got up to wash and dress.

As he began running the shower, he caught sight of himself in the mirror above the sink. The lower part of his face seemed to be covered in streaks of charcoal. He rubbed at one of them with a finger-tip and it smudged. He looked at himself and the image of his own puzzled eyes dislodged a memory from the back of his brain. He seemed to see a heavily made-up eye-lid winking back at him, and feel a pair of hard blue lips fastening onto his.

# PART THREE

# CHAPTER TEN

'MY NAME IS Richard and I'm an alcoholic.'

'Hi, Richard,' fifty voices murmured in unison.

'I don't usually share, but I just . . . I had to say something today because I'm so fucking angry.' The softly spoken Australian stared at the silent faces. 'I found out that one of my sponsees is using again.' He sighed and rubbed a bloodshot eye with his knuckle. 'I went round to his house and there was no answer, you know, and that's always a sign that somebody's using. I got someone to help me get in through the window. The place was a tip. The guy was still in bed – drunk, stoned. I mean, I could smell it on his breath. Then he looked up at me and said he hadn't touched a drop.'

There was a ripple of a laughter.

'*I* don't see anything funny in it. This fucking disease . . . It's a disease of *denial*. I just don't know what to do. We're all talking about road rage and people exploding with anger, but I just don't know what I'm *capable* of. When I saw him there, I just didn't know what to do.' The anger drained from his voice as he finished his sentence, and he sat down, defeated, and stared at his shoes. Half a dozen people raised hands to speak next.

Colefax had prised the ring-shaped top layer of his biscuit gently free from its base to expose a small smear of jam, which glinted in the light: a stained-glass window of sugary paste. As he worked at it with his teeth, it stuck to his canine like a tiny plastic cap, a little red riding hood. He picked it off discreetly with his finger, swallowed it whole, and looked around him.

Colefax enjoyed two things about these gatherings. One was the women. They were attractive and well dressed, and beneath the smell of perfume exuded a hint of something pleasantly *gamey*, which Colefax associated with damaged lives. Within the conventions of the meeting, ogling could be disguised as a look of understanding concern and was often met with a smile. He had shared this observation with his sponsor, the legendary rock guitarist Gideon Deck, who had explained that Narcotics Anonymous was even better for picking up women. Colefax had pictured a room full of fragile young heiresses with bitten fingernails, ready to discharge money and neuroses over a sympathetic man. Real head-cases, Deck had said. 'Self-esteem in negative numbers.'

The other thing Colefax enjoyed, and he surprised himself there, was the stories. Even Deck spoke like a character in a Chekhov play when he addressed the meeting.

'My name's Rebecca, and I'm an alcoholic.'

'Hi, Rebecca.'

'I missed your share, I'm afraid, because I was stuck in traffic and I got here late, but we're talking about anger and I just wanted to say how angry *I* am. My father's going away fishing this weekend and he's not taking me with him. And it makes me so *angry*. I feel as though all my life he's been holding back the things I want from me and . . . somehow . . . and . . . and . . .'

Colefax liked the moments in the meeting when the speakers ran out of the words they had prepared for themselves and began speaking more or less spontaneously, betraying more and more of their inner lives.

'It's as though he never thinks of me. And that *hurts* me. I can't tell you how much. It makes me angry and it makes me want to drink. When I drank, this was the feeling I'd drink on. And I'm angry that I *can't*.' Her voice was trembling. 'He's taking my brother with him and I want to call him up and say – why are you such an incorrigible old cunt? And I *would* say it – except, let's face it, I want his money. And I *deserve* his fucking money. I've suffered. I've earned his fucking money. Then I'll go fishing on my own.'

Colefax's oldest son Sebastian had been impressed to hear that Gideon Deck had befriended his father. Sebastian had a poster of the rock star on the wall of his room at Abingdon College. It showed him with a bush of frizzy hair and a kaftan, leaping into the air at the Isle of Wight festival, a lanky arm windmilling across his guitar. The picture had been taken more than a decade before Sebastian was born.

Deck, a lean, bespectacled man, wore understated clothes now: jeans, soft leather jackets, trainers. His substantial wealth was only obvious from his hair, which seemed to have been cut, strand by strand, with nail scissors and a micrometer; his invisibly bifocal glasses; and the sparkling crockery of his capped teeth. His rangy body had withstood so much chemical abuse that he was looked on with a kind of awed respect by a younger generation of musicians, as though he were the sole survivor of a horrific air disaster, or a Boer War veteran.

Colefax raised his hand. 'My name is Barnaby, and I'm an alcoholic.'

'Hi, Barnaby.'

'I haven't been coming here for long. My sponsor's warned me that the worst is yet to come, and judging by what I've heard, I'm sure he's right. But I wanted to say I found your share fascinating and it fitted in with a lot of the things that I've been experiencing.

'Two months ago, I wouldn't have thought it possible to go for a whole day without having a drink. I drank to give me enough energy to do my job. I drank to relax me after work, and I drank to get to sleep. Yet – and I suppose I still find this amazing – now that I've stopped, I have more energy, I feel more relaxed and I sleep better than I ever did when I was drinking.' He looked across the circle of sympathetic faces. Gideon Deck was chewing gum as if his life depended on coaxing a certain quantity of vitamins out of it with each chew.

'What I'm trying to work out now is what was it for. Booze filled a need, obviously. That need hasn't gone away. I was thinking about what the fairy godmother says in the story: "The kindest thing I can give you, my dear, is a little misfortune."'

There was a murmur of assent.

Colefax continued, 'I was reading a story to my youngest boy last weekend when he was back from school. He's a weekly boarder. It was a book of Norse legends, about a man who gets badly cut by his friend's sword. Well, you can imagine what Freud would have made of that.' Colefax joined in the good-natured laughter. 'That's not what struck me, though. In the story, the wound won't heal. So the young man goes to a healer. The healer says, "My son,"' or whatever it is they say in Norse legends, "my son, the only thing that will heal you is the sword that cut you. Make a paste of the rust from that sword and spread it on the wound." Now, I'm sure medical advice would be against that, and for very good reasons. The poor chap probably died of lock-jaw. But there is a bit of truth in that story.' He paused for a moment, and when he spoke again, he had exchanged the facetious tone for one of quiet sincerity. 'I feel we can heal our wounds if we're brave enough to confront the things that caused them. I just wanted to share that with you.'

146

There was silence. A woman on the far side of the room was weeping quietly and nodding. Gideon Deck put his arm round Colefax's shoulder. 'Words of wisdom, mate. Words of wisdom.'

At nine o'clock, Patricia Colefax picked her husband up from outside the church hall in Chelsea where the meetings were held. 'And what did you do at school today, dear?' she said, as he got in the car.

'Usual stuff. "My name's Barnaby, and I'm an alcoholic."' Colefax found not being able to drive strangely emasculating. Often, he would fidget in the passenger seat like a child and criticise his wife's diffident driving.

'I'm dying for a drink,' he said.

'Can you hang on until we get back?'

'I'm not sure if I can. Can't we stop off somewhere? Talking about it for an hour and half is a kind of torture. I don't know how the others manage.'

'Have a look down there. I think there's a hip-flask in the glove compartment. And listen, before I forget, there were two calls. *Woman's Hour* wants you to do a slot some day next week, and that ghastly fox man keeps pestering you about the arrangements for tomorrow. Norris. Is that his name?'

'Trevor.' There wasn't much whisky in the flask but it was a good single malt and Colefax savoured the flowery, peaty flavour. 'Trevor Diamond.'

What had upset Horace was not the thought of French-kissing a hatchet-faced Swedish transvestite. In fact, considering that the people of Great Much had always espoused a Levitical intolerance where anything to do with sex was concerned, he showed a commendable broad-mindedness about what had happened. What upset him was the idea that alcohol had released something inside him – a mischievous and perhaps sinister blue sprite that was capable of who knew what other acts. So when Trevor called about the slide projector for Colefax's press conference, the only thing that Horace wanted to return was reassurance. He wanted to be sure that the blue sprite was benign and would keep within certain boundaries. But if Trevor was sensitive enough to be aware of this, he gave no sign of it. On the contrary, he seemed to enjoy prolonging Horace's discomfort.

'I've been in the Merchant Navy, Horace,' he said, having phoned him up at work, 'and I thought I'd seen most things, but now I've seen absolutely everything.'

'Oh, come on, it was nothing.'

'If that was *nothing*, I'd like to see what you call *something*.'

Horace tried another tack. 'You know it doesn't mean I'm gay. I didn't enjoy it – I can hardly remember it.'

'Well, you looked like you were enjoying yourself to me.'

'Look, Trevor, I was really drunk. I could have been kissing a gnu.'

'Lucky we didn't get pissed at the zoo, then, eh?' said Trevor, his voice betraying his pride in his joke.

'You're enjoying this a bit too much,' said Horace, cupping his hand around the receiver as he hissed into it.

Trevor was still laughing. 'I'd love to have seen your face the next day.'

Horace tried to bear the mockery patiently.

'Oo, ducky,' said Trevor, and dissolved into laughter.

'You're not being very supportive about this.'

'Oh, *support*, very good.' Trevor chuckled at his mysterious *double entendre*.

'I don't get it.'

Trevor laughed so loudly that Horace had to move the phone away from his ear.

'It was your idea to go there,' said Horace.

'What's that supposed to mean?' The laughter stopped and Trevor suddenly sounded defensive. 'I wanted to get a drink. You didn't have to get off with anyone. *I* didn't.'

'Not that time, you didn't. But how many other times have you been?' Horace's voice sounded shrill and indignant.

Trevor fell momentarily silent. 'I don't know what you're trying to say,' he said quietly, 'but no way am I a *poofter*. That was just a bit of fun.'

Horace sensed that Trevor was uncomfortable and he relented. 'What about this slide projector, then?' he said.

'They should have it ready for you when you get there,' said Trevor. The rest of the conversation was brisk and businesslike. An unmistakable coolness remained until they hung up.

The next day Horace went reluctantly to carry out the favour.

The press conference was poorly attended. Only seven journalists bothered to turn up and one of those looked as if he had been sleeping rough. He had grass stains on his jacket and brazenly pocketed a fistful of the biscuits that Horace had been instructed to offer to everyone.

Colefax made the best of it, and in his introductory remarks he managed to imply that the low turnout was part of a media conspiracy, but even he seemed below par. 'The issues that I'm raising have been largely ignored or stifled by the press in this country,' he said. 'There has been no debate on these subjects, and the public remain woefully ill-informed about the impact this legislation could have. I hope today we may be able to light a small candle, a candle with which we can repel this – ahem – ill-conceived juggernaut.'

Horace stood at the back of the room, poised over the carousel of the slide projector. It was large and dusty, and a fan inside it made a humming sound when it was turned on. One button made the slides go forwards, another made them go in reverse. They made a clunking noise when they were depressed. Normally, Horace would have taken great pleasure in anything that required him to press buttons but he was fretting about the transvestite. He felt the whole episode was an indication of a loneliness he had been trying to avoid. He had got off with a man dressed as a woman, when he would much rather have been with a woman dressed as a woman, or even a woman dressed as a man. Or a woman dressed as anything. Or Betty Barmbrake. But a man was all there was, so he'd chosen that.

'Cheer up, Horace,' said a low voice in his ear. 'It may never happen.'

Horace looked up to see Jocasta smiling at him. He tried to

think of a riposte, but couldn't, and by the time his lips formed the word hello, she sat down a little way in front of him and dug out her shorthand pad.

Something about her seemed different. He tried to think what it was. The smile was new, but it wasn't just that. She looked relaxed and happy – that was definitely different. In his mind, he replayed the moment when he had turned towards her. *Cheer up, Horace. It may never happen.* There it was: the teeth, they looked whiter than usual. Even the whites of her eyes had a new brightness about them.

He leant over to her. 'You look,' he whispered, '*brown.*'

'I've been away,' she whispered in reply. 'First day back and I get this.' Her eyes flashed against her tan as she rolled them upwards.

At the other side of the room, the invited speaker had followed Colefax to the lectern.

'Thanks, Barnaby, for inviting me along,' she said. 'I'm going to give you some of the technical background. First, let me just show you what we're talking about here. Can I have the first slide, please?' One or two of the journalists glanced at Horace as he clunked through the slides to a blurry image of a pine-cone shaped object. 'The rabies virus, a member of the genus *Lyssavirus* and the *Rhabdoviridae* family . . .'

'Cheer up, Horace. It may never happen.' At the moment when she had said that, Jocasta had been close enough to him for her breath to make his ear tingle. It was still tingling now. Horace looked over Jocasta's shoulder to see that she was doodling shapes on her shorthand pad and cross-hatching the shadows with a ball-point pen. Her jaw slackened as she stifled a yawn with her fist. Horace yawned sympathetically into the sleeve of his jacket and felt his eyes fill with water.

'Now, once someone's been exposed to the virus,' said the doctor, 'it can take a few days or several years before symptoms appear. A lot depends on which part of the body has come into contact with it. But once those sumptoms are there, the victim is almost certain to die an agonising death.'

The words *agonising death* seemed to stir Jocasta out of her torpor. She looked up at the screen to see a slide of an African man in the throes of furious rabies.

'I'm sure you're well acquainted with the most common symptom of furious rabies,' said the doctor. 'That's hydrophobia or, literally, the fear of water. In the later stages of the disease even just mentioning the word can cause terrible panic in the victim. We're still not fully able to understand why.'

Horace was staring at Jocasta's thumb: it was tiny and the end of it splayed out slightly into a spoon-shaped pad where it pressed against the pen as she wrote. It was a lovely thumb. It was the thumb of a tree-dwelling primate, a fruit-peeling, branch-gripping thumb, and he wanted to touch it.

With her other hand, Jocasta lifted her hair up and away from the back of her head and her thin tanned fingers lingered in it as she frowned and scribbled on her pad. Horace imagined tracing the whorls of fine white hair on her neck with the tip of his finger to the smooth brown buttons at the top of her back, and how she would close her eyes as he slid his finger slowly lower and lower along the flesh-buttons of her body, and he imagined lifting her up softly and her saying his name, Horace, Horace . . .

'Horace?' The doctor cleared her throat. 'Horace, could we have the next slide, please?' Horace looked up in confusion and realised that all the eyes in the room were on his. He blushed deeply and advanced the slides too far and had to reverse them. For the rest of the talk, he tried to compensate for his slip-up by anticipating his cues carefully, but every now and then he stole a glance at Jocasta.

At the end of the talk, the doctor read her conclusion from a sheaf of index cards. 'Neither passports for pets nor the inoculation of the urban fox is in my view a reliable strategy. There remains a need for more research on the spread of fox-adapted rabies into domestic animals. Until the research is conclusive, one way or another, the only certain prophylactic would be to cull a significant number of foxes in the south-east, but I believe this would be politically and perhaps ethically unacceptable.'

At the end of the press conference, Colefax and the doctor took some questions from the journalists and then left. Horace stayed at the back of the room trying to avoid eye-contact with the journalists as they filed out. He still felt ashamed of his mistake.

Jocasta talked briefly with the politician. Then, after Colefax and the doctor had left, she came over to Horace as he was coiling up the cable of the slide projector and said, 'So, how did you end up doing the slides?'

'I don't really know,' said Horace. 'I just sort of got roped into it by a friend. Mr Colefax is the patron of his charity.'

'Really? A charity? And I always thought Colefax was such a cunt.'

Horace looked down at his feet. He felt himself blushing again. He found the unselfconscious way she swore erotic, but it also made him feel foolish, as though he were titillated by a peek of underwear, or the bared ankles of a Victorian dirty postcard.

'How much did I miss?' she said.

'Not much. Did you follow the argument?'

'No, not really.'

Two men in brown coats began wheeling away the coffee urn. The other journalists had left.

'You'll have to go somewhere else if you want to talk,' said one of the men. 'We're setting this room up for the spiritualists' convention.'

'There's a coffee shop downstairs,' added the other one.

'My grasp of the subject isn't that strong,' Horace said, when they were seated at a wobbly metal table in the empty tea-room.

Jocasta glanced at the press release Horace had given her. 'Barnaby Colefax is the Quarantine Bill's biggest opponent,' she read. 'What I don't get is all this stuff about foxes.'

'Well, what we're afraid of is that if rabies were to enter the country, it would spread into the fox population and become virtually impossible to eradicate. At least with quarantine in place there's no chance of it coming in,' said Horace. The explanation appeared to reach his mouth quite independently of his brain.

'Now, let me get this straight. The bill is proposing to do away with quarantine altogether.'

'Not exactly.' Horace watched himself in mild surprise as he illustrated his explanation with a repertoire of air-chopping hand gestures that he could only have picked up from Colefax. 'As I understand it, there'd still be quarantine for animals coming in from outside Europe.'

'Right.'

'Isn't this boring?'

'Yes. But unfortunately it's my job.' Jocasta looked up from the pad. 'Do carry on.'

'Well, there are various recommendations in the bill: that the animals should be tattooed or implanted with microchips, or that they should have passports.'

'Pet passports.'

'Right. The point is, we – that is us, the British – would be losing control of our borders. It *could* happen – it's not very likely – but an infected pet *could* get into Europe and once there it would be easy for it to get into the UK under the new rules. That's what Colefax is worried about. He's really got the best interests of this country at heart.'

'I see.'

'We haven't had a rabid animal in this country since nineteen seventy. We've been rabies free since nineteen twenty-two.'

'Really.' Jocasta had put down her pen.

'Do you want me to tell you about the warble fly?'

'Not unless it's absolutely necessary.' Jocasta took a packet of cigarettes out of her shoulder bag and hitched her hair round her ear. 'By the way, how's Harvard?' she added, offering him a cigarette.

'Oh, he's the new editor,' said Horace.

'No?' Jocasta froze with the unlit cigarette in her mouth and the match about four inches away from it.

'Yes. He's taking over from Pratt in a week or two.'

'Well, that's going to be very interesting.'

'It will.'

'Did the Pratt just decide to pack it in?'

'No, he got the sack.'

'The sack? Why?'

'Well, we had this telephone quiz, and I got punched by the father of one of the contestants. I had to go to court. It was all a bit ugly. And my great-uncle – Derwent – decided it was Pratt's fault. It was tough on him, really, because I did write the questions. Which were moronic.' Horace stared into the dregs of his coffee cup.

'A telephone quiz?' Jocasta looked thoughtful as she took a deep drag on her cigarette. 'I wouldn't feel too sorry for the Pratt,' she said. 'I hated him when I was training on the *Bugle*. He used to give Sneasby such a hard time.'

'I *hate* the way people give Sneasby a hard time,' said Horace, with vehemence.

'Me too.'

They looked at each other and laughed, and the sound of the laughter prolonged the moment of their agreement like a chord of music echoing in the empty tea-room.

'You're related to the Boothby's?' said Jocasta.

'Of course. How did *you* get to work at the *Bugle*?' Horace laughed. 'He took me on as a trainee in January.'

'What were you doing before that?'

Horace was absently tearing the corners off one of the press releases and putting them in his mouth. 'I wrote the odd review for a local paper in Otherbury but I spent most of the time looking after my grandfather. He was dictating me his memoirs.'

'Really?'

'It was sad. We left it a bit too late. His memory had started to go. He was losing his marbles. I'd bring him his breakfast and his pills and then he'd dictate to me all morning and I'd type it up in the afternoon. I'd write as fast as I could, but it was slow going. He'd chop about. Each day he'd start somewhere different so the

thing is almost unusable. I've got ten versions of some events –
him meeting Stalin, the first night of the Blitz – none of the
others. It's a mess. I brought it to London with me, but I can't
bear to look at it. It depresses me.'

'How long did you spend doing that?'

'Years. Literally, years. He got ill when I was taking my A
levels. After a while it got to the point where he just couldn't
bear to be alone.'

'He met Stalin?'

'Yeah. In the nineteen thirties.'

The woman behind the counter frothed up a jug of milk at the
steam jet.

'How do you like London?'

'I like it, but I seem to have had a run of bad luck since I came
here.'

'Like what?'

'Do you want to hear? It's a long story.'

'Please.'

Jocasta lit another cigarette and Horace told her about Jana
being deported. He explained how Lakshmi had run away, and
he recounted his adventure in the transvestite bar. Jocasta was
listening with an attention so complete that he felt like his
words were getting sucked out of him.

'I wouldn't worry about the transvestite,' she said, when he'd
finished. 'That seems quite a normal thing to do.'

'It's a bit grotty, though.'

'Oh, yes.' Jocasta nodded. 'It's the definition of grotty.' She
looked at him curiously and said, 'What happened to that canary
yellow jacket you had?'

'That?' said Horace, uncomfortably. 'It wasn't really *me*.' The
explanation was very partial. In fact, Horace had been reluctant
to wear any of his new clothes since Lakshmi's disappearance. A
sense of guilt had attached itself to the things he had bought on
the shopping expedition to the West End, and he was wearing
the old ones as a kind of penitence. Now, for the first time, he
noticed that his tweed suit was rather itchy.

Jocasta looked at her watch. 'Oh, fuck. My car's on a meter. I have to run. Nice to meet you, Horace. Give my love to Harvard. Tell him congratulations from me.' Her chair legs squeaked on the floor as she got up quickly from the table. She left the tea-room at a jog, rummaging in her handbag for her car keys.

Jocasta had got a parking ticket, but she drove to the offices at Canary Wharf in a surprisingly good mood. She kept thinking about Horace, and his odd clothes and his watchful face. He wasn't exactly *handsome*, but a haircut and a different wardrobe would transform him. And a spot of weight-training would fill him out nicely. Jocasta liked to transform men. It was sympathetic magic. As a relationship with Jocasta blossomed, unlikely bookish types would find themselves investing in contact lenses and pumping themselves up to unimagined proportions at the gym. Then, as the relationship withered and died, they would shrink back down to size, and someone else equally unlikely would begin his induction on the free weights and the stationary bicycle.

The *Globe*'s offices were very near the top of the tower, just above those of the *Daily Flag*. Jocasta was joined in the lift by an attractive young black woman. She was dressed smartly in expensive clothes and dark glasses, but betrayed a hint of awkwardness when she almost got out at the wrong floor.

'It's confusing. They say the building's got terrible *feng shui*,' said Jocasta.

The woman smiled. 'First day here. I'm a bit nervous,' she confided.

'It would be weird if you weren't,' said Jocasta.

The woman got out at her floor and Jocasta saw her going into the newsroom of the *Daily Flag* as the lift doors closed.

'Glad to see you've got your name in the paper,' said Harvard, the next day.

'I saw that,' said Horace. 'That's not quite what I said.'

'She's a former trainee here, Horace. You saying our methods are slapdash?'

'No. I'm saying I was misquoted.'

Jocasta's article was tucked away on one of the inside pages of the *Globe*. 'MP Warns of Fox Rabies Danger.' Horace's name appeared in the penultimate paragraph. '"One rabid animal getting into the UK could infect the entire population of urban foxes and prove impossible to eradicate," said Horace Littlefair, of the London-based charity Fox Outreach. "It's not a risk worth taking."'

'It's not even grammatical,' said Horace.

'Direct speech almost never is,' said Harvard.

The phone rang. It was Trevor, putting on a posh accent. 'I say, can I speak to Horace Littlefair of the London-based charity Fox Outreach?'

'Hi, Trevor.'

'Glad to see you got your name in the paper,' said Trevor. His tone was faintly resentful.

'I didn't know you were a *Globe* reader.'

'Barnaby faxed me the article. One of the local television stations picked it up and wants to do a story on us. OB job.'

'OB?'

'Outside broadcast. We're looking for a location. Someone who has foxes in their garden. You don't have a number for old Angie Kettle?'

'*Agnes* Kettle.'

'That's the one. I don't seem to have put her number in my computer.'

Horace gave him the number. 'I've been meaning to call her myself,' he said. 'I've still got some photos of hers.'

'You can bring 'em along if she says yes. Two birds with one stone.'

When Horace got home that evening, he found Mr Narayan had fallen asleep in front of the television. He had been watching golf, and even now the camera was panning across the grey sky in pursuit of an invisible ball.

The old man looked thin and unshaven. He was wearing a faded blue and yellow *lungi*, which clashed with the thick woollen socks he wore to keep his feet warm. A copy of the *Daily Flag* lay open at the TV page. Horace took it away and flicked through it idly.

'Britain's brashest columnist – exclusive to the *Flag*,' he read. Beside it was a photo of Raylena James, peering over a pair of glasses and nibbling suggestively on the end of a fountain pen.

# CHAPTER ELEVEN

AGNES KETTLE WAS making tea for the men in the satellite truck. She had to step over the cables that snaked from the van through her front door, across the lino floor of the kitchen and out of the back door into the garden.

Ivan the camera man had set up his gear already and was watching television in the front room with his hands folded over his paunch and his legs crossed. He looked like a surly Buddha.

'Why don't you sit on the sofa, dear? You'll be more comfortable.'

'Thanks. But I've got to watch my lower back.'

Agnes bore the two mugs of tea unsteadily to the van. 'I've brought some tea,' she said. 'Your friend didn't want any.'

A lanky, balding man wearing jeans and a Gideon Deck T-shirt leaned out of the sliding door. 'Cheers. He only drinks herbal. Let me give you a hand with that.'

'Ever been inside one of these?' said Dexter, sipping his tea.

'Oh, yes. I drove an ambulance during the war – not often, but I did.'

'Not quite like this one. This is your modern OB truck.' Dexter knocked on the wall of the interior. 'This is the picture we're sending back.' He pointed to a screen, which showed a shot of Agnes Kettle's back garden. The wooden fence that separated it from the field beyond ran across the picture. Her next-door neighbour's washing line was just visible on the far edge of the shot, flapping its load of socks and T-shirts in the light breeze.

'That looks awfully clever.'

'And that's the return,' Dexter explained, pointing at the screen next to it. 'Exactly the same except for one small difference: this one's travelled twenty-two thousand miles out to space and twenty-two thousand miles back.'

'Gosh.' Agnes felt no surprise at all. Scientific explanations were a matter of theology to her. She would have taken Dexter's word for it if he had told her the picture was hand-delivered by a team of invisible winged genies.

Trevor and Horace arrived in separate cars. Horace had driven one of the *Bugle*'s fleet of Minis. Discarded fast-food packaging had wrapped itself round his feet during the journey. Trevor was driving a new off-road saloon; a tiny fox was asleep in a cat carrier on its passenger seat.

The front door was open but they found no sign in the house of the old woman. Ivan ignored them as they passed him watching television in the sitting room. They wandered through the kitchen and out into the garden. Trevor peered at the camera, poised on its tripod.

In the satellite truck, Agnes Kettle watched Trevor's face

growing larger as he drew closer to the lens. 'Hallo, Mr Diamond.'

'He can't hear you,' said Dexter. 'Pinky, make sure Ivan knows they're out in the garden. We don't want his gear knocked over.' He glanced at Agnes Kettle. 'There's thirty grand's worth of camera sitting there.'

The reporter was the next to arrive. She was a young woman of about Horace's age with neat telegenic features and a helmet of sculpted hair the texture of extruded plastic. Her long turquoise jacket had segments of black velvet like naval insignia in the collar and cuffs. She carried a big hardbound notebook in the crook of her arm as though it were an artist's palette. Her name was Suzy Nimrod.

Agnes went off to make some more tea.

'She's always making tea,' said Pinky.

'*Nomen est omen*,' said Dexter. 'Stupid old trout.'

Miss Nimrod went to inspect the garden with Horace and Trevor, who was holding the fox in the cat carrier.

'Sweet! said Suzy Nimrod, poking her finger at the curled-up animal.

'I wouldn't do that,' said Trevor. He nodded towards Horace. 'He can tell you what that animal's capable of. If you put your finger in there, you'll know about it.' Trevor gestured at the garden. 'Now, what you have here is a typical urban-fox environment. If you come over here, you can actually smell where the foxes have been.' Trevor sniffed. 'Can you smell that?' Suzy's nostrils dilated slightly as she took a minimal sniff.

In the kitchen, the sound of a taxi pulling up came from the street. The door of the cab clashed shut and a faint aura of aftershave announced the entrance of Barnaby Colefax. He clasped Anges Kettle's twiggy hand in both of his and apologised for being late. 'I mistimed things slightly. I had to go to a taping at the BBC and had a hell of a time trying to get a taxi. How are your foxes?'

'They weren't too much bother for the last few months. Mr Diamond sprayed the garden and that seemed to do the job. But they've been making an awful mess in the garden next door and now they're getting up to their old tricks again.'

The light was still strong at five to six: great, slanting rays fell across the garden. Ivan, who had stirred himself off the couch, asked Horace to hold up a large hoop of silver cloth to even the light, which was casting a long shadow from Colefax's nose and making his face resemble a sun-dial. Trevor, meanwhile, stood off to one side, cradling the tiny fox in his arms. After the live introduction, he was supposed to give the fox to Colefax to hold for the duration of the interview. Ivan would zoom into a shot of the politician caressing the animal's head.

Pinky and Dexter were in the satellite truck. Every now and again, Suzy would communicate with them but their ghostly responses were inaudible to everyone except her.

'Ivan, can you give us some more head-room on the two shot? How's that? Better? Mr Colefax's face is still looking a little hot. Yes, I can hear you, gallery.'

Agnes Kettle stood at the other end of the garden, watching the mystifying tableau. They looked as stiff as mummers. Horace was flapping the reflector like a punkah-wallah, chasing shadows across the politician's face. 'Keep that still,' said Ivan. Impassive, at the heart of the scene, were Colefax and Suzy Nimrod. She was sweating imperceptibly through her pan-stick, trying to ignore the dazzle Horace was directing into her face.

'Coming to us in thirty,' said Suzy Nimrod. Close up, her make-up looked crude and bright like grease-paint, but from where Agnes Kettle was standing she exuded an orange glow of health and confidence.

'In ten,' said Suzy Nimrod. Her hands, which held the notebook, were shaking slightly. Horace could feel himself getting more and more nervous as he counted down mentally to zero, but he tried to keep the reflector steady.

'Good evening, John.' Suzy Nimrod's voice was unnaturally loud and its random inflections parodied the natural gravity of speech, and dropped at the end of each sentence. 'Ordinary gardens like *these* are the natural habitat of London's urban *foxes*. Few Londoners can be unaware of the animals which have adapted so well to urban *life*. But some fear that urban *life* could become urban *death* if the Quarantine Bill is allowed to become law.' She stared fixedly into the camera for about five seconds, then relaxed. 'We've got two minutes in tape. Pull out to the two shot, let's get the fox over here.'

Trevor seemed unwilling to part with the animal at first. Suzy called to him sharply, 'Don't fuck about, we don't have long.' The animal curled up in Colefax's arms, gave a slight yelp, and then urinated down the politician's trousers.

'I think it's your aftershave,' said Trevor.

'Christ. Can we keep that stain out of shot?'

'Hold it up a bit higher.'

'Twenty seconds to go. Are you sure it's out of shot?'

'It's a wild animal,' muttered Trevor. 'What d'you expect?'

'Shut the fuck up,' said Suzy Nimrod. 'Ten seconds.' Horace noticed her shift her weight to her left leg because the right one was shaking.

'I'm joined now by MP Barnaby Colefax, who's making it a one-man mission to beat the bill. Mr Colefax, why do you see the Quarantine Bill as such a threat to this country's well-being?'

'As you said, Suzy, foxes like Tigger are part of London's urban landscape. But what we have to realise is that these foxes could act as a reservoir, if you like, for the rabies virus if it entered the country.'

'What do you –'

Colefax steam-rollered her attempt to interrupt. 'Now, don't get me wrong. Quarantine is unpleasant. I love pets. But if rabies gets into this country we'll have to put down not only wild animals like Tigger here, but domestic ones as well.'

'What do you say to people who accuse you of pandering to xenophobia to rebuild your parliamentary career?'

'Oh, that's nonsense. I really can't understand it when people apply the word xenophobia to people who are brave enough to stick up for British interests. This country is rabies free and has been for almost a hundred years. We've got a peace of mind that most Italians and Frenchmen and Germans would give their eye-teeth for.' The volume of Colefax's voice was unsettling the fox, which was scrabbling against his lapel. 'I hope that every animal-lover in the country will sign my petition to stop the bill.'

'Barnaby Colefax, I'm afraid that's all we have time for right now. Thank you very much indeed. John?' Her face was frozen in its professional rictus for a further five seconds. 'All right, everyone, that's a clear.' Colefax was dabbing at his trousers with a handkerchief. The fox had trotted off to disturb some of Agnes Kettle's plants.

'Well, they do say never work with children and animals,' Ivan offered amiably, as he detached the microphone from Colefax's tie.

'Was that okay?' Suzy was still staring into the camera and talking to her invisible controllers. 'Yeah, yeah. I'm sorry. We had a bit of a commotion with the fox. Nothing serious. As long as it wasn't obvious at your end.' She exhaled loudly. Ivan took the reflector out of Horace's white-knuckled hand and folded it up.

Agnes Kettle watched the tableau dissolve. Dexter and Pinky wandered back into the garden and started coiling up cables. Trevor put the fox back into the cat carrier. Ivan slouched past with his huge camera.

'Mrs Kettle. Thank you ever so much for putting up with us.' Suzy Nimrod hugged the notebook to her chest and offered the old woman her hand.

'Not at all. The pleasure was mine. Are you sure you won't have another cup of tea before you go?'

'It's been a long day. I think I'll just head off home.'

'Thank you for being so accommodating,' said Barnaby Colefax to the old woman. 'Suzy, I don't suppose you could give me a lift back towards central London?' He and Suzy Nimrod disappeared, Colefax guiding her with his arm.

Trevor gave her departing back a cold look.

'She's got a fucking attitude, I'll tell you. Rule number one: you do not treat a wild animal as though it's a pet.'

'I thought she ambushed Colefax with that second question,' said Horace.

'Nah. She was a fucking lightweight. Didn't you see her hands shaking? He's a big lad. He can take care of himself. I'm off, then. Need a lift?'

'I've brought one of the staff cars.'

'Right you are, then, mate. Let's go have another piss-up soon. Next time no transvestites.'

'Right.'

Horace and Agnes Kettle sat in her dark front room with fresh cups of tea. 'I brought your photos back,' said Horace.

'Oh, thank you, dear. I'd completely forgotten.'

'This one. The one you said was me. I think I know who it is. Without the beard. It's Joseph Littlefair, my grandfather.'

'Let me see. Yes, that's right.' The old woman angled her head so that she was peering through the thickest part of her glasses at the photograph. 'Fancy that.'

'Did you know him through the Boothbys?'

'Joseph? No, I met Derwent through *him*. Now, I think I met Joseph for the first time in nineteen forty. Would that be right?' She paused and calculated the date, using her fingers and the arm of the chair as an abacus. 'We had a lot of war round here, you know.' In her memory, the smell of caramel drifted over the city from the bombed docks. 'It's odd how it comes back to you.' She was silent for a few moments. 'There was a lady in our street, Molly or Mary. I can't remember which. She wouldn't take any notice of the war – "As far as I'm concerned, it isn't happening." She was a Christian Scientist. I don't know. It was stubbornness. If she didn't believe in it, perhaps she thought it wouldn't happen to her. She was in the street when the bomb fell. She worked in Harvey Nichols, I think. Women's fashions. She told me once she'd served Gandhi. What on earth he was buying, I've no idea.'

She saw it more clearly now: brick dust rising from the collapsed building; the scrape of rubble and shouting. Water leaked from links in the hoses.

'It flattened two houses, at least. I ran down the street to help. I told them I was a nurse. It was a shock to me because at the hospital we only treated the ones who had a chance. It was terrible stuff: bits of bodies and things. I just held one boy's hand while he bled to death. After that my hand was shaking too much to put in stitches. I remember Joseph saying, "I can deal with any of it, but it's when I see the children." I knew what he meant. They brought them out without a mark on them, but their lungs must have been destroyed by the blast.' She wrung her hands as she spoke. 'You tried not to think too much about it. But you couldn't help it. Especially the tiniest ones. Then there was the other side of it: feeling ever so alive. It seems awfully cruel to say it, but it did that to you. It was the opposite of feeling so fearful all the time.'

'You met him at this bombing?'

'Yes. I think that was the first time. He worked for the Auxiliary Fire Service.' She sipped her tea. 'He was fun. A terrible tease. He talked non-stop, but that was part of his charm. He'd been abroad ever such a lot. He told me he'd met Stalin and, of course, I thought he was just being a show-off, but then he brought me a photograph to prove it. Well, he was being a show-off, but it was true.'

'I think he met Stalin a couple of times.'

'Yes. We had that in common – we'd both travelled. I remember thinking, I wonder if I'll ever leave England again, because then it was pretty desperate, you know. And I miss abroad. There was no orderliness about life in London then. But I didn't go abroad again until long after the war.'

'Were you quite close?'

'Close? It depends what you mean. We weren't *lovers*. Good heavens, no. We were both married. I know a lot of people did, but not us. He was quite a bit younger than me.' She was peering at the photograph again. 'I can't for the life of me remember when this was taken.'

'Did he talk a lot about politics?'

'Oh, he never shut up about them. He never stopped. He tried to get me involved, I remember. I think I may have gone along to one of his meetings but I'm afraid it would have been over my head. I'm not very clever with things like that.' Agnes paused and looked down at the floor.

'I didn't see him much after the war. He was very busy then. He went overseas a lot. I did get a letter from him after my divorce. That was a terrible time.' The old woman gave a rusty laugh. 'My husband ran off with someone else. She got her claws into him and that was it. It was the first time that I felt glad I hadn't had children. I went back to nursing. And I didn't see him for a long time after that.'

She fumbled with one of the lamps beside the sofa and then sat for a while in the pool of light it cast.

'We had an Italian doctor in the area. He'd been a POW. He couldn't practise here officially, but . . .' Agnes's tone changed slightly, it sounded like a plea for understanding. 'You have to remember what those days were like. You would go into a mortuary and see the same thing, time after time. There was always one lilac-coloured corpse. That was coal-gas poisoning, deliberate or accidental. And you would always see a pretty young thing, lying there with the baby still inside her, dead of a soap embolism, or Dettol, or whatever they'd used to douche her. Of course, it was different if you were rich. You just needed a trick-cyclist to write a letter saying it posed a risk to your mental health. But the people we saw didn't have the choice. We had a great big suitcase. Open it up with a clean surface, a sterile surface. It was a good deal safer than letting them loose on the tender mercies of the local handy lady. Gin and a hot bath, or whatever they used. Knitting needles. We didn't *advertise*. But women share information with each other. I've no idea if men are the same way. A lot of it is wrong, of course, especially when you're younger. But it happens your whole life. Everything from removing a tablecloth stain to aborting a child. You can find out the details, if you need them.'

Horace was silent, wary of puncturing the memories that seemed to surround her. The old lady moved her head as she spoke as if the scenes were being enacted in the air between them.

'It must have been fifteen years later that I saw Joe again. Someone rang me on the telephone. It was a young woman. She said she was in dreadful trouble, could she see me right away. Now, I was working less and less then – I was getting on myself, you know – but I said she could come to see me. She was a tiny thing, in her twenties, I suppose, but she looked much younger. Red eyes, hair all a mess. A lot of the women we used to see were married. That was quite common. At the hospital I remember treating a woman who'd had seven or eight miscarriages. It was on her medical report. I asked her about it. She said, "If you had five children, wouldn't you?" That was the attitude of some of them, you see. I don't suppose some of them would have known what to do with birth control. So she said, "I'm Nadya Littlefair" – it was rather a lovely name, I thought. Russian. I asked her what was the matter, though I could make a pretty good guess myself. She told me she thought she was pregnant. I said, "Do you want to keep it?" It was the only thing we ever asked, really. She said, "I don't know." Well, "I don't know" isn't enough, not when you're dealing with a thing like that. She was terribly sniffly, so I gave her my handkerchief and told her to go away and think about it. I suppose it was a couple of days later that she came back, with Joe this time. I hadn't seen him for years and years. His hair was thinner. I can't remember if he had a beard then. I think he may have. I didn't find out much about his life because we didn't get the chance for small-talk. His face was like this.' She set hers into a frown. '"Hello, Agnes," he said, like that, you know. Face like thunder. And *she* was looking down, not saying a word, poor thing. I suppose she was frightened. It felt like he was egging her on. "Go ahead", you know, he was like that, he could be. She didn't lift her head, kept her eyes on her feet the whole time. She just said, "I've thought about what you said to me. I've thought it over. And here I am." But her voice was quiet, ever so quiet. I said, "Are you sure?" She didn't say a word. Then Joe said, "She's sure." I knew that something wasn't right. I said, "I'd like to hear it from *her* if you don't mind. Now, are you sure?"

'It was pretty obvious to me that she wanted to keep it. People tend to be businesslike about it. They're obviously upset – most people are a bit funny about any kind of operation – but they try not to let it show. I looked at him and I told him I wouldn't have anything to do with it. And that was it. It would have been wrong. He said, "Come on," and off they went. My heart really went out to her then.'

'That was the last I heard of him. Derwent wrote to me when he died, but that was all. Never a card, nothing.' The old lady smiled.

'But this pregnancy. Did she have the baby?'

'She had the baby, all right, but they gave it up for adoption. It must have broken her heart.'

'If she'd wanted to keep it.'

'It was a boy. He would be . . . let me think. Gosh, at least thirty by now.'

Brother, thought Horace. And in the silence that fell he could feel the invisible pulse that half connected him to a stranger in the earth.

'Did they know who the father was?'

'Joe's girl? I suppose she must have, but I don't think she let on. Perhaps Derwent knows.'

'I doubt it,' said Horace.

'They were never close. Joe thought Derwent was a boor. Well, he is, isn't he, really? Though he's done very well for himself. He's done very well.'

'He has.' Horace thought for a moment. 'What happened to the baby?'

'They sent him up to a couple in Doncaster, I believe. My sister was in touch with them for a while. Poor thing.'

'The child?'

'I was thinking of my sister.' Agnes smiled at him. 'You must think I'm terribly indiscreet. I go on terribly. I'd say it was my age, but the truth is I've always been like this. I'm an awful chatterbox.' Agnes giggled. '"Agnes Kettle makes the most noise," that's what they said at school. It's the way I am. Now, you're in newspapers, aren't you?'

'That's right.'

'That's interesting work. I used to take a newspaper, but I find that nowadays it just depresses me. I don't know whether that's my age, or if things have really changed. I read and look at the television. The lady who brings me the library books says you must get terribly bored. But I tell her how can I be bored with all these wonderful memories? I remember things from so far back it surprises me. And yet I forget the names of people I've met yesterday. That's age, I suppose.' Her knees creaked as she stood up.

Horace held her mottled, papery hand. 'It's been a pleasure.'

'I'm sure I've bored you silly.'

She gave him a wave from the doorway as he drove off. The warm weather had broken and it was starting to rain.

# CHAPTER TWELVE

'WHAT DO YOU mean he's *pulled out*?' The odd, mid-Atlantic accent of the new features editor, Ms Nonni Theramin, was rough with age and cigarettes. She had frozen in the act of painting her toe-nails, with one chubby foot drawn up into her lap, and a bottle of dark blue nail polish standing on the edge of the desk. She was bug-eyed with indignation.

Jocasta closed the door and sat down in the extra chair. 'Just that. He's pulled out. I think he decided it would harm his career.'

'What fucking career?' said Ms Theramin. She looked down

and began applying the polish to the ridged nail of her left big toe. 'So who's left?'

'Just Angie Deck and the film producer's son, Wertheim.' Jocasta glanced at the editor's toe-nail: she thought the colour was ill-advised. The finished toes were a varicose shade of blue –almost frostbitten, or as if someone had dropped a piano on Ms Theramin's big pale feet.

'Christ Almighty. Two's not a trend. We need at least three.'

'I thought you said it wasn't a trend piece.'

'I said no such thing, Jocasta, and let me tell *you* something – some people hate dogs, some people hate firemen, *I* personally hate contradiction, and won't stand for it. *One* is a profile, *three* is a trend, but *two*! Two is just embarrassing. We need more.'

Jocasta thought hard. It seemed an age since she had been on holiday, when it was really no more than a week. Work and London had reclaimed her within days of arriving back. Her tan was gone, though there was a little sand in the bottom of her handbag.

Ms Theramin had been brought in to attract younger readers to the *Globe* and had immediately singled out Jocasta as an ally since she was both the youngest person in the newsroom by about ten years and the only other woman. At first, Jocasta had been keen to work with her. She wanted nothing more than the space and freedom to pursue more interesting stories in detail. But she had quickly grown disillusioned. Ms Theramin, who was nudging sixty herself, had rubbished all her story ideas as 'old hat', or 'too newsy', or she simply pulled a face that was supposed to suggest something like the smell of rotten herring. On the other hand, all the stories Ms Theramin wanted to cover were suspiciously alike; so alike, in fact, that they seemed to belong to a single genre. Its requirements were simple. The protagonist always suffered a tragic reverse – through drugs, crippling disease, or bereavement – but overcame it to reach a more exalted stage of their personal development. The trouble was, the genre also demanded that these stories were true.

Unfortunately, the chapped red feet of the ugly sisters had as

172

much chance of getting into the glass slipper as the average life had of conforming to the tight specifications of Ms Theramin's features. Lives were just too shapeless and unwieldy. They had to be coaxed in and braced to stay there. The troughs of failure and the peaks of success had to be too marked. It wasn't enough that the dyslexic child had learned to read, she had to write poems in *ottava rima* and beat grandmasters at chess.

'What about that junkie from the Aussie soap? I think he's an osteopath now. Or a chiropractor. Something in backs,' said Jocasta.

Ms Theramin waved her hand impatiently and didn't bother looking up from her toes.

Jocasta's eyes roved across the walls of the office as she tried to think of candidates for the piece. So far, she had been to see just one person: Angie Deck, the former wife of the legendary rock guitarist Gideon Deck, for an article on overcoming the effects of celebrity, which was due at noon the following day.

Angie Deck had been exactly as Jocasta had imagined her: an unblinking blue stare; flowing clothes; big hair; expressive gestures. She had come to the door in bare feet, and ushered Jocasta into a large sitting room that was decorated like a Moorish palace, and which overlooked a leafy street near Holland Park. They each drank two of the strongest cups of coffee Jocasta had ever tasted.

Mrs Deck was a co-operative interviewee because she had something to sell. She had just begun marketing a range of flat-pack furniture that had been assembled by amputees in third-world countries. The items were of indifferent quality, but that wasn't the point. The products and the advertising were supposed to appeal to the prospective customer's conscience. 'Give someone a hand with that chair,' was the slogan that would shortly be appearing on billboards arond the country, above a black and white photograph of a limbless man staring reproach-fully at passers-by.

Unfortunately, Jocasta couldn't persuade Angie Deck to elaborate on the years of mythological excess with Gideon. She

173

talked instead about a recent trip to Mozambique to set up a factory where victims of land-mines could make croquet sets. It was enough for the piece. But what Jocasta wouldn't be able to say in the article was the thought that struck her most forcibly: Angie Deck was completely insane.

'Ring around.' Ms Theramin waggled her freshly painted toes to dry them. 'Our dicks are on the chopping block on this one.'

Horace was at his desk when the phone rang.

'Look, I know this is tragic, and I'm scraping the barrel, but I wondered if you might have some thoughts on overcoming celebrity you could share with the readers of the *Globe*,' said Jocasta.

'Overcoming celebrity?' said Horace.

'You said your grandfather had met Stalin.'

'That's true. Twice.'

'Well, what's it like being the grandson of a famous communist?'

Horace was silent for a moment. 'God, I don't really know. What's it like being the grandson of anyone else?'

'Mmm. Yeah. Good point.' Jocasta flipped urgently through her address book.

'Can I ask *you* something?' Horace picked up a printed invitation from the edge of his desk. He blinked nervously: something that had hatched in his mind much earlier was fluttering its wings and pecking the back of his eyes.

'Of course.'

'Are you busy tomorrow evening?'

'I'm not thinking that far ahead at the moment,' said Jocasta. Events beyond noon the next day had begun to seem as hypothetical as quarks and curved space.

Horace fingered the piece of card. 'The thing is, the Museum of Garden History have invited me to an open evening. I wondered if you'd like to come as my guest.'

'That would be . . .' Jocasta wasn't sure of the word she wanted.

'I was going to ask my friend Trevor, but he's not been himself lately. It starts at seven.'

'Seven?' Jocasta was distracted by a promising name in her address book.

'Great. See you there.' Horace hung up the phone and rubbed his hands.

'How's it going?' asked Ms Theramin, when she returned to her office from a lunchtime shopping expedition.

'No celebrities,' said Jocasta, 'But I've managed to bag an invitation to an open evening at the Museum of Garden History.'

'Another thing you should know about me, Jocasta, is that I don't appreciate that brand of irony.'

Horace was too excited to get back to work straight away. Since he didn't smoke, he couldn't use the excuse that he was going for a cigarette to get outside the fusty newsroom. Instead, he had to go to the toilet to have time alone with his thoughts.

Horace had thought about Jocasta often since the press conference, and more often since he had found out about his brother. His discovery had made him feel isolated, in part because he realised that there was no one to discuss it with: Harvard was giddy with his imminent editorship; Mr Narayan had been virtually monosyllabic for months; Trevor was – well, he didn't feel like speaking to Trevor. He might have told Lakshmi, he thought, if he had known where she was.

The new knowledge also made him feel isolated from his past. His grandfather had been dead less than a year, but these new facts about him made it seem as though he had been dead much longer. Horace was full of questions, but there was no way to drag the old man back from the dead to cross-examine him about his other grandchild.

So Horace knew he had a brother, but it was oddly purposeless knowledge – there was nothing he could do about it. And yet the implications of it radiated back through his life. Someone very like him had been in the world already. And this other life had

175

been secretly parallel to his all along. And that fact, the fact of having a forerunner, made him, if for no other reason than that it meant he was not alone, feel both a little better and a little abandoned. It was difficult to accept that something which might have made all the difference in the world made none.

Horace had heard no more from Trevor or Colefax since the outside broadcast at Agnes Kettle's. He assumed they were busy with Quarantine Bill business, as references to it multiplied both in the newspapers, and in the letters that he received from readers. He was surprised by the language of this correspondence. Some people wrote as though containers of rabid animals stood on the quays of French ports, ready to be loaded upon ships once the bill had become law. The most deranged suggested quarantine should be extended to include foreign humans. But Horace recognised the opinions as well: they were Trevor's — xenophobic, sentimental, distrustful. For all of the people who wrote to oppose the bill, isolation was the same thing as being an island; and the truth of it went far beyond etymology.

Horace wandered back to his desk and carried on with his work. Summer brought with it a raft of gardening events and the Rambler dutifully advised his readers of all of them. He found it heartening that in a city where the most obvious feature was the traffic, and where the air on hot days was hardly breathable, people cultivated sweet patches of green behind their houses, or on their roofs, or windowsills. The back gardens of Glenburne Road were quilted with tidy lawns and strips of flower-beds. One hot night, Horace had slept with the window open. Rain fell while he was sleeping, hissing quietly down onto the still city, and when he woke up, the bedroom was fragrant with flowers and wet grass.

A hand tapped Horace on the shoulder.

'Mr Sneasby? What are you doing here?'

Mr Sneasby looked uncharacteristically spruce. His newish maroon blazer and a couple of shaving nicks by his nostirls suggested an appointment of unusual significance. For a moment, Horace thought he must have been fired.

176

'I never miss a leaving do,' said Mr Sneasby.

'Whose?'

'Pratt's, of course. Tomorrow's his last day, officially, but he's not planning to come in. Didn't you sign the card?'

'That? No, yes, I did.'

Mrs Doolaly had been round earlier with the card and an empty treacle tin for contributions. Horace had guiltily dropped a couple of pounds into the tin, and then he had agonised over the card. He wanted to write something memorably witty that would somehow make light of his early humiliation at the hands of Pratt, while also suggesting that he had risen above it and could show the departing editor a degree of manly sympathy. In the end, he settled for 'Good Luck! Horace.'

Horace looked at his watch. It was five o'clock. 'Right. I've just got to read through the last of these letters.' He held up the unopened envelopes. 'I'll be along in a second.'

Mr Sneasby wandered over to the opposite side of the newsroom, where half a dozen sales and marketing people from the top floor were milling around with prawn sandwiches and plastic cups of wine.

Horace was a slow and fastidious reader. He still had several letters to go when he heard Harvard raise his voice and address the gathering.

'When someone has given as much of himself to a place as our editor has,' Harvard was saying, 'it's always difficult to say goodbye. I'm sure everyone joins me in wishing Dennis Pratt all the best for the future.'

Horace made his way over to the throng, and along with the others he raised his little white plastic cup and toasted Pratt dutifully.

'Mr Boothby has sent his *apologies*,' Harvard said, prolonging the word in an obvious imitation of Boothby's voice. 'I suggest we adjourn to the Taurus Arms and let our absent owner and publisher stand us the first round.'

There was a heartfelt cheer.

'These are some small things to remember us all by,' said

Harvard. He gave Pratt the leaving card and a mock-up of the *Bugle* that announced the editor's departure as front-page news. Mrs Doolaly gave him a book token, which she had bought with the money donated by the employees.

Pratt was trying to smile as he received the leaving presents. His lips moved sideways and separated slightly, making his mouth look like the slot in a post-box. 'Thanks, Harvard. Just one or two words, really. It's been a cracking good laugh. I think I've managed to turn one or two of you into proper journalists. The rest of you will have to carry on muddling through without me. Anyway, you lot needn't worry about *me*. I'm looking forward to doing a bit of real journalism for a change.' He made a secret inward smile and enjoyed the silence for a moment before continuing in a tone of voice that seemed to herald a joke; 'Still, it's a pity Derwent Boothby couldn't make it along. I wanted to remind him that there's a difference between making paper and owning one. It's for making paper that you start with a load of *dead wood*.'

One or two sales and marketing people laughed. The journalists were uncomfortably silent, except for a single person who said, 'Shame!' Pratt seemed not to care. He sat there rubbing his earlobe between his thumb and forefinger, looking pleased with himself.

Harvard tried to make light of the remark. 'Well, with that endorsement ringing in our ears, I suggest we all go to the pub,' he said.

But before anyone could leave the newsroom, Mr Sneasby cleared his throat tentatively and raised a trembling hand. 'I'm really not used to seeing the newsroom so full,' he said. His voice could only just be heard over the raucous whispering. 'I've known Dennis for almost fifteen years. I wanted to mark this, well, *historic* transition with a small memento. Here you go.' Sneasby took a small parcel from his pocket and passed it to the outgoing editor.

There was a quiet muttering as people pressed around to watch Pratt unwrap Sneasby's present. He looked puzzled as he let the paper fall to the ground. It was a book: a second-hand paperback of *Nineteen Eighty-four* with a battered orange cover. Pratt held it out at arm's length and looked at it suspiciously as though it might explode in his face.

'What is it?' someone called out. Pratt held the book above his head, but he lifted it too abruptly, and as he did, the ancient binding broke apart and the pages fluttered down, turning in the air as they floated across the room, or fell in bunches at Pratt's feet. The people nearest to him began collecting up the scattered leaves of paper. Sneasby had drifted to the back of the room and was standing there motionless in his maroon jacket, pinching his nostrils together with his fingers as though to suppress a fit of laughter.

Sneasby's mysterious gift did seem to break the tension in the room. People began drifting off to the pub, whispering to each other that Sneasby had finally lost it and didn't that speech just prove that Pratt was a wanker. Horace stooped down to pick up a handful of fallen pages, but he was pulled away from the scene by the sound of his phone ringing.

'Horace?'

It was a woman's voice. His first thought was that it was Jocasta, calling to beg off the visit to the Museum of Garden History. But as he listened, he realised it was Lakshmi's. From the noise in the background, Horace guessed she was in a station somewhere.

'Horace? Did you get the money?' she said.

'The money?'

'The hundred pounds.'

'No. Where did you send it?'

'To your job.'

Horace rummaged around in the papers on his desk. In all his imagined encounters with Lakshmi, he had never foreseen this happening. He found himself saying: 'What kind of envelope was it in?'

'A sort of peachy-coloured one.'

Horace found it and tore it open. The money was inside a

179

birthday card. 'You shouldn't send cash through the post,' Horace said, then he caught himself. 'Forget that. Where on earth are you? What am I going to tell your dad?'

'Don't worry about me. I'm fine.'

'How fine?'

'Very fine,' said Lakshmi. 'Like the apple juice.' She giggled. 'I'm pregnant.'

'Oh,' said Horace. 'Congratulations.'

Most of the journalists had already left the Taurus Arms by the time Horace arrived. Pratt had stayed for only one drink and Sneasby hadn't bothered going at all, apparently satisfied that his point, whatever it was, had been made. Horace didn't much feel like going either. He was full of worries and knew he wouldn't enjoy the forced conviviality of the pub. But the alternative was to go straight home, and he was certain that if he bumped into Mr Narayan, the old man would take one look at him and see the image of his heavily pregnant daughter hovering above his head like the thought-balloon of a character in a cartoon.

Lakshmi had made Horace promise not to tell anyone. *Anyone* – she said it twice; he translated it as *my father* and felt a stab of pity for the old man. 'I'm just not ready to tell him yet,' she said.

To Horace, it seemed that her leaving was a kind of theatre. It was exile and rebuke. It was a kind of punishment that showed she was beyond scolding; was, in fact, a woman. It was cold-hearted, too, but he envied her certainty: she knew exactly what she wanted and that in itself was a gift.

Lakshmi had talked excitedly until the money ran out and she promised to call again.

Horace found Harvard sitting at the bar. 'I think your friend Sneasby's finally lost it,' Harvard said.

'You always say that,' said Horace, quietly. 'It's a good book.'

'I've no doubt. But that particular edition of it had seen better days.'

180

'That may have been a much-loved heirloom,' said Horace.

Harvard made a snorting noise. 'It all got a bit mean-spirited. Pratt left this behind. Look.'

Pratt's leaving card was on the bar-top beside them. Horace drew it towards him and found that the cardboard was slightly damp with beer. He opened it up to read the remarks. Several of them were openly rude, and one mocked the quiz questions that had brought Pratt his dismissal: 'Is Pratt's departure (a) undeserved (b) unwelcome (c) unexpected (d) none of the above?' it read. Someone had ringed Horace's message on the card and written 'arsekisscr!' in a drunken scribble next to it.

'Why do you think he did it?' said Horace, closing the card and remembering the pages of the paperback fluttering across the room.

'Who? Pratt or Sneasby?'

'Sneasby.'

'Pair of bitter old hacks, both of them.'

Horace thought he was right about Pratt, but not Sneasby. Would he really have gone to the trouble of wrapping up the worthless book and delivering it in person on one of his days off just for the pleasure of watching its pages fall out? He puzzled over it on the walk home but came to no conclusion. But who understands the daily calvaries of a million unhappy people, and the fairytale reversals that make their wan lives bearable?

The Museum of Garden History was housed inside a deconsecrated church next to Lambeth Palace. Horace killed time looking at the exhibits. 'What on earth is that?' said Jocasta, when she arrived. She was wearing strappy sandals and a long, straight grey dress that left her arms bare and made her figure seem flat and angular. She took a glass of white wine from a table by the door.

'It's a vegetable lamb,' said Horace.

'It looks disgusting.' The vegetable lamb stood on four spindly legs. It was mossy and moth-eaten like the remains of a mummified cat.

'It's not an animal at all. It's the root of a kind of fern. Look:

> 'Rooted in earth each cloven foot descends
> And round and round her flexible neck she bends
> Crops the grey coral moss and hoary Thyme
> Or laps with rosy tongue the melting rime;
> Eyes with mute tenderness her distant Dam
> Or seems to bleat a vegetable lamb.

'It's from the *Oxford Book of Vegetable Lambs*.' Horace looked up from the placard. 'That was a joke.'

'Thanks.'

'Do you want to see the collection of gardening tools?'

'Joke?'

'No.' Horace seemed surprised. 'They've got some weird ones.'

'Not in this life. Can I smoke here?'

'I don't think so. Let's go outside.'

'It was lucky you called. It's no fun coming to these things by yourself,' said Horace, as they walked out of the church. Part of the graveyard had been turned into a geometrical garden with benches and fountains, but it was so close to the South Lambeth Road that the noise of the traffic never let up.

'Yeah. I got into a little difficulty at work. One of the people I had lined up to profile dropped out.' Jocasta hovered in her long dress over the tombstone of Mr Vincent de Cleve. '"Here lies an honest man, To say more would be unnecessary." Sounds like he led a fascinating life.'

'My grandfather's said, "I am a stranger in the earth, hide not thy commandments from me."'

'Was he religious?'

'No, not at all.' The two of them walked at slow, conversational pace along the path. 'But he liked the mystery of it. He liked to say he didn't believe in God but he did believe in organised religion. I think the epitaph was his idea of a joke. Did you find somebody who had overcome celebrity in the end?'

'Sort of.' Horace stopped and turned to her. She continued

speaking. 'I ended up talking to Angie Deck, Wertheim – the film producer's kid – and the sister of Lydia Skin.'

'The supermodel?'

'Yeah. And I got some quotes from a psychologist about the corrosive effects of fame. Went down to the wire, though. I was hoping the stress would kill my boss. Maybe next time. Christ. Is that *the* Captain Bligh? Speaking of bastards.'

The captain of the *Bounty* had the biggest tomb in the garden. It was a large stone bulkhead, in which were interred the remains of the captain, his wife and child.

'How is Harvard, anyway?'

'Busy. Changing things.'

'It must be strange. Shall we sit?' Jocasta sat down on a hard stone bench and Horace sat beside her. Jocasta's cigarette smoke rose up over them to mingle with the traffic fumes.

'It's better than having Pratt in charge.'

Horace's clothes, Jocasta noticed, had an odd smell about them: not unpleasant, but faintly musty, an old-man smell. They sat on the bench together in silence for a few moments.

'We had Pratt's leaving do yesterday,' Horace went on. He found her spikiness was not unfriendly and that he was less awkward than he had imagined.

'That must have been a treat.'

'It was strange.' Horace explained what had happened and then said, 'So Pratt made a nasty remark and Sneasby gave him an unreadable book. It sort of makes you feel sorry for both of them.'

'It certainly must be easier to feel sorry for Pratt now that he's gone. I don't recall feeling much pity for him when he was kicking my arse around the newsroom,' said Jocasta.

'Pratt kicked you?'

'No, stupid, not *literally*. He was a bully, that's all.'

'Well, I suppose you need someone like that in charge,' said Horace. He pointed at the tomb ahead of them. 'A Captain Bligh. Blighs make good leaders.'

'I don't think so,' said Jocasta.

'He was a great sailor,' said Horace. 'Christian stuck him in an open boat in the middle of the Pacific and Bligh managed to get it all the way to Indonesia. It's one of the great feats of navigation. He didn't even have a sextant.'

'But he was a bully.'

'Probably. There was another mutiny against him when he was governor of New South Wales. He can't have inspired much love in his men if they were trying to overthrow him the whole time. But it's a bit more complicated than "Was he a nice bloke?"'

'I think that's bullshit. Everywhere I've worked there seems to be a Captain Bligh in charge. Some idiot who thought his job was his life and resented people who reminded him that there were other things in life besides work. Ask Harvard. People who want to exercise power over other people. It comes out of a kind of weakness.' Jocasta took a long drag of her cigarette. Horace was close enough to smell her: the soapy smell of her hair and dress, the sharpness of her cigarettes. His arm tingled where it was near enough to feel the warmth of her body.

'What about you?' said Horace. 'What do your parents do?'

'My dad works in confectionery.'

'Sweets?'

'Chocolate factory. He's sort of a sixties' drop-out made good. My mum's just a housewife. I suppose I shouldn't say *just*. No brothers and sisters. You?'

'Don't know anything about my dad. There's a blank on the birth certificate. That's why I'm a Littlefair. Never having had one, I don't think I miss him very much. Didn't know my mother. Didn't know my brother. In fact, I didn't know I *had* one, until last week.'

'Really?'

Horace recounted the story he had heard from Agnes Kettle.

'Wow,' said Jocasta. And she had to ignore Nonni Theramin's voice in her ear saying, *Two more and it's a trend.*

'I never knew he was so ashamed about it. There's something very *bourgeois* about that.'

184

'I know what you mean. My dad was all peace and love, man, in his wild years. Now he's pinstriped suits and pipes of port. Why does that happen?' Jocasta lit another cigarette. 'You must feel weird about it all.'

'I don't know. I wonder if it's possible to miss someone you've never met. It shouldn't be, really, It doesn't make sense. But since I heard about it, I imagine him walking about, seeing the same things I see, feeling the same way about them.'

'A double.'

'Exactly.'

'Well, he's your brother, not your twin. And probably a half-brother. Even full siblings can be completely different from each other. Look at Cain and Abel.'

'I know what you mean,' said Horace. 'It's more the *idea* of it. *Someone.* Do you see?'

'I think so.' There was a pause that seemed to be prolonged by the silence that followed a break in the traffic. 'I've seen enough of the Museum of Garden History,' said Jocasta brightly. 'Let's go to the pub.'

On the way, she told him about bumping into Raylena James in the lift. 'You know what the funniest thing is?' said Jocasta.

'What?'

'Her column is really good. She's ten times better than the It-girl they had doing it before.' Jocasta bought them both pints of Guinness. She smiled at him as she came back from the bar. Horace wanted to say: *I could talk to you all night.* But he didn't. His rush of happiness was overtaken by the anxiety that it would all suddenly end: she'd run away, or die, or be deported to Poland and he'd be left alone in a city full of unhappy men.

'So what's Colefax like?' said Jocasta.

'You know how certain people have a kind of charisma – a sort of quality that makes you think, I have a lot to learn from this person?' said Horace.

'Stop right there. Listen to this. I worked on a colour supplement for about a week when I was doing my degree. The most interesting job I did was a story on celebrity barbecues. You

185

know, *What is Angie Deck having on her barbecue this summer?* This may come as a surprise to you, but celebrities eat the same things at their barbecues as the rest of us. They just ask for the condiments more rudely.'

'Well, of course they do. But something sets them apart . . .'

'Money and fame?'

'A kind of authenticity. They're *different*.'

'I disagree,' said Jocasta.

After another pint of beer, Horace broke his promise to Lakshmi and told Jocasta why she'd run away.

'Oh, God, the poor thing,' said Jocasta. 'I ran away from home once. I hid at the end of the road with my scooter and my white patent-leather handbag. I think I must have been about six. What I learned from that was that if you scare your parents badly enough they don't tell you off. I think that probably remains true for the rest of your life.' She stopped, and puffed a cigarette, and said, more seriously, 'The thing is, did she run away because she was pregnant, or did she get pregnant to run away?'

'I'll have to think that one over,' said Horace. He went unsteadily to the toilet. When he came back he half expected to find that she had disappeared, but she was still in the same place, studying one of the beer-mats. She looked up at him and smiled, then she said, 'I'm going to have to go in a minute. My flat-mate's having some people round.'

'Oh, fine. I'd better get back too.' Horace looked at his watch.

'Listen, a load of us are going to Cosmic Tribe tomorrow. Do you want to come?'

'Cosmic Tribe?'

'The club.'

'Right. Yes, I'd love that.'

'Good. My friend's the press officer. She'll get us on the guest list.'

'The press officer?'

'Yes.'

Horace extrapolated Cosmic Tribe from his previous experience of nightclubs. He imagined the dance-floor of the Manhattan and doubled it in size. He peopled it with clones of Darrell and Lakshmi and added some extra staff to help cope with the increased demand for onion bhajis. 'What do they need a press officer for?' Perhaps she worked in an office above it, notifying the media of forthcoming guest beers.

'Mainly, she has to issue press releases whenever someone boils to death behind one of the speakers.' Jocasta imagined Horace with gaiters and an Ordnance Survey map, squashed in among thousands of sweaty, bare-chested ravers on a dance-floor that was vibrating as if for take-off, with smoke pouring out of vents in the ceiling, bathed in multicoloured flashing lights and out of his mind on drugs.

'It sounds dangerous,' said Horace.

'It is. You'll like it.' Jocasta got up, kissed him very lightly on each cheek, and then left.

Horace sat finishing his drink. The barman cleared away her glass, and swept the caul of Cellophane and the ashtray of faintly marked butts into a dustpan.

'How was Percy Thrower?' said Tamar.

'Fine. Coming along to the Tribe on Saturday.'

'No? Tell me everything.'

'Not much to tell. He's very nice.'

'*Jocasta.*'

'What?'

# CHAPTER THIRTEEN

Jocasta was leaning against a gravestone with a glass of white wine in her hand. Each time she opened her mouth her words were drowned in a hum of unintelligible noise, like sounds under water.

'I'm not sure I follow you,' Horace kept saying, and Jocasta would try to explain again.

'I said . . .' she began, but the rest of it was lost.

Horace couldn't place the noise. Was it a plane engine? Traffic? He had already been awake a few seconds by the time he realised that the sound was the theme tune of a children's television programme that was burbling under the door of his bedroom. He raised himself into a sitting position and scratched his scalp.

Next door, Mr Narayan sat morosely in his pyjamas watching Saturday morning television. In between the cartoons, thirty-year-old presenters with foetal faces and bouncing adult breasts urged children over an assault course of foam hurdles. The old man watched without pleasure or comprehension; he just gave his brain up for possession, letting the manic energy of the programme overwhelm the anxiety in his synapses. He hadn't shaved for a while, and his white bristles made his face look jowlier, like the folds of an old brown handbag.

On the screen, the studio audience squealed encouragement as two small boys floundered through a paddling pool of non-toxic slurry.

Lakshmi had sent her father a brief card to say she was fine, but she made no mention of her pregnancy. Mr Narayan took the news with apparent indifference. '"How sharper than a serpent's tooth it is to raise a thankless child,"' he muttered to himself. He had drunk a cocktail of bitter disappointments. What bothered him most was the thought that Lakshmi had surrendered her academic ambitions.

Hopes for Ashok and Madhu's university education had been written off as one of the costs of emigration, like the factories that had reverted to the government and were rusting unused in some corner of Kampala. Both his sons had left school early to go to work. Madhu was gradually taking over the running of the newsagent's. Ashok had bought a share in a fruit and vegetable stall on the High Street that sold speciality food to Indian restaurants: spiny green jack-fruits that burst open to yield yellow pods tasting of bubble gum; palmyra, with their sweet, opalescent flesh like the eyes of a sea monster; tamarinds; rough green drumsticks for *sambhar*; mangoes and rambutans; every conceivable dhal.

There was no doubt that Ashok and Madhu had the knack of making money. And if her brothers had thrived with the legal

189

minimum of higher education, Lakshmi had once argued, she could too. *What do I need A levels for, Dad?* But it was a bad tack – Mr Narayan was ashamed of his under-educated sons. Business acumen was a deformity they'd all had to evolve to survive a desperate transition. Only Lakshmi had been spared.

Horace was pulling on his tank top as he passed the door of the sitting room. He was doing his best to avoid the old man altogether. Mixed in with the sounds of hysterical children were klaxons and buzzers, which marked the various laps of the assault course. A huge hooter brought the game to an end. As Horace began picking his way past the creaky treads on the stairs, he heard a familiar voice emerging from the babble of sound.

'Do you have a pet, Wayne?' said the voice.

Horace paused.

'What kind of pet?' the voice continued.

Horace went back up the stairs, stepping on all the creaky ones this time, knocked on the sitting-room door, and went in.

'A dog,' said Wayne.

Mr Narayan murmured a greeting without taking his eyes from the television, where Barnaby Colefax was perched on the bonnet of a red plastic racing car and saying to a small black child, 'Really? Well, I have a dog too. What kind of dog is yours?'

'Alsatian,' said Wayne.

'And what's its name?'

'Sherry.'

'Cherry?'

'Not Cherry, Sherry!' Wayne shouted at the politician. Colefax gave a strained smile, and in the safety of his trouser pocket his hand bunched momentarily into a fist.

'I don't expect you'd like it very much if Sherry got bitten by a rabid fox and had to be put to sleep for ever, would you?' said Colefax.

Wayne shook his head theatrically.

Colefax and Trevor, who was holding a tiny fox cub, were sitting on the stage surrounded by half a dozen children, picked from the larger studio audience on the basis of cuteness and racial diversity. They all wore badges with their names on them.

The gimmick of the stage set was that it represented the contents of a child's toy box, enlarged by a factor of one hundred. At least, they were the toys the programme's producers were familiar with from their own toy boxes, not the sleek electronics and muscular androids of contemporary childhood.

Trevor was leaning against the muzzle of a giant ray-gun. His expression was grim as he held out the little animal to be fingered by the children. 'Stroke it, don't poke it, or it'll have your fingers off,' he muttered darkly at a frightened child.

Standing in the sitting room, Horace was surprised that Trevor had told him nothing about this programme and wondered for a moment if it had come up at short notice. Then he remembered Trevor's slightly wounded tone the last time he had spoken to him: 'Nice to see you got *your* name in the paper,' Trevor had said. But if Trevor couldn't bear to share his foxes with Horace, how long would he share them with Colefax?

Colefax was now looking mildly irritated as one of the presenters put a wireless microphone in Trevor's face. There was something proprietorial in the way Trevor shielded the fox from the television camera as he said, 'What I want to say to people is this, you have nothing to fear from the urban fox . . .'

'Foxes have as much right to be here as you or I.' Horace's words dubbed over the movements of Trevor's mouth and Mr Narayan looked round the wing of his armchair. 'Scrabble later, Mr N?' said Horace, who felt guilty when he was confronted by the dark bruised orbits of the old man's eyes.

Mr Narayan punched a button on the remote control to reduce the din and nodded laterally in a movement that Horace now had no trouble in recognising as affirmative.

'Say, four?' said Horace.

Four was fine with Mr Narayan.

Although it was a Saturday, Horace had promised to go to the office to help install some new equipment. After much argument, Harvard's first achievement as incoming editor had been to persuade Boothby to upgrade the facilities of the newsroom. Boothby had managed to find another company that was shedding their outdated computer terminals and proposed taking them off their hands. The manual typewriters the newspaper no longer needed had been offered to its employees for ten pounds each. Horace and Sheila Doolaly had bought one each. The others had been carted off by a sniffy rag-and-bone man for nothing.

Harvard was in the newsroom, supervising the installation. 'They're a bit tatty,' he said, surveying the secondhand terminals, 'but at least I've dragged this place into the information age.'

Horace and two of the other journalists did most of the lifting. Out of their week-day suits, crawling around in the grit dislodged by moving the furniture, they established a camaraderie that was absent during the week. Mr Sneasby sat at the news desk taking intermittent bites out of a browning apple with the air of a man who had seen off his nemesis.

'Bet you were sorry to say goodbye to the Pratt, Victor,' said Harvard, as chairs and desks squeaked into place around them.

'Life's too short to bear a grudge,' said Mr Sneasby, and munched his apple with slow patience, like a tortoise chewing a leaf.

By two o'clock a green-grey terminal was sprouting from every desk. Horace switched one on and it came alive with a ghostly ping. The cursor blinked on and off in the top left-hand corner of the empty screen. Horace pressed a variety of keys but none of them produced any discernible effect. 'Is that it?' said Horace, unable to hide his disappointment. 'What about the Internet? What about Cyberspace?' His expectations had been whetted by articles he had read in the paper: he was hungry to tour the art collections of the Hermitage and downland bomb recipes from disgruntled separatists in the United States. He also wanted to send messages to Jocasta.

'The system's not up and running yet,' said Harvard. 'The rest is up to the nerds who are coming in on Monday. In any case, you won't be able to get on the Net from here.' Then, in a voice dripping with irony, he said, 'Well, I'm glad you like it, Horace.'

'No, obviously, it's great. This is really going to make a big difference to the way I work.' Horace's fingers rippled over the keys as he pretended to be sweating under the pressure of an important deadline.

'Are you making fun of me, Horace?' said Harvard.

'Me?'

Harvard couldn't tell if he was joking.

With the exception of Sneasby, everyone trooped off to the beer garden of the Taurus Arms for lunch. Saturday and a spell of bright weather had flushed crowds of people onto the street, to sell or shop or wander. Horace stopped to chat to Ashok at his stall then caught up with the others at the pub.

The beer garden of the Taurus Arms was more beer than garden. There were a few picnic tables, dingy umbrellas sticking out of fat plastic stands and potted plants. But the sunshine redeemed it. Customers basked in it, smiling, with their heads tilted back and their eyes squeezed shut against the light.

Horace sat down with his lager shandy in the middle of a heated discussion. Romford, one of the sports reporters, was explaining his blueprint for the perfect Saturday evening. 'You can't beat a quiet night in, a couple of tins, a smoke, a Ruby Murray and *Match of the Day*,' he said, rubbing his hands at the thought of that much luxury.

'Boring! said Paula, who was a trainee like Horace.

'You'll be in trouble when the season ends,' said Harvard.

'I'm dreading it, man, I tell you. No joke.'

'What about you, Paula?' Harvard was directing the conversation like a chat-show host.

'My ideal? This would come close: tiger prawns and spaghetti with truffle oil on a beach in Thailand with one of the Chippendales. Oh, yeah, and oysters, loads of oysters.'

'See?' said Romford. 'I'd get in trouble if I said something like that.'

'Food again?' said Harvard. 'All you lot want to do is eat.'

'I'm bored of going out all the time,' said Paula.

Horace sipped his drink uncomfortably. He was wondering what he would answer when his turn came. What *did* he do at the weekend? All the true responses sounded a bit pathetic: play Scrabble with Mr Narayan; sit alone in my room reading the newspaper; go out with Trevor and accidentally cop off with a transvestite.

'As your new editor,' said Harvard, 'I have to point out that it's not bored *of* but bored *with*.'

All of them groaned in mock annoyance at his pedantry. Romford wanted to know what he would be getting up to that evening.

'My usual,' said Harvard, in a tone of deliberate mystery.

'Which is?'

'The opera,' he announced, giving the *r* a slight trill.

'Bollocks!' said Romford, in a voice choked with lager and derision.

'Another drink?' said Horace, who could feel his moment approaching. There were no takers.

'A glass of single Speyside malt,' Harvard went on, 'opera on the stereo, libretto in my lap. *That* is the way to spend a Saturday evening.'

'Libretto sounds nice,' said Romford, winking at Paula. 'I like foreign birds. They've got more class.'

Harvard looked at Horace. 'What about you?'

Horace had seen a way through the forest. 'Tonight I'm going to Cosmic Tribe with a friend,' he said.

'I thought they'd closed it down because of drug-dealing,' said Paula.

'They did,' said Harvard, 'but I think it's open while they appeal the closure order.'

'I've never actually been before.' Horace was having to back-track: his remark now appeared to have been almost too successful.

'Oh, you'll like it,' said Paula.

Romford made a face. 'White man's dance music,' he said.

'What are you going to wear?' said Paula.

'What am I going to wear?' Now he was stuck. Fudge, man, fudge. 'I haven't decided yet.'

The queue for Cosmic Tribe was at its longest between eleven and twelve in the evening, after the pubs had shut and before the ticket prices rose at midnight from ten to fifteen pounds. From the outside the building was indistinguishable from the late 1960s shopping centre which it abutted and in whose car park its patrons parked their parents' cars on Friday and Saturday nights.

Jocasta and her friends arrived in their own cars. They were part of an older crowd who had started clubbing a bit later and stuck with it a bit longer. They looked down on the mainly teenaged ravers who went to Cosmic Tribe. In other, smaller, London clubs, the punters dressed better and carried themselves with more sophistication. But Jocasta's friend could get them all on the guest list whenever they wanted and there was something intoxicating about the sheer size of the place and the singlemindedness with which the younger clubbers set out to enjoy themselves.

Jocasta liked to tell the story about the time she gave a sixteen-year-old girl half her precious seat in the packed chill-out room. Drugs were fizzing through the girl's blood and she clung to Jocasta's wrist with a hot, damp hand as her eyelids fluttered open and shut over her saucer-wide eyes. 'I'm scared,' said the girl, as Jocasta reassured her. 'I've never had a whole one before. I shouldn't really. I'm two months' pregnant.'

In the side-street outside the club, four or five hot-dog stands were setting up for business and puffing out onion fumes. It was ten past eleven and Horace had been waiting for fifteen minutes to one side of the queue that was building along the pavement.

Jocasta and her friends left their cars on the fifth floor of the car park above the shopping centre. They descended to ground level in a clanging lift that smelt of piss.

Horace hardly recognised her. She was wearing patent-leather boots, a jade green miniskirt and a short jacket that looked as though it was made of black ostrich feathers. On her back, she was carrying a miniature rucksack like a tiny parachute. She pecked him on both cheeks and introduced him to her friends. 'You didn't have to dress up,' she said.

Horace was wearing a pair of baggy brown trousers and a shirt he had ironed that evening. He'd also brought a cardigan in case it got chilly later.

'Why are you limping?' Jocasta asked.

'I dropped a typewriter on my foot.' The clanky old manual had slipped from his grasp as he carried it from the office that afternoon. Horace's new trainers were aggravating his injury. The shoes were identical to a pair Lakshmi had coveted, except they were a different brand, slightly more crudely made and a tenth of the price. He had congratulated himself on his prudence.

One of Jocasta's friends was a handsome mocha-coloured man called Dylan who had crimped his hair into porcupine quills. 'First time here?' he said to Horace. Jocasta was attracting the attention of a security guard.

'Yes.'

'Jocasta says you're a journalist.'

'Yes.'

'Cool.' The fronds of Dylan's hair waggled slightly as he nodded.

The guard waved them through the door, stopping briefly to tick Horace off for his appearance. 'Make a bit of effort next time, mate. People have come here to enjoy themselves. All right?'

Horace couldn't understand it: the shirt and trousers had

taken ages to iron. And why wasn't the guard concerned about the polyester T-shirts of Jocasta's friends? Tamar was crammed into a top so small it left a couple of inches bare around her navel, which was pierced with the kind of brass stud used for sealing parcels.

The narrow corridor veered sharply to the left after a few yards and passed the ticket office. As they went down it, the distant thumping grew louder and started to insinuate itself into their movements. Jocasta's jaw was working, chewing gum on the beat. Dylan was waving his fronds in time to the music.

Jocasta spoke to the languid attendants in the ticket office and waved them all through the double doors. The music was so loud that she had to put her lips next to Horace's ear to say, 'Dylan's a musician. Tracy's PR company represents his label. Can you check this in for me?' She gave Horace her feathery coat to leave at the cloakroom. 'I'll be right back.'

The room they were in was some kind of antechamber for the main club. Most of it was taken up by the queue for the cloakroom, which was longer than the queue on the street outside. The attendants were dancing in jerky movements as they took the coats and handed over numbered paper tickets. Jocasta went off towards the source of the pounding, through a doorway that was intermittently lit up with flashes of light. To Horace, the noise was an impenetrable din, like the sound of a building site or a car factory.

He checked in Jocasta's coat and bag, and his cardigan. Apart from Dylan, he wasn't able to recognise any of Jocasta's friends. Every other person in the club seemed to be wearing a too tight polyester T-shirt.

Jocasta came back with a handful of pills and a bottle of Cosmic Tribe mineral water.

The doorway into the next room was blocked up with people waiting to pass into or out of the main part of the club. Dylan, Horace and Jocasta had to push their way through the throng. On the other side was a vast, hangar-like space with a central dais where a handful of dancers were urging the crowd on. Here, the music was so loud it had a physical presence: the deepest bass notes induced a sympathetic vibration in Horace's gut.

There was motion everywhere: in the marionette movements of the dancers on the stage and the purposeful flows of people moving from room to room. Even the music had an urgent forward momentum. Jocasta said something but her voice was inaudible over the noise. Horace asked her to repeat it. 'I said, it's *mental* in here.'

Horace agreed. Some of the dancers did look like the inmates of a lunatic asylum. Groups of boys were dancing together, stripped to the waist, jaws contorting round their chewing gum, their eyes as wide and unblinking as a herring's. Others had the dark, drained faces of the lobotomised. Some were shrieking above the noise.

Jocasta nibbled one of her pills and quickly took a sip of water. 'Bitter.' She grimaced. 'Want some?'

'I'm not sure,' said Horace. 'Will I boil to death?'

'Unlikely.'

The pill was the texture of chalk and left an aftertaste so bitter it made him shiver. He tried to rinse it away with the water. Dylan also took one.

'Let's go to the chill-out room for a bit.' Jocasta led the way through the crowd.

The chill-out room was less noisy than the dance-floor. The music was softer: undulating planes of electronic sound. The three of them squashed onto two seats of a sofa. 'The others have gone off to dance,' said Jocasta. 'They'll come here when they feel like monging.'

There was an odd lack of libidinal energy in the atmosphere. For all the bare flesh on show, there was no sense of sexual intent: no stiletto-heeled women at the bar waiting to be bought a drink, no men sharking around for partners. People had come in groups or couples and were contentedly self-absorbed with their pills and bottles of water, like day-trippers at the seaside with sandwiches and Thermos flasks.

Horace bought two beers and a bottle of water at the bar and perched on the edge of the sofa. So far he hadn't noticed any effect of the drug that couldn't be put down to the volume of the music and the size of the crowd.

Jocasta shouted in his ear, 'Dylan was just saying he got harassed by the police this evening.'

'Really?'

'Stopped my car, innit. Forty-five minutes they were talking to me. They said you look tasty. I said I'm answering your questions but if you put your hands on me there's going to be trouble. I'm not having any of that custody in death shit.'

'Custody in death?' asked Horace.

'Yeah.' Dylan looked aggrieved.

'It's like what Colefax said.'

'Yeah, but the thing is, politicians are only waking up to it when it happens to them.'

Jocasta told a long story about being arrested aged fourteen for being drunk on the platform of Earl's Court station.

'I got stopped by a policeman today,' said Horace. 'He thought I'd stolen a manual typewriter.' He was going to explain what had happened to him but suddenly didn't feel like it. The muscles in his neck felt tight. His palms were sweaty. There was a flutter of anticipation in his stomach. Behind the repetitive thumps of the beat was a rushing oceanic sound that appeared to move across the room. He closed his eyes to hear it better, as it slid first one way and then another across the ceiling like something in flight. He shivered. He was staring at a spotlight with his eyes shut and watching the rosy penumbra on the inside of his lids. He squeezed his eyes closed tighter and chrysanthemum blossoms flowered behind his eyelids.

It was like basking in sunshine. He could feel the heat of it on his face and craned his neck towards the light. He *was* basking in the sun. He was on the beach at Lyme Regis with his grandfather. The oceanic roar of the speakers was the sound of the waves. He thought, *The peace that passeth all understanding.* He wanted to stay there, with the old man, staring out to sea. He wanted to think about nothing else. He felt unutterably calm.

Dylan and Jocasta also had their eyes shut. 'So, what about this manual typewriter?' Dylan said slowly.

'I said, I wouldn't buy a copy of the newspaper while I was out burgling houses,' said Horace, smiling to himself as he spoke, even though he knew he was mangling the anecdote. 'And he said it could all be part of a cunning ruse.'

'He said that? Cunning ruse?'

They were all silent for a while. Then Jocasta said, 'Cunning ruse,' and they all giggled.

'I have to use the toilet,' said Horace. 'Don't go away.' He opened his eyes and looked at Dylan and Jocasta. He'd only just met Dylan, but he felt an odd rapport with him. He was sorry to have to leave them to go to the toilet. He patted Dylan's hand.

'We're not going anywhere,' said Dylan.

The toilets were crowded and silent. A line of men were waiting to fill up their water bottles at the sink. The handles of the taps had been removed and they gave out a slow unvariable trickle. The queuers were as placid and wide-eyed as a herd of cows, ruminating on their chewing gum. The music had diminished to a vague thud. Horace felt frail and unsteady. He kept licking his dry lips. He sat on the toilet sweating with his head in his hands, fragments of his beach dream recurring.

When he felt able to, he joined the queue for water, which inched along the wet floor. Some of the men poured it onto their heads and chests. A man wearing plastic armour butted into the queue next to him. 'Is that all right, mate? I've got to get something to drink.' His eyes bulged. He was trying to blow air upwards onto his red face. '*Nil desperandum*,' he said.

'I'm sorry?'

'Someone nicked my crown.'

'That's a shame.' Horace smiled, he felt full of benign understanding for this man with his plastic armour. 'That's a nice suit of armour.'

'It's just a bit of a laugh, innit. The once and future king and all that. Albion. Where are you from then, mate?'

'Near here, Wandsworth.'

'Wandsworth? Don't think I know that.'

'It's where we are now,' said Horace.

'Oh, right.'

'I met Arthur Pendragon in the toilet,' said Horace, as he slid in between Jocasta and Dylan.

'I'm ready for a bit of a shuffle. You coming?' said Dylan.

'No way.' Jocasta's eyelids were fluttering as though she was on the edge of sleep.

'I'm gonna mong later. I'll find you here.' Dylan set off, after giving Horace a fond pat on the cheek.

'God, these are strong,' said Jocasta. 'I'm rinsing my brain out. What would your grandfather say about this?'

'I think he'd say, "Things are going badly in this wicked world."' Horace closed his eyes. He saw his grandfather's head carved on the belfry of the church at Great Much. It detached itself with a forlorn whoop and flew over the churchyard like a bat. He flew with it for a while, over the road towards Otherbury, past the houses and fields he knew. Then he opened his eyes. In front of him, a man was stripped to the waist and dancing with gestures that were aimed at Horace like blows. Horace smiled at him. The man just grinned, his eyeballs were bulging like a terrier's. His arms were chopping the air just in front of Horace and Jocasta as though powered by galvanic energy. Jocasta smiled at him too, hoping he'd stop it. More than anything, the situation seemed socially awkward. 'We're just talking,' said Horace.

'Yes,' said Jocasta. 'We're just talking.'

'You don't want to talk,' the man shouted, in a hoarse voice. 'You want to *rush*.' The electrical charge powering his muscles propelled him to the dance-floor.

The rhythms that had seemed invasive when Horace had first entered the club now seemed almost unnoticeable. Instead of fighting to be heard above the music, he felt as though he were suspended in it: a womb of pulsing noise.

Jocasta's ear was about six inches away from Horace. It was as pale and pink as the inside of a seashell and smelt very faintly of perfume. Just in front of it, the light hairs that were too short to be pulled back with the others stirred slightly from his breathing. He moved closer to kiss it. 'Don't,' said Jocasta. 'That tickles.' She kissed him on the mouth and flicked her pointed pink tongue, which tasted unbearably sweet from the chewing gum.

'Look at these two,' said Dylan's voice above them.

'I'm snogging Horace,' said Jocasta.

Jocasta drove Tamar, her boyfriend, Ashley, and Horace back to their flat. They had to leave early because Tamar had started to feel sick. It was about four in the morning. 'Jo,' she moaned from the back seat, 'I'm all pilled up.' Ashley didn't say anything.

Horace sat in the front seat with a street map on his lap. He had lost the ability to distinguish reliably between left and right. Even the red of the traffic lights seemed oddly ambiguous. Jocasta drove extremely slowly. 'Look at that,' said Horace.

'What? What?' Jocasta was trying to keep her eyes on the road.

'Over there. Slow down a bit.'

They were alongside Clapham Common, heading towards Brixton. A fox was trotting across the road. '*Vulpes vulpes*,' said Horace. 'The urban fox.'

The others leaned forward to peer out of the window. The car was practically at a standstill. The fox paused in the headlights and seemed to look straight at them. Its eyes glowed green.

'Fucking weird,' said Ashley. 'Did you see its eyes?'

The animal continued to cross, then as Jocasta put her foot on the accelerator, it changed its mind and trotted back into the path of the car. There was a soft thump under the left front wheel.

The fox lay at the side of the road. It wasn't visibly marked, but it trembled slightly and made no effort to move. Horace called Trevor on Jocasta's mobile phone. Tamar and Ashley stayed in the car listening to music. The accident and the fresh air seemed to have cleared Horace's head, but when he looked at the street-lights, they had aureolas in the shape of giant orange moths.

The streets were clear of traffic and Trevor took only about ten minutes to arrive.

'Been to a party?' he said, with a tinge of envy. Horace thought he meant to make him feel guilty. Music was still tinkling out of the car.

'Club,' said Horace, following him round to where the fox lay.

'Let's have a look at you, then. Don't worry, my dove.' He touched the fox gently with a gloved finger-tip. 'She's a goner, I think.' He straightened up. 'Yeah. PTS job. This is my second RTA this week.' It was as if he couldn't say *put to sleep* in case it upset the fox. He took a syringe from a kit in his car and injected the animal with barbiturates. 'Easy, my dove.' Jocasta leaned her head on Horace's shoulder.

Horace suddenly had a thought and grinned. 'Hey, Trevor, I saw you on TV. "Stroke it, don't poke it!" '

Trevor looked at him as though he had belched in a crematorium. 'Horace, an animal is *dying* here.'

'Yes,' said Jocasta. 'Don't be so insensitive.'

'You've done the right thing, calling me,' said Trevor, as he walked gravely back to his car. 'Don't worry about it, love. It can't be helped. One thing you could do, though. I have to pay for the materials I use. A contribution would be appreciated.'

'Yes, of course,' said Jocasta. She let go of Horace to dig in her purse for first one twenty-pound note and then another. 'I feel terrible about this.'

'You needn't. Unfortunately, this happens all the time. It's the number one enemy of the urban fox. At least, apart from those twats in Brussels. Right, Horace?'

'What's that? Oh, yeah, right.' Horace had been drifting off: the music stole out of the car and set off that oceanic feeling. He wanted to sneak into the back seat and insert himself between Tamar and Ashley and close his eyes, like a cub in a litter.

Trevor frowned at him. 'You all right? It's been a long night, hasn't it, mate? You don't look all there.' He directed his attention back to Jocasta as if to punish Horace for not listening. 'You've done the right thing, love. If anything like it happens again, you can reach me on this number.' He went over to gather up the body of the dead animal. 'I'm not saying that it will, but I know lady drivers, eh? And you'd better look after Dozy here. He looks about ready for bed.' He directed a long-suffering look at Horace and set off to his car.

Jocasta got in the car and pummelled the steering wheel, half seriously. 'I can't believe it. What an annoying git! I feel like running *him* over.'

Horace was feeling secretly pleased that Trevor had made such a bad impression with his misplaced gallantry. 'He's got this bad habit of saying the wrong thing,' he said.

Jocasta looked at him in disbelief. 'Unbelievable. He should be in a museum with a label saying "Unreconstructed Northern Sexist".' She pulled away from the kerb. 'At least I don't feel so guilty about his fox.' Then she added, 'Poor thing.'

When they got back to the flat, Tamar and Ashley went to bed. Horace and Jocasta sat on the sofa drinking glasses of wine. 'I don't know why she takes it,' said Jocasta. 'It just makes her anxious. How are you feeling?'

'Excellent.' Horace felt relaxed. They sat in silence listening to the stereo. Jocasta smoked.

'I'm not very good at this,' she said.

'What do you mean?'

'You know.'

Horace nodded.

'I'm quite dozy. I think I'll go to bed after this.' She blew out a cloud of smoke.

'Do you want to stay or not?'

'If you don't mind . . .' Horace said.

'On one condition.' She balanced the cigarette on the edge of the ashtray, then yanked out the tails of his shirt and, unbuttoning it at the collar, pulled it over his head. Then she took off his trousers, squashed the clothes into a ball and threw them into the bin in the kitchen. The lid clanked down and she came back into the sitting room. 'I've got something you can wear in the morning,' she said, and led him by the hand to the plum-blue darkness of her bedroom.

# PART FOUR

# CHAPTER FOURTEEN

'THE SON?' SAID Harvard Machine.

'Apparently so.' Marcus Hennessey offered his new editor a little grey pellet of nicotine chewing gum.

Harvard pointed to the patch on his forearm. 'Well. I'd never have thought it.' He was remembering that day at the offices of the *Dinakaran*, the son's hoarse voice saying, *I saw the body, it was a professional job*. Even if he was the murderer, the grief could still be unfeigned. 'I'd like you to make it to the arraignment,' he said, finally. 'Frankly, I'm a little incredulous.'

Hennessey chewed his gum in bursts for punctuation. 'I

talked to one of the blokes at the station off the record. It seems to have been some sort of dispute over money. He ran the paper like a family shop. You know, rather informal financial arrangements, everyone pitching in and doing their bit. He liked to keep a firm grip on it all. They think the son just got tired of waiting for the old man to retire, slipped someone some money and bang, the old man's all over the front of the office.'

Harvard remembered the photographer scuffing the blood off his shoe. 'And all that stuff about the Tamil Tigers?'

'Red herring. Maybe he thought the police would get hung up with that and never get round to suspecting the family. I feel sorry for the poor sod who spent months translating all the back issues of the paper. Mind you, it's a better story – politics of the sub-continent and all that.'

Harvard ruminated. 'I suppose it's obvious. You're more likely to get nobbled by a member of your own family than a Sri Lankan hit squad, whoever you are.'

'It's too bad you weren't the detective leading the inquiry, Harvard. They'd have wrapped things up much sooner.'

'You're still on probation, Hennessey. Take a photographer with you.'

Hennessey grabbed his coat and headed out of the building. He was one of three new reporters Harvard had recruited from the agencies. It had meant a huge battle with Boothby, but he didn't mind that. The only drawback was that Boothby had demanded something in return.

'Our local MP is getting behind an issue of national significance, Harvard. "Rock the Fox" fits in with the campaigning traditions of the *South London Bugle*. I know you don't have a high opinion of Colefax, but I think he's with the angels on this one.' Boothby delivered the words pompously and slowly as though to remind Harvard that he was, after all, the proprietor and editor. Harvard had tried to remain respectfully intransigent.

'There's a strong intellectual case for the lifting of quarantine as well, you know, Derwent. It's just that when English people hear the word "rabies" they start to froth at the mouth. It's Pavlovian.'

'It's not a question of taking sides on this issue. The "Rock the Fox" supplement will be a service to our readers. It'll be a guide to who's playing at the concert.'

Harvard took a deep breath. 'The thing is, Derwent, I don't see how we can publish a guide to the concert without implicitly endorsing Colefax. And I, for one, don't feel that I can endorse the man's frankly xenophobic opinions.'

Boothby made a noise like an engine backfiring. 'I am your publisher, Harvard.'

'Let me think it over.'

Having thought it over, Harvard decided it was still a bad idea, but agreeing to this request was the only way to secure the new employees. Harvard swallowed his principles and decided to scratch Boothby's bristly old back this once, as a matter of self-interest.

Since Pratt's departure, the paper had begun to put on readers. It was nothing miraculous, but there had been a change of atmosphere, and it was reflected in the finished product. Some of the gloom had lifted from the newsroom. The most jaded of the old-timers had been let go, and the greenest of the proposed replacements had been vetoed in favour of more experienced, more expensive journalists. Harvard encouraged a bit more risk-taking with the fetaures and a bit more discipline with the news.

But the change that had come over the paper was nothing compared to the change that had come over Horace Littlefair. He was a man transformed. Gone were the fusty old clothes; gone was the otherworldly wistfulness; gone was the solitary man with a preference for weekends spent in the office. In his place was a dapper figure, dressed in a charcoal grey suit and peacock blue tie, who owned a personal stereo and spent two evenings a week at the gymnasium – exertion that he secretly despised but did anyway because it seemed to make Jocasta happy.

And here, perhaps, was an irony. For a while Horace had caught up with the world, the world was already beginning to move on. Jocasta kept a stack of fashion magazines in her toilet, and from them one thing was clear. Fashion editors, who organise the nation's wardrobes on the principle that no style of dress remains ridiculous for ever, had instigated a craze for retro-rural chic. Lydia Skin had appeared on the cover of Italian Vogue in moleskin breeches and a gardening bib. A 1950s tweed suit was precisely the outfit that every person of taste now coveted.

As for Trevor, Horace had thought little and heard nothing of him since the night-time meeting over the fatally injured fox. He assumed Trevor had been too busy running errands for Colefax, who had been ubiquitous since winning permission to stage his concert on Clapham Common. Then, as Hennessey brushed past his desk on the way to the arraignment, the phone ran. It was Trevor.

'Hello, mate, been trying to get hold of you for days.'

'Really? I've been here.'

'You're like me, you are, only contactable when you want to be. So how's things?'

'Not bad.'

'How's that girlfriend of yours? Run over any more animals?'

'No.'

'Everything all right? You sound a bit odd.'

'No, no. I'm trying to finish off a bit of work. What's on your mind?'

Trevor had hoped to sidle up to the favour he needed and was discomfited to be asked straight out. 'It just so happens that the next issue of our newsletter is due out and I promised our friend Colefax we'd have some copies for the concert.'

'Right.'

'Thing is, he needs it yesterday, if you get my meaning. I need to take it in to him tomorrow at the latest.'

'Right.' Horace had been planning to spend the evening with Jocasta.

'I could really do with some help. You know, you're the words man.'

Pathos and flattery together were irresistible. 'All right, then,' said Horace.

'Nice one. I'll take you and your missus out for a slap-up this weekend. See you this evening.'

Horace knocked on the door of Harvard's office. He had decorated it with a poster of Scotland's 1978 World Cup team and some postcard scenes of Lvov. 'Come in, have a seat, success hasn't changed me,' said Harvard. But it wasn't quite true, he seemed to be thriving on the pressure and the battles with Boothby.

'Hi, there. I've got a favour to ask.'

'Ask away.'

'I've promised the fox bloke that I'll give him a hand with a special issue of his newsletter for Colefax's thing on the Common.'

'"Thing on the Common" hardly begins to do it justice. You are referring, of course, to the Rock the Fox extravaganza.'

Horace carried on through the irony. 'He wants to run off about five hundred copies. I told him I'd type it and photocopy it.'

'No problem.'

'We could pay something for the copies. I don't know what it would cost.'

Harvard sometimes wished Horace would take things without asking, exploit those near him and abuse the few privileges of his underpaid job. He worried that, despite his growing confidence, Horace didn't have the streak of ruthlessness necessary for survival in a world of Pratts and Boothbys. 'Don't be crazy, Horace. Just use it. You know, whoever said, "There's no such thing as a free lunch," had never worked in journalism.'

'That's great. I appreciate that.'

'Better still. Forget the typewriter. Lay it out on one of the terminals here. How long's it going to be?'

'Four pages, I expect, if that.'

'Do it here. Don't type the sodding thing. You're breaking my heart. I've got the computers in here so we can move into the next millennium only a few decades behind everybody else.'

'Thanks, Harvard.'

'Don't mention it. I hope this guy's paying you.' Harvard followed him out to the newsroom.

'He is, sort of. He's supposed to be paying me in kind.'

'What's that? A couple of foxes?'

'Something like that.' Horace smiled lamely.

Horace and Trevor struggled with the newsletter from seven in the evening onwards. Trevor embraced the suggestion of using the computers to produce it, but they soon found them frustrating. The software for laying out pages was baffling and old-fashioned. Bits of work kept disappearing into electronic limbo. Eventually they decided to print out the text in simple columns and glue them to A3 sheets.

Trevor wanted to reproduce line-drawings from books he had brought with him, and was disappointed to hear that copyright laws made it impossible, or at least illegal. Eventually, the two of them compromised on some photographs from Trevor's own collection that reproduced fairly clearly on the photocopier. Horace sketched a passable fox for the masthead. Even then, the projected four pages were less than half full, and it was already ten o'clock.

They had been held up with the writing of the editorial. Trevor had composed a long and fawning endorsement of Colefax's work against the bill: 'People can waffle on as much as they like, but at the end of the day it takes someone with the "guts" to stand up for what they believe in . . .' And so it went on. Horace attempted to rewrite it but secretly he knew he was simply making it worse.

For the inside pages, Horace wrote a short piece explaining the merits of quarantine. Underneath it, he stuck Trevor's selection of 'Fox Facts'. And, seized by whimsy, he wrote a crossword based on trivia questions about the life-cycle of the fox.

The last item was a sponsorship form. It had three columns for the donor's name, address and size of their contribution. There was, ambitiously, room for thirty sponsors, though the directions for using the form were obscure. By this point, however, Horace didn't want to raise any objections that would prolong their working day. They had been in the office together for five hours.

When they had finished pasting up the cut strips, the logo, the photographs and the hand-drawn crossword, they photocopied it onto both sides of a sheet of A3.

'These columns are a bit wonky,' said Trevor. 'And this photo has come out blurry.'

'They always do on a photocopier.' Tiredness was beginning to make Horace snappy.

'It's not bad, though. It'll do.'

They photocopied five hundred of the outside pages, put all the sheets back into the machine and photocopied the inside pages onto them. The photocopier complained and trembled like an old mule being driven up a moutainside. Some of the copies were spoiled because, in his tiredness, Horace had put them back in the wrong way up. 'That's not much use, is it?' Trevor opened one of the defective issues to show its upside-down inside pages. 'I think the toner's a bit low.'

'I think we're allowed a couple of double-yolkers,' said Horace. There weren't more than thirty that were unusable. And once Horace and Trevor had folded all the good ones and packed them into a cardboard box, they looked at the evening's work with something like pride. Horace gave the box a paternal stroke and agreed to go with Trevor to Colefax's office in five hours' time.

'I think you must be my first Horace,' said the young man in a suit who took them up in the lift.

'Well, you're definitely his first Tarquin,' said Trevor, 'and mine.'

'Yes,' said Tarquin. 'I get a lot of that. Still, better than John

Smith, isn't it? You'll have to excuse the disarray but we've had to get up and running from a standing start in less than three weeks. Barnaby's still shuttling between here and Westminster and his surgery.' The wood-panelling of the lobby imposed a deferential silence on Horace and Trevor, who was carrying the big box of newsletters. The elderly receptionist greeted Tarquin, who said, 'It's all right, these two are with me.'

The office smelt of fresh carpet and new computers. Well before nine o'clock, its enthusiastic occupants were buzzing around the room, talking in loud young voices. Tarquin stopped by a man who was absorbed in his computer terminal. 'This is Hugh, he's designing the web-site. Barnaby's keen to have this as cutting edge as possible.' An overweight girl with her long hair in an Alice band was on the phone next to him. 'Tiggy Wigmore. Tiggy's just back from a *stage* in Brussels.' Tiggy gave them a little wave. 'We're lucky to have her with us: she knows how the enemy thinks. Now this is the person you need: Cassandra Thorfinnsdottir. The communications director.'

Cassandra was a pretty young woman of about twenty-one who had been studiously ignoring the visitors.

'Thorfinnsdottir,' said Horace. 'Is that an Indian name?'

'Iceland,' said Cassandra, and gave him a smile so chilly it might have frozen vodka.

'We've brought the newsletters,' said Trevor, plopping the box onto her desk.

'The newsletters?'

'Did I stutter?' said Trevor. There was a prickling unease in the silence after he spoke.

Cassandra laughed nervously and lifted out the top copy. In this bright, well-lit office, the newsletter suddenly looked hideous: the reproduction poor, the logo ill-drawn, the columns clearly crooked. Cassandra looked up from it. Her puzzled expression seemed to say: Give me some help here, why have you put this rubbish on my desk? Trevor looked blankly back.

'I think Mr Colefax knows about this,' said Horace. 'He's been working very closely with Trevor in the campaign against the bill. Trevor endorsed him a long time ago. And I think Mr Colefax asked him to produce some kind of newsletter to coincide with the concert. That's right, isn't it?' Trevor nodded his assent.

'This is the first I've heard of it. The thing is, we've just had these back from the printers.' Cassandra reached down beside her desk and lifted up her own cardboard box. 'These are our infopacks.'

Horace picked one up. It was the size and weight of a woman's magazine and as sleek and glossy as the bonnet of a new car. A full colour photograph of a baby fox cub and tiny Labrador puppy filled the front cover. It opened to reveal two cardboard wallets stuffed with booklets and fact sheets, more colour photographs, pie charts, graphs, badges and bumper stickers.

'How many of these have you got?' said Trevor.

'Several thousand more.'

'Well,' Trevor continued, 'we can run off some more of these on your photocopier and we'll just slip one of ours in each of yours. You can give us a hand.'

Cassandra laughed. 'Well, we can't just do *that*. This has been designed. I mean, the whole thing has a kind of integrated, graphic *look*. I'm afraid these would just let down the whole tone of the infopack. The pack is complete as it stands. Barnaby has said nothing to me about a supplement.'

Trevor was leafing through one of his own newsletters. 'What about this stuff? Fox facts. A crossword. Yours doesn't have a crossword.'

Horace edged the typed sheets away from the glossy bindings. He saw Hugh looking over from his computer. Trevor and Cassandra were about to begin rowing when Tiggy arrived to conciliate them with her expansive smiles. 'Barnaby's just called from a taxi to say he'll be in any minute. Do you want to wait over here? Now, can I get you some coffee?' She parked Horace and Trevor at an empty desk and gave Cassandra a knowing look as she went off to make it.

Horace wanted to take the box of newsletters and leave immediately. But Trevor was determined to stay there. 'Bloody infopack. Stupid tart doesn't know what she's going on about. I'm not going to be spoken to like that by a Sloane on the phone.' Horace wasn't sure how much of it was bluster to hide his embarrassment.

Colefax picked up one of the newsletters and twirled it absently. Horace willed it to burst into flames in his hands. 'There must have been some misunderstanding. When we said we needed an information pack I didn't mean you should do it yourself. I hope this hasn't meant a lot of wasted effort.'

'Why don't you just slip them into your infopacks or whatever they're called?' Trevor was sitting directly opposite Colefax. Horace was at one side, moving his head to follow the conversation like a spectator at a tennis match. Colefax was being firm but consoling.

'Well, I'm afraid I rather agree with Cassandra there,' he said. 'She's gone to a lot of trouble to have these things made. I don't think they're quite made to go together, do you?' He held up an infopack in one hand and the newsletter in the other. 'In another way, I'm not altogether sorry this has happened because it illustrates something that's been on my mind –'

'Excuse me, sorry, but Gideon Deck's on the phone.' Tiggy's head and arm had appeared in the doorway.

'Thanks Tiggy. Can you tell him I'll call back?' The door shut with a thunk. 'This campaign has taken off more than I could have imagined, and I'm sure more than you ever expected. We have all sorts of backers, sponsors – very keen to see this bill stopped. You wouldn't believe the depth of the support we've received. Just to take one example,' he pointed through the glass wall of the office, 'that lot. Not one of them is paid. They're doing this because they love the work and they believe in it.' The politician went on, 'The point I'm making is this, Trevor. Each person should do the thing he knows best. I think it's time for *you* to concentrate on your core interest – the fox – and leave the rest of it to us. Believe me, I won't forget your help.' He stood up and gave them a smile. 'Don't forget these.' Horace took the box of newsletters. 'While I'm thinking of it,' Colefax pressed a device on his desk, 'Cassandra, do you have any more of those backstage passes for Rock the Fox? Can you see Morris and Trevor get a couple? Well, I'll see you both there. Trevor, keep up the good work. You know that none of us would be here without you.'

'Let's face it. The newsletter was quite shit. It's not surprising Colefax wanted nothing to do with it.' Jocasta pulled up her long skirt to let the sunlight fall onto her pale legs. It was after seven in the evening, but slanted shafts of yellow light shone through the trees. The foliage everywhere was unkempt and excessive, like the ornamentation on the Victorian tombs around them. Cherubs, angels, urns, wreaths, columns and plain sarcophagi vied with vines and long grass. The bric-à-brac of death was half buried under the greenery; the monuments of a forgotten north London necropolis. Jocasta took a swig from the bottle and gave him a winy kiss. He moved his head in mock-annoyance, ignoring the hurt look she gave him.

'That's not the point.' He was about to say more but someone was approaching. Jocasta straightened her skirt. The two of them squinted up into the yellow light and smiled a bit foolishly. They were as far away from the main avenues of the cemetery as it was possible to be. This was their first interruption. 'That's not the point. We had no time to do it. Trevor said it was needed urgently. Then it turned out it wasn't needed at all.'

'Sounds like it was Trevor's fault.'

'I think he was trying to be more involved. He's oddly sensitive. He likes to be stroked.'

'So do I.' She looked up at him, immediately regretting that she'd said it. It felt corny. But Horace carried on talking and began running his hand through the long hair close to the nape of her neck. She closed her eyes. She remembered: she didn't have to weigh everything she said for wit and originality with

Horace. His unflagging approval relaxed her and dissolved her prickliness.

'It must have been embarrassing for him,' he said. 'I think it upset him to be so left out of the organising. In a way, he imagines the foxes belong to him. He resents other people being involved.'

'Maybe he thinks he's a fox.'

'There's a bit of that too.'

'Well, you got those passes out of it.'

'Mmm.' Horace leaned his head against the warm marble. Long grass tickled his ear.

'Who are you going to take?'

'I'm trying to narrow down a long list.'

Jocasta punched his arm.

'Ouch. You. You, if you'll let me.'

She rubbed the place she'd just hit and said, 'I've met his wife, you know.'

'Colefax's?'

'No. Gideon Deck's.'

'You mentioned.'

'Very strange woman. But I suppose you would be if you were married to a rock god.'

The wine and the sunlight were sending them to sleep. Horace closed his eyes. 'The weird thing about Colefax and Trevor is that they should ever have got involved in the first place.'

'How did it happen?'

'Colefax befriended him really, gave him money for Fox Outreach in return for a kind of endorsement.'

'Well, now that he's got the BMA and RSPCA behind him, poor old Trevor is pretty irrelevant.'

'But Colefax is still friendly with him.'

'How long have they known each other?'

Horace took a swig from the wine bottle. 'It was around the time I got to London. Colefax read an article I wrote and got in touch with Trevor after that, so that would be some time towards the end of January.'

'This year?'

'Yeah.'

'That was about the same time Colefax got caught with my friend Raylena.'

'Right.'

Jocasta rolled over onto her stomach. 'He can't have had a lot of time on his hands for working with wildlife groups.'

'So?'

'It's odd. He's about to be nailed for soliciting and probably deselected – that's if he isn't made to resign immediately. What does he do? He starts laying the groundwork for a campaign against a bill that's going to be debated *months* after his court appearance.'

'That's strength of character. He wasn't going to just give up and assume it was all over.'

'It still seems odd.'

The sun was dipping further. It was getting cold. 'So,' said Jocasta, 'are you glad I brought you here?'

'Really. It's amazing. I'm surprised more people don't know about it.'

'It's one of the city's secrets. There are lots, you know.'

Horace smiled. 'So I've heard.'

'I think we should go back to your house tonight.'

Horace imagined her in his tiny room. 'That's not the best idea. My landlord is pretty old-fashioned.'

'This is the guy who drove his daughter away?'

'That's a bit harsh.' Horace got up and helped Jocasta to her feet. 'Also, you won't like my flat.'

'Who says?'

'Believe me. I'm sure about this.'

'So move. Get a place I can stay at.'

'It's not the best time. Mr Narayan's very depressed. He's not getting on with his sons. I'm more or less the only person who talks to him.'

'This is absurd. You can't stay there because of your landlord.'

'No?'

'You get rid of one demanding old man who won't let you leave, and six months later you've found another.'

'My grandfather wasn't demanding.'

'No? What would you call him, then?'

'He was just old.'

Their arguing voices carried over the graves of the empty cemetery as they walked to the front gates. They stopped by her car. 'Are you all right to drive?'

'I'm *fine*. I only had about two swigs.' She was flushed and her hair had come loose from the clip where Horace had been stroking it. There was something touching in her indignation.

'Just asking,' he said quietly, and bent to kiss her on the lips.

'Jocasta thought you'd be interested,' said Horace, winding up his story. Harvard had listened quietly.

He called Hennessey in from the newsroom. 'Tell him what you told me.'

'It's not much,' Horace began. 'I was just mentioning to Harvard that – how can I explain this –'

Harvard butted in. 'It's a question of dates. Our pal Colefax started his nonsense about the urban fox back in January, at exactly the same time he had his hands full with his court case. Do you follow me? He calls this bloke –'

'Trevor,' said Horace. 'Trevor Diamond.'

'Right. He starts taking an interest in *wildlife*.' Harvard said it was incredulity. 'Why?' He raised his hands in bafflement. 'Horace doesn't think there's anything in this. But then he's rather a fan of Colefax, aren't you?' Horace ignored the teasing. Harvard went on, 'I think it's worth taking a look into this. Do you know anyone in the Streatham vice squad? What about the bloke who stopped them?'

Hennessey shook his head. 'He's moved on. They got a lot of stick after the court case. Threats. They made out the whole

222

squad were racists. You know how these things work. We're not too popular down there ourselves.'

'Why's that?'

'Colefax's column. Apparently he was rather scathing about the police after his trial.'

'It was quite measured, I thought, considering,' said Horace.

Harvard thought for a moment. 'Do this, look. Hennessey can call the lads in Streatham. See if you can find out where this bloke's gone. But don't let on to anyone else what you're up to. I don't want to have to explain to Boothby that we're investigating his star columnist.'

'Right, then.' Hennessey went back to his desk.

'Good man. Horace, why don't you have a chat with your fox man?'

'I will, but he's cagy. I don't know if it'll do any good to ask him straight out.'

'You don't know that until you've tried it. Probe, probe. Now, off you go.'

Hennessey came back to see Harvard half an hour later. 'I need a bigger *A to Z*,' he said. 'He's been moved to Ongar.' He leafed through the book. 'Bloody hell, he's miles away.'

'Nip off and have a wee chat with him. We'll get someone else to cover for you.'

It took two hours to drive to Ongar. PC Woolrich was off-duty. He was also teetotal. 'It's very rural here,' said Hennessey, filling his lungs with air and breathing out. 'Feels like the countryside.' The policeman gave him a look that suggested further observations on that theme would be unwelcome. The two men went for a cream tea in a café that was also an antique shop.

'I was stitched up. Simple as that. And there's not a *thing* I can do about it. You'd be bitter too.' Woolrich slathered clotted cream on one half of a scone.

'How, though?'

'I don't know. Well, I *do* know. It's obvious what happened. He nobbled the tart.'

'Paid her off?'

'Must have been. Now he's flavour of the month, she's earning a packet in newspapers and I'm in Ongar. It's been terrible. I've put on more than a stone since they moved me out here.' He sighed and bit into the scone. 'It's the stress.'

'The problem is,' said Hennessey, 'from our point of view, how do we go about showing she's been nobbled? She's not going to say anything. And nor is he.'

'There must be someone else involved,' said Woolrich, through a mouthful of food. 'A go-between. That's what I reckon. He wouldn't have risked making contact with her off his own bat – not at first.'

'Really?'

'That's my guess. But you've got no chance of finding them. It would be the last person you'd think of.' He polished off the last of his food and eyed Hennessey's plate. 'Is that all you're going to eat?'

'Yeah. You have the rest.'

'Do you mind? Cheers.' Woolrich slid Hennessey's scones onto his own plate. The transaction seemed to brighten his mood.

Horace chalked his cue. 'You think I should move in with her? I've only known her a month.'

'You can only ask.' Trevor took a big draught of stout and scanned the table for his next shot.

'I don't want to upset my landlord. That's the thing.'

Trevor pumped the final red into the pocket, stunning the cue-ball for a clear shot on the black. He acknowledged Horace's remark with a grunt and played his last shot with a feathery lightness, just shaving the black to tuck it into the centre pocket. 'Play again?'

'Yeah. It's my round as well. I'll get some change.'

'Don't bother. There's a fifty and a twenty here, look.'

Horace could hear the zip of the coin slot and then the

hailstorm, as the balls came thundering out of the table's innards. He returned with two dark pints of stout, still settling under their creamy heads. 'So,' he said, 'seen anything of Colefax lately?'

'Your break.' Trevor licked the foam off his moustache. 'No, the last time I was with you. When we met Tarquin.'

'I didn't think much of his assistants.' Horace potted a red on the break, but on his second shot drove the cue ball aimlessly up the table. Trevor started circling the table one way and then the other, like a matador taking the measure of his bull.

'Them? They were the biggest bunch of arseholes I've ever met.' He looked Horace in the eye and put on a strangled Lord Haw-Haw voice. '"Oh, *no*, that would spoil the tone of the *infopack*." Infowank, more like.' He began annihilating the yellow balls.

Horace watched him, and then as casually as he could, he said, 'What do you think the truth is about Colefax and the prostitute?'

'Put it this way. It's not my job to know. It's not my look-out. Maybe she was telling the truth, maybe she wasn't. It doesn't bother me. As long as the contributions keep rolling in, I'm not bothered.' Trevor tried a tricky double to negotiate his way to the black through a maze of red balls.

'He keeps donating?'

'Shit. Two shots.' He backed off from the table with his pint. 'Oh, yeah. He keeps paying me.' Trevor looked absently at the configuration of the balls. 'It makes you wonder, though, doesn't it?'

'I'm sorry?'

'It makes you wonder what people are like.'

'I'm not sure I follow you, Trevor.'

'People have secrets, don't they? But it doesn't make them any the worse for that.'

Horace wondered if Trevor was on the verge of his confession. He tried to look casually curious.

'Take me,' said Trevor. 'I've got secrets that I wouldn't want everyone to know.'

'Really?' Horace was chalking his cue.

'Oh, yeah.'

Horace avoided Trevor's eyes. 'Like what?'

'You going to use that cue or just chalking it for the future?' said Trevor.

Horace stepped up to the table. 'What kind of secrets?' he persisted.

Trevor took a sip of his drink. 'Well, since you ask . . .' he began.

Horace found himself momentarily distracted by a pleasant fantasy in which, dressed in a dinner jacket, he was approaching a dais to collect an award for investigative journalism. Jocasta was sitting in the front row, applauding. Improbably, Barnaby Colefax was being dragged away from the prize-giving in handcuffs.

'. . . a tiny little baby fox, it was,' Trevor was saying. 'My dad had found it on the way home from work. This was when we lived in Doncaster. And I said, "Where's its mum and dad?" And my mum took me and explained that sometimes your real parents aren't able to look after you, so someone else has to.'

'Right,' said Horace. 'Obviously.' He waited for more.

'That was their way of telling me.'

'Telling you what?'

'Telling me that I was adopted, you wassock. Sometimes you're not with us at all. Earth to Horace, are you receiving us?'

'So that's it? The secret?'

'Yes.' Trevor looked at him in surprise. 'Pardon me if it's not interesting enough for you.'

Horace tried not to sound disappointed as he watched Trevor line up his cue for another shot. 'That's amazing. Thanks for sharing it with me,' he said, wondering meanwhile how he could get back on to the subject of Colefax. 'So you never knew your real mother?'

'My parents are my real parents, as far as I'm concerned. I'm not bothered about anyone else.' Trevor failed to pot anything this time and was cross. 'Come on, raise your game, son,' he muttered to himself.

'You'd never try to track them down?'

'No way. They might be some twat, some Tarquin. I know as much as I want to. My real mother's dead, anyway. She was killed by falling masonry.'

Horace fouled his shot: the cue ball hopped off the baize and bounced along the parquet floor of the pub. 'How do you know that?'

'The adoption agency told my mother after it happened. I remember her telling me. I pretended to be sad because I thought I should, but it didn't bother me.'

'Falling masonry?' said Horace. 'That's weird.'

'Too right,' said Trevor, as he downed the rest of his drink. He adjusted the position of the cue ball. 'Two shots for me.'

'My . . .' Horace began. *My mother was killed by falling masonry* was the sentence on his lips, but a terrible thought had struck him. Two sets of masonry and two mothers? One set of masonry and two mothers? Or just one of each? He saw a heavy stone pineapple topple from the cornicing of a Victorian house and plunge towards the pavement. A woman in a headscarf wheeled a pram beneath it. Her burl arms were covered with tattoos. A neat little moustache curled over her upper lip. A fox cub was asleep in the pram.

Horace looked across at Trevor who was staring at the pool table and scratching his behind. He knew this, because the crotch of Trevor's trousers was rising and falling in time with the movements of his arm.

Horace had never imagined what his brother might look like. He thought of his forerunner only in the vaguest terms, but drew comfort from the mere idea of him: a presence, faceless and yet benign – an angel, almost. He did not expect to meet him. He did not want to find him scratching his bum in a pub in Southwark. He did not want him to be Trevor.

'My round, I think,' he said finally.

'No argument, there,' said Trevor. 'I could murder another.'

# CHAPTER FIFTEEN

AGNES KETTLE WOKE up at dawn and watched the grey light spilling from under the curtain. The radio beside the bed was turned to the BBC World Service and the terse headlines resonated in the cold bedroom. The news reader spoke of floods, earthquakes and elections; but the place-names had a pleasant and unfamiliar music: Lilongwe, Tegucigalpa, Vitebsk. It wasn't news as much as an elaborate calendar: the interlocking wheels of names and interminably repeating disasters that marked time over the years with endless recombinations.

The old woman got out of bed and shuffled down the carpeted

stairs, holding tight to the banister. In the kitchen she made tea and put two pieces of bread under the grill, then sat on the stool staring at the marigolds on the wallpaper until their gold heads seemed to blur into wheels. The petals of the painted flowers meshed like the teeth of cogs and moved round in tiny increments. It had a sound of its own, this marigold clock: its ticking was the dripping of rain outside and the faint throb of her own pulse.

The smell of smoke brought her to: the bread under the grill was on fire. Slowly, unhurriedly, she pulled out the tray, then waved out the flames with a mottled hand and opened the back door to let out the smoke. The fumes went swirling past her into the garden and made her cough. The morning air was faintly damp. She flapped a tea-towel to clear the smoke from the kitchen, but stopped suddenly. A pair of amber eyes was following her movements from the bottom of the garden. 'Goodness,' she muttered, holding the tea-towel to her breast. 'You gave me a fright.' The fox watched her. Its body was poised to move and it went forward like a spring unwinding, then stopped.

The old woman felt a pain in her chest and caught her breath sharply. She grabbed the door-jamb as she staggered inside to the kitchen table, where she sat down, pressing the tea-towel against her face. Beneath the soap powder, it smelled of cooked fat.

Helping herself up with one hand, she went to the phone, but it rang at the other end with no reply. She hung up and sat down again at the kitchen table. The back door stood ajar. The fox had come half-way into the kitchen. Its forepaws rested lightly on the coir welcome mat and it was gazing at the old woman. This time she got up from the table to shoo the animal away, but as she stood up her vision was flooded with white light. The face of the fox was preserved in negative in the flash: patient, unblinking, unafraid.

The old woman fell awkwardly and struck her head against the kitchen table. The fox recoiled, but after a while it returned,

230

pulled its hind legs inside, and trotted over to where she lay. The impact of the table had broken the skin on her forehead. Small beads of blood welled up through the cut. The fox sniffed at the body: it lay face down, with the hand holding the tea-towel turned under it; the head to one side, the mouth ajar. The gas flame in the grill sighed quietly.

Lakshmi peered out of the front window and waved at Horace as he rang the bell. The roar of a lorry behind him was as loud and sudden as a plane passing. Over Vauxhall Bridge the traffic had virtually stopped, a sluggish river of metal oozing forward by inches. The door opened. Horace took in as much as he could – hair chopped to the neck, a loose dress that hid any change in her shape, an amber pendant – then she hugged him and pulled him inside by the arm.

The hallway smelt of joss-sticks. A plump red-haired girl with a nose-ring poked her head round a door. Lakshmi introduced her as Gillian. Her feet were bare and an ankle chain tinkled as she came out to shake his hand. Pinned to her T-shirt was a tiny badge shaped like a triangular road sign with a silhouette of a fox. 'I got it from a friend who works for an MP,' she explained.

'Barnaby Colefax?'

'That's right.'

Lakshmi tugged his arm. 'Do you want tea or coffee?'

'Coffee, please.' Horace followed her into the kitchen. 'What's his name?'

'Hugh – he was at college with me. Lakshmi's met him. He's designing a web-site for them.'

'Hugh's pestering Gillian to move in with him but she's not interested,' said Lakshmi.

'Unlike you, I'm not ready to settle down,' said Gillian. The tinkling sound of her anklet followed her round the room as she opened the fridge, took out a carton of milk and sniffed it. 'This one's all right.'

'Don't listen to her, Horace.' Lakshmi poured the boiling water into the cafetière. While it was steeping, she took three small bowls from a stack of bright-coloured crockery above the stove. 'We prefer to have it in these,' she explained.

Horace looked around the kitchen. Gillian went over to the window-frame and picked at something on the paintwork. 'It's nice here,' he said. The walls and woodwork seemed uneven, but everything had been stripped or freshly painted with a pale orange glaze. Potted herbs stood by the window. A dented pressure cooker like a medieval helmet had been washed up and lay on the draining board.

'You should have seen it when we moved in,' said Gillian. 'I've been here almost two years now. The last person to live here was an old man. It hadn't been cleaned properly since he died – the council wanted to knock it down. You wouldn't believe the mess. There were copies of *Picture Post* and cat-shit everywhere. The oven was just disgusting – it was like something had crawled inside and died.'

Lakshmi had been heating milk on the stove and arranging biscuits on a plate with a pointed thoroughness. She brought the coffee to the table. Gillian took hers away to her bedroom.

'How did you meet Gillian?' he said, when they were alone.

'She's a friend of a friend.' Lakshmi lifted her bowl with the finger-tips of one hand. 'This is how they drink coffee in France. I forgot to ask you, do you take sugar? Gillian won't have it in the house but Darrell smuggled some in for his tea.'

'No, I'm fine.' Horace sipped his coffee, gripping the rim of the bowl with his fingers. 'It doesn't feel very stable.'

'You'll get used to it. How's your job?'

'You know, fine. Not bad. You're working, right?'

'Yeah, for a bit longer. I like it. You look well.'

'Thanks. So do you.'

They both took a sip of coffee. After a while, Horace said, 'Will you be staying here, then?'

'I'm not sure. The council are supposed to be putting me in a flat. Gillian's been helping me to hassle them. But I think I'd rather stay here.'

'What's Gillian like?' Horace asked.

Lakshmi lowered her voice to whisper, 'Everything she cooks is brown.'

'You mean brown rice, brown flour?'

'No,' said Lakshmi. 'It's not brown to start with, it just all ends up brown. I don't know how it happens.' Then she raised her voice to its normal volume. 'Come on, let me show you the rest.' She stood up and took him round the house with a proprietorial enthusiasm, explaining the origins of each piece of salvaged furniture. It was an old, rambling building, with crooked floorboards and window-frames. Lakshmi's bedroom was upstairs at the back of the house. An enamel jug filled with dried flowers stood in the fireplace. 'I stripped the wallpaper,' she said proudly, 'and this was undernearth.' It was a fragment of a Victorian wallcovering, yellow with age and decorated with faded roses that matched the glaze on the walls. She sighed. 'I'll be sorry to leave this behind.'

'It's bigger than my room,' said Horace.

Lakshmi laughed. 'It's scandalous, what you pay my dad. You could share and get a nice two-bedroom place in Hackney or somewhere. Honestly, Horace, living alone isn't economical. You should look in the papers. Or talk to Gillian about squatting. You'd save so much money.'

Horace looked at her, and felt foolish for thinking that somehow he'd come to help her. 'You're right. I am thinking of moving, but . . .' He tailed off. He couldn't say, *I feel bad abadoning your father.*

'Listen, I've written my dad a letter.' She turned to take a white envelope from the mantelpice and gave it to him. The outside of the envelope bore an indecipherable squiggle.

'What's that?'

'It says *appa*. It's Tamil for *father*.'

'I didn't know you spoke it.'

'I don't. The letter's in English. That's one of six words I know how to write.'

'I'll give it to him.' The two of them walked down the staircase to the kitchen.

'Mind the step at the bottom,' she said. 'It's rotten.'

Trevor had left his house before first light to deliver two cubs to the animal sanctuary in Staines. He had woken up too early to feel hungry, but on the way home he stopped at a drive-through Mister Egg for breakfast. He decided to stay and eat his food there over the newspaper.

Only the most dismal parts of London had drive-through fast-food restaurants, because the great aprons of tarmac they required were too expensive to site anywhere else. The Old Kent Road's Mister Egg faced a vast factory outlet for office stationery.

Trevor didn't need to look at the laminated menu the assistant gave him. 'I'll have the early bird special number two, please.' The assistant punched the worn plastic keys of the register. The American conglomerate that owned Mister Egg had recently replaced the lettered keys with pictures: food ideograms. But they wore out quickly and the till operators had to memorise the position of each item like touch typists.

'How do you want your Mister Eggs?' she asked, in a bored voice.

'I'd like them fried.'

'It'll be two minutes to freshly cook your order, sir.'

'Fine.'

'Thank you for coming to Mister Egg.'

Trevor sat down. He had his car keys bunched in his hand. Behind him, four builders at a table together had just collected their Mister Eggs. 'He's got pace,' said one. 'That's what we've been so badly lacking in midfield.'

'*And* he's naturally left-sided.'

'Not bad for two hundred and fifty grand.'

'You know why, don't you? The other clubs only want the finished article.' He was gesturing with his fork. 'They'd rather pay five million quid for a Ravanelli or a Vialli or whatever his name is than go for a twenty-one-year-old whose first touch might need a bit of working on.'

One of them hadn't spoken yet. He was absorbed in a copy of the *Daily Flag*. 'Bloody hell,' he said now. 'This is outrageous. Look.'

'What?'

A voice came over the Tannoy. 'Early bird special number two.' Trevor went up to the serving counter brandishing his receipt. The assistant handed him his food on a styrofoam tray. As he returned to the table, he could hear his neighbours discussing the article.

'It's not *them* that's the problem – it's selfish humans that's the problem . . .'

'No. No. No . . .'

'They'd be fine if it wasn't for us.'

'Let me get a word in edgeways. What's more important? What's more important? A human life or an animal's?'

'He's got you there.'

'I'm not saying I agree with this article . . .'

'Just answer . . .'

'He's got you . . .'

'I don't know why they're making such a fuss. Foxes are vermin. End of story.'

Trevor laid down his plastic knife and fork on his styrofoam plate. It wasn't the end of the story, because after a tiny pause the man had resumed speaking.

'If they killed enough of them now, right, then there wouldn't be any risk . . .'

'It could still come in. Rabies could.'

'Yeah, but it wouldn't stay.' He filled his mouth with scrambled egg. 'I'm just telling you what *I* would do.'

'We should stand up to Europe, *that*'s what we should do.'

Trevor turned round. He knew instantly which one had been holding forth: a red-faced man with dusty overalls and a prodigious beer-gut. He was about to start speaking again, but Trevor interrupted. 'Excuse me,' he said. The man smiled: for a moment he thought Trevor was after the salt and pepper. Then Trevor said, 'I have never heard so much *shit* spoken by one person in all my life.' All four turned to look at him with incredulity. The red-faced man had stopped chewing and his mouth hung open, displaying the remnants of his scrambled Mister Egg. Trevor went on, his anger rising, 'If I were you, I'd keep my mouth shut about things you know fuck all about.'

Now one of the other men intervened. He raised his hand warily and said, 'All right, mate.'

Trevor stared at the red-faced man and said, 'Eh? Eh?' Then he shook his head and went back to his seat. After a few moments he threw away his plate of food and left the restaurant. The four men watched him go.

'Fucking nutcase.' The red-faced man started eating again.

'I reckon he was one of them animal-liberation blokes.'

'Did you get a look at his shoes?'

'No, why?'

'Well, if they're leather, he can't be animal rights.'

'If he *was* animal rights, what's he doing eating at Mister Egg?'

'What are you on about?'

'Battery hens.'

'Are they?'

'Of course they are, stupid.'

'Oh. I didn't know that.' He looked at his plate. 'Here, do you want the rest of mine? I only eat free range at home.'

When Trevor got home he checked his answering-machine for messages. There were none. He picked up the receiver and rang to get the number of his last caller. 'You were called today at oh five thirty-six . . .' said the recorded voice. He made a note of the number and pressed three to redial it but the phone at the other end rang without answer. He hung up.

Outside Tooting Bec station a dark-haired man in a double-breasted suit was whistling the theme music from a film about gangsters. Horace glanced at him as he came out of the station and walked to work. Harvard waved to him from the office. Hennessey was already in there. Horace sat down in the spare chair.

It was often said about Marcus Hennessey that he looked like a plain-clothes policeman. It was something about his cropped hair and preference for plaid shirts. He was reading from his shorthand notes and elaborating in a policeman's ponderous voice. *'Weight problem,'* he read. 'Yeah. He's blow up like a balloon – says its the stress. He doesn't drink, which is a bit unusual for a vice-squad boy. I got the feeling he might be a God-botherer.'

'More importantly, did you think he was telling you the truth?' Harvard was sitting on the edge of his desk and kicking his feet slowly back and forth. Horace was mesmerised by the flash of Harvard's black loafers. He had got up early to see Lakshmi and wanted to go back to bed.

'Very much so.' Hennessey cleared his throat. 'I thought he was on the level. And I've heard good things about him elsewhere.'

Harvard stopped his feet in mid-swing. 'Who else do you think he's talked to?'

'Anyone who's bothered asking, I imagine. He feels very hard done by. He wants people to know he was telling the truth. The trouble is, how do you prove it?'

Harvard turned to Horace. 'What about Trevor Diamond?'

Horace felt guilty. He had been too flustered by Trevor's revelation or press him any harder on the subject of Colefax. 'Trevor's sort out of the loop with Colefax. He's an odd bloke and the people Colefax is using now are very clean-cut, posh types. Trevor doesn't fit in with them, and I don't think Colefax really wants him around. All the same, Colefax has been giving him money for months. Officially it's all donations for Fox Outreach, but in Trevor's mind, the distinction is very blurry.'

Harvard's feet started moving again slowly. 'It makes sense. Colefax needs to contact the tart before the trial. He can't go himself in case he's seen – she's probably being staked out. So he sends someone he can rely on. Someone who he has a very tenuous link with, but who he has another reason for knowing.'

He paused. 'I'm just worried that nothing will come of it. Three, four people at the most, know the truth of this. And not one of them has a good reason to talk to us.'

'Except for old fatty in Ongar,' Hennessey butted in. 'And he would, wouldn't he?'

Harvard nodded. 'That's right.'

Trevor had been putting off odd-jobs in the flat. One of the cubs had pissed on the carpet in the bathroom and it needed replacing.

He knelt down with a stanley knife in one hand and began ripping up the flooring, thinking, as he did so, about his quarrel with the man in the restaurant. He leaned against the bath to prise the carpet apart from the underfelt. The plastic side panel of the tub sighed and bent in.

It was just what he had been afraid of: Colefax had made the foxes into a national issue, and now that they were visible, they were vulnerable. They'd been better off before; ignored, protected by the handful of people who had their best interests at heart. Take those kids who were working for Colefax for free. For free! The carpet gave way suddenly and he pricked the back of his thumb with the stanley knife. A drop of blood sprang up. He put his knuckle in his mouth and went to get the medicine chest. It was in the kitchen. Ginger was asleep on top. 'Shoo, you,' said Trevor gently. The cat opened its slumbrous green eyes and slid off the box with a miaow. Trevor unlatched the box and rooted through it for some plasters. It had been designed for fishing tackle, and its plastic trays held medicines, bandages, syringes for feeding, and boxes of the powerful sleeping pills he needed to neutralise the jarring pain of his knee, which throbbed, as it did now, when he was preoccupied, or kneeling too much, or overtired. He cleaned the tiny wound and covered it with a plaster.

A portable radio stood on top of the fridge. Trevor clicked it on and wheeled the dial through the scraps of noise: a snatch of 'Lillibullero', a sound like a sea-gull's shriek, hysterical audience laughter, a French disc jockey, and then a familiar voice saying, 'We're urging everyone who opposes this mad piece of legislation to come along and lend their support. Apart from anything else, it should be a lot of fun.'

'Barnaby Colefax,' said the presenter, 'thank you very much *indeed*.' But the last word was lost as Trevor spun the dial back towards the quiz show. He thought for a few moments and then went into the sitting room with the telephone number he had jotted down earlier.

His computer sat at the far end of the room covered with a plastic sheet. Trevor unveiled it and switched it on. Its fan started up with a quiet hum. The pointer on the screen had been customised to look like a tiny paw. He slid it over to open his list of clients. They were represented on the screen as a stack of index cards; one hundred and seventy-three of them. Trevor clicked the word *search* and typed in the phone number. *Searching, one moment please,* appeared in a little box on the screen. Then the computer returned the matching entry: Kettle, Agnes.

Horace sat at his desk, drinking a cup of tea and trying to look busy. The rest of the staff had been pressed into service to produce the Rock the Fox supplement in time for the concert. Harvard had apologised to everyone: 'I'm afraid I've delayed in the hope that an act of God would prevent this concert taking place. Sadly, my prayers have not been answered.' Most of them went about their work with good humour, but Horace and Hennessey had been left alone to get on with the Colefax story. Hennessey had said he was going off to talk to some of his *contacts* in Streatham. He gave the word a mysterious emphasis. At this moment, he was playing pool with some off-duty policemen and drinking subsidised lager.

The phone rang. It was Trevor. 'I've got a little bit of a problem here,' he said. 'Agnes Kettle – got a call from her this morning. I've been ringing away but can't get her to pick up the phone.'

'Really? What did she want?'

'I didn't speak to her. I was up at the crack of dawn, down to Staines with some cubs. Did a last number redial when I got in and it turned out it was hers. I thought you might have an idea where she was.'

'None. Let me think.' Horace remembered the last time he'd spoken to her. She'd been frail and animated, her pale face hovering in the darkened room as she talked. 'We should probably go round there in case she's had a fall.'

Horace told Harvard he was going out to see Trevor. 'That's it,' said Harvard. 'You're getting the idea. Keep *on* at him, keep *on* at him.'

By the time he arrived Trevor had been standing on her doorstep ringing the bell for a couple of minutes. Horace peered through the letterbox. 'Hello!' he shouted. There was no answer and he could see nothing through it. The spring on the brass letterbox was stiff and it snapped shut as he let go of the flap. 'Shit. What now?'

Trevor motioned him out of the way. 'I'll put my shoulder to it.'

'Bad idea. It's much too solid – and it's probably on the chain. You'll hurt yourself. There's that low fence at the back, I'll go round and get in that way.'

Horace ran round the block to where the iron bollards marked the entrance to the playing field behind. From the rear, all the houses looked identical. He jogged past them until it became obvious that he had gone too far, then he ran back. He knew he was looking for a house with a kitchen door on his right and a tidy garden of its own but a messy one next to it. There were several that fitted the description but the first had a child's plastic tricycle upturned on the lawn; the next had its kitchen door open. Horace vaulted the low rear fence and ran inside.

The gas flame still hissed above the grill. Bloody tracks criss-crossed the linoleum floor. The old lady's feet faced the door, one slipper hanging off and her toes pointed at an awkward angle. The pool of blood by her head was so dark and luminously red that Horace didn't know at first what it was. Most of the skin had been torn away from her face. A single, grotesquely round eye stared out of the raw flesh. Horace took off his jacket and laid it over her face, then he went into the hall and opened the front door. Trevor looked at him. 'What?'

Horace shook his head. 'Don't go in there. We'll call the police. Have you got your mobile?'

Trevor insisted on looking at the body for himself. He lifted up a corner of the jacket and winced. 'Someone's made a right mess of her.'

Horace avoided the mutilated face with its staring eyeball. 'We'd better not touch anything. It might be evidence,' he said.

They waited outside for the police to arrive. Horace had left the gas on, thinking that it was best to leave the scene as undisturbed as possible. Trevor smoked. Neither of them said anything. Inside, the horror of the crime was too present; outside, in the street, it was somehow too absent. Horace wanted someone to acknowledge the awfulness of what he had seen, but there was just the street, the bland houses and the odd passer-by.

It was a relief when the police cars and ambulance finally arrived. 'Which of you found the body?' the officer asked. Horace explained what he had seen.

'I can't be one hundred per cent positive about this,' said the officer, 'but it appears to me that the mutilation occurred after death. The pattern of wounding on the face and the tracks on the lino suggest that a wild animal of some description's been at the body. We won't be able to say for sure until we've ascertained the cause of death.'

'It's so sad,' said Horace. 'I just don't know what to say.'

'It *is* sad,' said the policeman. 'Regrettably, in situations such as these, it is very difficult to know what one *can* say. Would you know if she had any relatives?'

'Her sister was a teacher in . . . ,' Horace glanced at Trevor. 'Her sister was a teacher in the north of England somewhere but I'm sure she's dead.' He had a bittersweet recollection of the old woman saying in her raspy voice, *I don't know if she was what you'd call a lesbian.*

'It could have been a fox,' said Trevor. He was on his second double whisky. 'But that's the nature of a wild animal. To you or I, that's a dead body lying there, right. To an animal, that's its next meal.'

'What if she wasn't dead?' said Horace. Drinking was making him feel worse: by diminishing his sense of unreality it lulled him into feeling that things were normal; then he remembered the torn red mask of the old lady's face.

Trevor didn't seem to be listening. 'Even then it's unlikely,' he said. 'A fox is naturally terrified of humans. Think about it: she's ten times the size of a fox.'

'It's a wild animal, Trevor. How can you know what it would or wouldn't do?' Horace finished his drink. 'I'm having another.'

When he came back from the bar, Trevor said, 'I suppose you're going to put this in your paper.'

'That's a point. You mean *Murdered OAP Mauled by Fox*?' Horace looked at him unsteadily. For the first time, Trevor was unsettled by something in his tone. It might have been antagonism, or sarcasm.

'They're getting a very bad press at the minute. There's lots of people thinking that getting rid of one or two foxes might not be a bad idea.'

Horace looked at him. It was monomania: this seeing the world in terms of one thing. If you said to Trevor, there's more to life than foxes, what would he say?

'There's more to life than foxes, Trevor.'

'What's that supposed to mean?'

'What it says.' Horace could see Trevor was uncomfortable. 'Isn't it irrelevant? No one's going to blame the animal.'

'That's where you're wrong.' Trevor sounded almost plaintive. 'You know as well as I do that foxes are persecuted creatures.'

'It's *nothing* to do with foxes.' Horace surprised himself by his vehemence.

It was almost midnight when Horace got home. He had decided to leave the car behind and collect it the next day. He had called Jocasta from the pub but her housemate had told him she'd gone out and it was too late to ring again now. She would be crabby if he woke her up.

The curtain of his bedroom was open. He needed to put more money in the meter for electricity but for now the moonlight was bright enough to change by. He dumped the contents of his trouser pockets on the plastic desk: coins, keys, a pen, *papier-mâché* balls of laundered Kleenex. As he took off the jacket to put it on the back of his chair, he remembered Lakshmi's letter. It had been sitting in his inside pocket for more than twelve hours, and its corners had wilted sligtly. He smoothed them out on the desk.

Horace was thinking about Trevor. It hadn't occurred to him to ask him any more about Colefax: too much else was on his mind. Now that he was more relaxed, he regretted not asking.

He found Trevor more, not less, annoying since they'd had the conversation about adoption, and he was glad that he had kept silent that evening in the pub in Southwark. The only repercussion of his discovery – if a discovery was what it was – had been an odd dream in which Trevor was putting pilchards into Horace's mouth and saying, 'His stomach's the size of a thumb-nail.'

He had told Jocasta the dream, but not the cause of it. 'There's something about you and Trevor you're not telling me,' she had said, with sudden seriousness. 'You were lovers, weren't you?' Then she had burst out laughing.

'Lovers?' Horace had laughed with the relief of it.

He got into bed. People weren't any the worse for their secrets, he thought. Trevor had said so himself.

# CHAPTER SIXTEEN

JOCASTA CAME OUT of the changing cubicle wearing her bikini and carrying her clothes in a big straw bag. The cubicles ran along one side of the lido for about fifty yards. The wooden doors of each one had been painted a different colour. The enormous pool was only crowded at the shallow end – a hundred yards away – but the sounds of children screaming and splashing carried all the way to the entrance. Every so often, a train rattled through the cutting that ran a few yards behind where Horace was sitting. It drowned conversation for a moment and sent tiny ripples through the blue water.

Jocasta walked gingerly over the bricks in her bare feet, picking her way through the towels and oiled white bodies. She looked tall and pale in the sunlight. When she reached Horace she rummaged in her bag and took out a pair of enormous round sunglasses. 'My old boyfriend said these made me look like the thing in the Roswell incident,' she said, as she sat down on the towel.

'What's that?' Horace propped himself up on his elbows. He was wearing a pair of Madras check trunks and arranging chess pieces on a tiny board.

'Well, if you don't know, I'm not telling you.' Jocasta took a tube of sun-tan lotion out of her bag and squeezed too much of it into her hand. 'I'm not giving you any ammunition to use against me.'

'Which old boyfriend was that?' Horace had had to get used to the presence of various undead boyfriends from Jocasta's past – some as sources of humorous anecdotes, others of troublesome phone-calls. 'It's an occupational hazard of the modern mating rituals,' she had explained. 'It's customary nowadays to have sex with someone before you find out if you like them. Our parents did things the other way round. That had perils of its own.'

'Fabio,' she said.

'The one who got caught smuggling cocaine in packets of chicken noodle soup?'

Jocasta smiled. 'No.'

'The American bodybuilder?'

'No. He was the Italian one.'

'Which Italian one?'

'The junkie.'

'With HIV?'

'That's right. Those are his shorts you're wearing, in fact.' She turned her face into the sun.

'Oh, thanks a lot.'

'I knew you'd have brought Speedo trunks or something equally ghastly so I took precautions.'

'Mine are better for swimming in.'

246

'Yes, dear. Do you want some of this?' The tube made a farting sound as she squirted it into her hand. Horace slid forward and let her rub sun-tan lotion into his shoulders. A small child ran past them, arms propped into the air with water wings, panting and dripping water. 'We're supposed to call it sunburn cream now, aren't we?'

'Will you come to this funeral with me?'

'If you want me to. When is it?'

'Next Wednesday.'

'Of course. If you want me to.'

'She knew my grandfather quite well.'

'You mentioned.'

Horace was looking at the shimmering blue water slopping into the run-off at the side of the pool. It was so big that it moved with the wind like a tiny ocean. Jocasta complained that swimming lengths in it made her sea-sick.

'Maybe she'll come back and haunt you,' she said.

'I doubt it.'

'Why's that?' Jocasta had finished with the sun-tan lotion and was arranging herself on her towel. The straps were undone on her bikini top so she clasped it on with one arm.

'I don't believe in ghosts.'

'Really?'

'Of course not. Do you?'

'I think I do,' she said. 'Will you do me now?' Horace wiped his palms on the towel and squirted the tube into his hand.

'Eight?'

'Eight's fine for my back. I have to use fifteen on my face.' She lay flat with her chin on her hands. 'I went to Belize on a freebie with a friend. It'd been laid on by their tourism ministry. We spent three days on one of the keys scuba-diving. The guy who drove the boat had always lived on the island. That's nice.' Horace was rubbing the cream into her lower back. 'He had that thing of being young but seeming old. People in small communities sometimes do. I don't know what it is – having to grow up faster, I suppose. Anyway, he talked about how quiet it had been before the tourists had come – when they still used oil lamps for light and had no electricity. It wasn't long before we were there: ten, fifteen years maybe.

'He said it was so quiet then that they used to see and hear things that you couldn't see anywhere else. "Like what?" I asked him. He said, "Well, my cousin drowned when we were little, and when we were playing we used to see him quite a lot." I thought, yes. The past must be like that, present all the time, but faint, like starlight or something.' Jocasta was silent for a moment. 'You must have had ghosts in your village.'

'We had a screaming skull.'

'Really?'

'It was supposed to belong to one of the families who'd lived there longest. They'd made their money from sugar plantations in Jamaica. The story was that it belonged to a slave boy who'd died in the house. It screamed because it wanted to go home. I saw it once. It was brown and small.

'Did it scream?'

'Not while I was in the room.'

'Poor thing. Why didn't they send it home?'

'It was just a story. We never heard the thing screaming.'

'Don't you ever want to go back and visit?'

'Great Much? I suppose I will. There's not much there for me now.'

'I'd like to visit it.'

'Well, perhaps I'll take you one of these days.' He paused. 'I sometimes wish now that I hadnt spent so much time there, that I'd left earlier. I'm in no rush to go back.' The water glinted. A faint vibration in the brickwork turned into the noise of a passing train. 'Are you going to have a swim before we go?'

'It makes me feel ill. You swim. I'll watch.'

Close up, the water was less pristine. Invisible currents roiled a few twigs and leaves at the bottom of the pool. It was also cold. Horace jumped in and swam off from the side, breathing out a steady stream of bubbles under water as his arms pulled him along. The water running past his submerged ears tinkled faintly like a wind-chime.

Jocasta and Horace drove back to Glenburne Road to pick up the backstage passes and invitations. Colefax and his wife were hosting a party for a selected group of guests at their house after the concert. Horace had been invited, along with the Boothbys, Harvard and Trevor.

Mr Narayan was serving someone in the shop and bracing himself for the Saturday afternoon onslaught of lottery customers. He beckoned Horace and Jocasta over. Freshly shaven for the first time in ages, he seemed to have shed years.

'Horace, I'm trying to explain your plan for reforming the national lottery to Mrs Dennis. Remind me how it works.' He gave him an encouraging nod. Jocasta looked on in bemusement.

'Right,' said Horace. 'Well, the idea is to replace it with a one-off lottery –'

Mrs Dennis cut him off. 'I'm happy to carry on as I have been,' she said. 'Can I have twenty Bensons as well, please, Vivek?' She folded her lottery slip away in her bag.

'Certainly.'

When she had left, Horace introduced Jocasta and Mr Narayan properly. Once they were safely exchanging pleasantries, he ran off to get the tickets. It had become a point of honour not to let Jocasta see his room, all the more so since he had seen how much of a home Lakshmi had made of the condemned house in Vauxhall. But his caginess only made Jocasta more determined to see it. She asked him if his room hid some dreadful secret.

It wasn't such a bad place, he thought, as he rummaged through the drawer of the desk for the tickets. The sunlight was coming in from the garden. It was just the weird bath – kitchen arrangement that spoiled it . . .

'So this is it, Bluebeard's chamber.' Jocasta stood in the doorway, smirking. 'Can I come in?' She walked in slowly and peered around her curiously, like an archaeologist entering a tomb.

'Okay. Very funny.'

'I don't know why you've been so touchy about this,' she said. 'It's just a bit unorthodox, that's all.' She felt a surge of affection for him when she saw the bowl and spoon on the draining board. 'Give me a kiss.'

'Take care of your English rose, Horace,' said Mr Narayan, as they left. Jocasta accepted the compliment with a gracious wave.

'Now, why is he allowed to patronise you and Trevor isn't?'

'It's all in the delivery. He likes women, Trevor doesn't.'

'Oh, I see.'

'He was saying some nice things about you while you were upstairs.'

'You were only alone for about thirty seconds.'

'That's plenty of time.'

'What did he say?'

'I'm not telling you. I don't want you to get big-headed.'

The notes of the soundcheck fuzzed out from the giant speakers and spread over Clapham Common. The crowd had been trickling in all day, but now the main body of the audience had started to arrive. Police marshalled them all the way from the Tube station and towards the space that had been set aside around the stage.

Much earlier a small tribe of people with multicoloured dreadlocks had set up an encampment on the common. Now, their men were jamming on bongo drums and didgeridoos while their children played tag with one another. Smoke rose up from food-stalls that had sprung up around the encampment. Instead of the usual lip-burgers and horse-dogs, they sold faecal-looking dhals, spring rolls, jerk chicken, fresh doughnuts and coffee. A tiny girl sat on the ground having her hair woven into little plaits by her mother.

An hour or so earlier, Colefax had wandered around the groups of people sitting on the grass. He had ended up being photographed playing frisbee with a kaftaned traveller. His supporters had fanned out across the common to give away leaflets and collect signatures against the bill.

It had been a day of perfect sun and a few high clouds and the feeling of sunburned contentment spread through the crowd. An old couple who had been out for a walk surrendered to the atmosphere. They added their names to the petition and accepted free leaflets and little triangular badges in return. They were wandering happily among the food-stalls, eating mung-bean curry, watching the bongo-players and feeling broad-minded.

Horace recognised a photographer, from the *South London Bugle*, who was sprawled on the grass and trying not to get barbecue sauce on his tie. He had decided it was too early to get the obligatory photograph of a policeman dancing with a plump black woman. He gave Horace a wave. 'Been here long?'

'Just arrived.' Horace squatted down. 'Big turn-out.'

'And more on the way. I've just been listening to this to find out what's going on.' He had brought a portable radio with him. 'Harvard's here somewhere. I think he might have gone round backstage.'

'Really? Well, we'll go along and see if we can find him. Maybe see you later.'

'Yeah. See you.'

''Bye,' said Jocasta.

Horace and Jocasta pressed on into the thickest part of the crowd until they came to a policeman. When they flashed their laminated passes at him he peered at them for a moment, then turned away and conducted a brief conversation with the crackling radio on his lapel. Turning back to them, he said jovially, 'Right, sorry about that – first time I've seen these. If you make your way towards that dirigible . . .'

They looked over to where he was pointing. A small airship was tethered to the ground at one side of the stage. Small inflatable animals were hanging from it and twirling slowly in the air like shapes on a mobile.

'Just below that,' the policeman went on, 'you'll find the VIP tent.'

'This is staggering,' said Jocasta. 'Look how many people have come.' They worked their way through the crush, trying not to step on toes, and worming past indifferent backs. 'The weird thing is who they are. Travellers *and* the green-wellie brigade.'

It was true. All the tribes of the city were represented: the tribes of the dreadlock and the dog-on-string; the tribes of the urban off-road vehicle with child safety seat; the tribes of the rag-rolled wall; the tribes of the satellite dish; the tribes of the Internet; the tribes of the houseboat and the loft apartment.

Two schoolboys from Abingdon College were self-consciously smoking a parsnip-sized joint. Herby clouds of smoke drifted over the crowd bringing with them the smell of burning privet.

A guard at the entrance to the VIP tent was checking their passes. It was a large marquee that had been set aside for the musicians and the invited guests. Inside it was hot and smelt of cut grass. Gideon Deck was in one corner with a band from Zimbabwe called the Chimurenga Brothers. He looked relaxed and was swigging from a bottle of mineral water.

'That's her, look.' Jocasta dug Horace in the ribs. Raylena James was being escorted by an elegant young film critic. She was laughing at something he'd said. Her white teeth flashed and her fingers twinkled. 'They're engaged,' said Jocasta.

'No,' said Horace, remembering the opportunity he had not taken and why. 'I never confronted him about it. I never seemed to get the chance.'

'That's what I mean,' said Jocasta. She leaned her head on Horace's shoulder. 'If anything, I'm slightly more impressed by Colefax than I was before.'

'I see you're looking at love's young dream.' Harvard had appeared at their side. 'They make a nice couple, don't they? I always said Colefax was too old for her.'

Raylena caught sight of Jocasta and gave her a wave. Then she turned back to her companion and carried on laughing.

'She's got a lot to laugh about,' said Harvard, 'but not as much as him.' He pointed his thumb at Colefax, who was mingling graciously among the musicians, his wife in tow. 'At this moment, he should be learning the ropes at a second-hand car dealership. Instead, he's the most popular politician in the country. I'm sorry, the *only* popular politician in the country.'

The Chimurenga Brothers had left the tent. Flashing lights preceded their entrance onstage and the crowd suddenly went silent. Guitar arpeggios tinkled out of the speakers.

'Are you going outside to watch?' asked Horace.

'I can see it from in here.' Harvard pointed at a row of monitors inside the tent.

Jocasta bent down and picked up one of the many Rock the Fox supplements that littered the floor. 'Come on, Harvard. Listen, "Uplifting dance music from the original World Music wonderband".'

'I know, Jo. I wrote that.' Protesting weakly, he allowed himself to be dragged out of the marquee.

The crowd was on its feet, dancing in the fading sunlight. 'See what you would have missed.' The mobile twirled above them in the blue sky. One of the Abingdonians was bouncing happily in time to the music. His friend lay comatose on the grass.

Jocasta had put her sunglasses back on and was twirling around. Horace reprised the Mr Tither dance he had invented at the Manhattan. It seemed to suit any music that demanded lots of quick, intricate steps. Harvard leaned over and shouted in Horace's ear, 'I was having a chat with your mate.'

'My mate?'

'Trevor.'

'Is he back in there?'

Harvard nodded.

'I'll go in and get him.'

Trevor was standing in a corner of the marquee, looking uncomfortably hot in his tie and jacket, talking to Cilla Boothby. 'Last thing I did was a big clearance job,' he was saying. 'They're putting in a multiplex cinema across the road from me and wanted some earths clearing out.'

Mrs Boothby saw Horace approaching. 'Mr Diamond was telling me how you found poor Agnes. It must have been a dreadful shock.'

'It was a shame.' Horace caught Trevor's eye. He hadn't wanted to subject his great-aunt to the details of what they had found in the kitchen. He wasn't sure if Trevor shared this delicacy, but he guessed that he wouldn't recount anything that showed foxes in a bad light. 'I came to see if you wanted to join us outside.'

Cilla said she'd better stay with Derwent. He was suffering from the pollen and she was carrying his inhalers. But before Horace left, he found himself accepting an invitation to dinner.

Trevor wandered outside and loosened his tie.

'Are you all right, Trevor? You seem a bit down.'

'Not at all. This isn't my kind of music, that's all.' But the sight of the vast crowd seemed to pain him. He shaded his eyes and looked up at the mobile. One of the animals suspended from it was a bushy-tailed fox.

The Chimurenga Brothers played for forty-five minutes and then went off without an encore. By nine o'clock it was starting to get dark. Lights began swirling over the stage. The silence was punctuated by isolated shouts and whistles, then a roar went up as Gideon Deck appeared onstage with his trademark white guitar, playing the distinctive opening riffs of 'Devil Rider'. He bantered briefly with the crowd between songs as he worked his way through the blues staples of his early years, songs like 'Wine Spodeodi', a couple of the pompous heavy metal numbers from the album *Ragnarock*, then the later ballads. He was joined onstage by the Chimurenga Brothers for the first encore. As the applause died down, Deck said, 'Finally, let's not forget why we've come here. Ladies and gentlemen, I want you to give it up for a good friend of mine: Barnaby Colefax.'

Colefax jogged onto the stage from the wings, waving at the crowd with both hands. He had taken off his jacket and tie and rolled up his sleeves. He unyoked the microphone from its stand. 'Thank you, Gideon,' he began to say, and feedback howled through the speakers. The crowd covered their ears. 'Sorry about that.' The wailing had stopped. Colefax's voice boomed across the common. 'Just shows I'd better leave it to the professionals.' A few people in the audience tittered. He could make out faces in the front row smiling appreciatively. 'I'll keep this short. I just wanted to say a word before Gideon and the Chimurenga Brothers wrap up the day.' Colefax had jotted down a few notes but he knew he wasn't going to need them. He allowed himself a little pause, closing his eyes and breathing in the adulation as though it were alpine air. Christ, he thought, if only they could bottle this.

'I'm touched and staggered by how many of you have come today. I can't tell you how heartening it is for me. I look out from here, and I see a nation, people who differ from each other as much as people can, but who are united by certain beliefs.'

'He obviously can't see me from where he's standing,' said Harvard.

A woman a few rows in front of him turned round angrily and hissed, 'Sh!'

'We take certain things for granted: the security that comes from being an island nation, the closeness between animals and humans that's so much part of our national character. Now the government wants to jeopardise those things. Why? Because it's shortsighted, and it's busy trying to ingratiate itself with its European chums. Well, you're too clever to be taken in!' He looked across the crowd. 'We're here today to give them our answer! N, O, spells no!'

The crowd cheered. A man threw his arms in the air and knocked Trevor's drink out of his hand. Trevor gave him a baleful look until he apologised.

Colefax's voice rose over the cheering: 'You've shown the world we're not about to relinquish our traditions without a struggle. Thank you all!'

With those words, Gideon Deck struck up the band and led the Chimurenga Brothers in a rendition of 'Born to be Wild'.

Patricia Colefax came onstage to stand next to her husband, who was gamely trying to keep time on a tambourine.

Balloons were released over the audience from a net above the stage. Horace watched them rise up in a thin stream, like bubbles from a fish. Harvard put his arm round his shoulder. 'How much longer do you want to stay here? I'd like to return to reality fairly soon.'

Colefax's huge garden backed onto a private park, which was enclosed completely by the block of houses that included his home. The park sat hidden in the centre, like an atrium, a private wilderness, a secret emerald. The front of Colefax's house faced the common and the bench where Horace had spent his first night in the city.

For a long time, shame had closed him off from the recollection of his arrival. But now he could remember it in detail: the texture of the bench that had been almost petrified with wind and weather, the belisha beacon winking between the toes of his shoes. He imagined telling Jocasta the story of it, making her laugh with it, and turning it from a painful memory into harmless folklore. But now wasn't the time.

Jocasta was footsore and tetchy. The crowd had dispersed slowly towards the pubs and Tube stations, leaving behind it food wrappers, squeaky polystyrene dishes, and tattered Rock the Fox supplements. There seemed little chance of getting a minicab, so Horace suggested they walk. Trevor was morose and silent, but his presence alone was enough to put Jocasta in a bad mood. Harvard hadn't spoken since the end of the concert. He was still reliving the moment when Colefax returned to the stage alone to punch the air in front of the adoring crowd. Only Horace was enjoying the evening.

The four of them passed dining tables set out on the pavement of Battersea Rise. A day of sunshine seemed to have painted the city in fresh colours. Red-faced men and women splashed wine in each other's glasses. Honey-coloured boys hung around the bus-stop. The night sky was bluer than usual.

'I thought you said it was close.' From Northcote Road, the pavement pointed uphill. Jocasta was fed up with walking.

'It's about half a mile from here.'

'Half a mile?' She stopped and looked at him incredulously.

'It'll only take us five minutes to walk it.'

'Next time you say it's not far I'm taking a minicab.' She began trudging up the hill.

'You're behaving like a spoilt child,' said Horace.

By the time they had reached the common, the four were spread out like a column of advancing commandos, with at least five yards between each of them. They regrouped at the entrance to Colefax's circular driveway. Harvard seemed to wake up. He took Jocasta's arm and led her into the house, leaving Horace to go in with Trevor.

Out in the garden, Colefax's sons were being introduced to Gideon Deck and the Chimurenga Brothers. Deck was drinking an orange juice. 'Your old man tells me you play the guitar a bit yourself,' he said to the older boy, Sebastian.

'Only classical,' put in the younger. His brother glared at him.

Catering staff circulated with trays of food. A young girl diffidently offered some to Harvard. 'What do we have here?' he asked in an avuncular tone. 'I see, baby vegetables wrapped in a piece of smoked salmon.' Then, injecting his voice with the faintest hint of threat he said, 'Was this your idea?'

The girl blushed madly and insisted it was not.

'Harvard,' Jocasta admonished him. 'Thank you, they look lovely. I suppose you'd prefer a Ginster's slice and a couple of bottles of Pschitt?'

'I like Julian Bream,' Gideon Deck was explaining. 'Especially his lute stuff. And Drip, Drip, Drip are a good band. Good old-fashioned numbers. I just don't get a lot of this new stuff coming out now. It sounds like a car-wash to me.' Sebastian Colefax mentally resolved to tear down his Gideon Deck poster as soon as he got back to school and replace it with one of someone who had died at a respectably early age.

Horace wandered to the foot of the garden and peered over the wooden wall at the back. Tall trees fringed the park, blocking the view of the open space at its heart, but he could sense it behind the foliage, which was rustling in a breeze as soft as respiration.

'We have a bonfire party in there each year.' Colefax was at his side. 'It's wonderful to have all this green space in the city. It's Morris, isn't it?'

'It's Horace, actually.'

'So sorry. Terrible.' Colefax was still crackling with the success of the concert. It made him feel expansive. 'You've been working with Trevor.'

'Yes.'

'You've done great stuff, great stuff.' He jangled his coins in his pocket. 'Sorry about the balls-up about the newsletter. I think Trevor must have got the wrong end of the stick.' He paused. Horace's silence had unsettled him slightly. He was relieved when his wife appeared to drag him off to another corner of the garden.

'Best to give the fox weirdos a wide berth,' she said to him.

Horace looked at the guests gathered in the garden. He could see Harvard and Trevor some way away from the main group, chatting to each other. The Boothbys were talking to one of the Chimurenga Brothers. Gideon Deck was talking to a group of people he didn't recognise. Jocasta was talking to one of the young women who worked for Colefax.

'I've been having a chat with your friend Trevor.' Harvard had been drinking all evening but he didn't seem drunk, though his eyes were slightly shiny. 'You'll never guess what he told me.'

Horace looked across to see Trevor having his glass filled. Trevor turned away from the waiter without a word and drew a mobile phone out of his pocket. 'No idea,' said Horace.

'He says he was running errands for him back in February – taking money to the country's most penetrated columnist over

258

there.' Raylena James was deep in conversation with Gideon Deck.

'He owned up to it?'

'He arranged a meeting between them in Richmond Park, he says.'

'What should we do about it?'

'Do?' Harvard laughed. 'Nothing. Aside from repeating the story to as many people as possible, there's not much we can do. She won't talk. She's got no reason to. Maybe he had a hand in getting her the column. *He*'ll never talk, obviously. And Trevor can say as much as he likes, but he can't prove a thing.'

'So that's it?'

''Fraid so. This is the end of the story, my friend.'

'Nonsense. It can't be.'

'What do you want me to say? That there are photos? That there's a fourth person involved? That there's an incriminating document somewhere, proving that he's a liar and a perjurer? You know what he's like now. That's enough. That's all.'

'It's not. It can't be. Trevor could go to the tabloids.'

'He *could*. A disgruntled former employee with a fox obsession. How credible does he look to you?'

Horace looked across the darkened garden. Trevor was checking the messages on his answering-machine. He snapped his phone shut. He was swaying slightly. His eyes had a bleary, puzzled look. 'No messages,' he reported, when Horace approached him. His right eyelid closed when he spoke.

'Harvard told me about you and Colefax,' said Horace.

'He's been a big disappointment,' said Trevor. 'Big, big disappointment.'

'You've done all right out of it.'

Trevor screwed up his face. 'Where's the waiter?'


'I'm sure he would have told you if you'd asked him. Maybe you didn't want to know.' Horace and Jocasta were sitting on the bench under the horse-chestnut tree. 'You never asked him directly.'

259

'No.'

'If anything, I'm slightly more impressed by Colefax than I was before.'

'You sound like Harvard.'

'"Blighs make good leaders".'

'It's completely different. Bligh was an autocrat, not a liar.'

'I'm surprised at you. What kind of person did you think he was, for God's sake?'

'I thought he had principles.'

'Well,' she said, 'I don't know where you got that idea.'

Trevor had been sent home in a minicab after trying to touch up one of the waitresses. Harvard had taken him into the kitchen and tried to sober him up with black coffee. Nonetheless, for some reason, Trevor insisted on stopping the cab and getting out well before his destination. He would wake up the next morning on a building site near Southwark Bridge. The Boothbys gave Harvard a lift home. Horace and Jocasta sat on the common for almost an hour, talking.

Jocasta broke off their conversation when she saw the orange lamp of a black cab making its way down Trinity Road.

'Quick,' she said.

'Don't I know you?' Horace said to the driver, who had a pony tattooed on his forearm.

'Not me, squire. I'm new to this game.'

# CHAPTER SEVENTEEN

'A PENIS SHEATH, you say?' said Mr Garbedian, exchanging glances with his wife. 'How fascinating. What made you want to buy that?'

Derwent Boothby looked slightly discomfited. 'Hang on a second,' he said, with affable bluntness. 'I'm not one of your patients. Don't start with your psychic claptrap. This is just a souvenir. Give it here. That's going back on the shelf.'

Cilla Boothby was regaling Jocasta and Mrs Garbedian with her husband's medical history.

'He looks perfectly well to me,' said Mrs Garbedian.

Jocasta was finding it a very long evening. She couldn't understand how the Garbedians had ended up there. But then she didn't appreciate Derwent Boothby's gift for turning a coincidence into an acquaintance, and an invitation into an obligation.

'So you're off to Europe tomorrow?' said Mrs Boothby, changing the subject. 'How are you getting there?'

'Driving,' said Jocasta.

'Will you be coming along to the march?' said Cilla.

'Unfortunately not. Horace is supposed to be visiting some friends in the afternoon. Besides, neither of us feels very strongly about the quarantine issue.'

'Pity,' said Cilla. 'Derwent's one of the speakers.'

Horace was standing stiffly by the bookcase, not paying attention to either of the conversations around him. He had been preoccupied during the meal and had excused himself for what seemed to Jocasta like a very long time. She wondered if he was having second thoughts about going on holiday with her. Two weeks was a very long time to be alone with one other person without the distractions of work, friends and comprehensible television. Of course, that was supposed to be the good thing about it too.

'Please excuse me,' said Horace, quietly, and slipped out of the room.

'Naturally, Derwent, what interests me is not quarantine *per se*, but the *idea* of quarantine,' said Mr Garbedian.

Jocasta fiddled with one of her bracelets and decided to pursue Horace to the toilet for a quick snog. She excused herself and went to find him, not sure if Juanita Garbedian's glance at her had contained a plea for mercy or if she'd just imagined it.

A rim of light surrounded the heavy oak door of the toilet. Jocasta gave the handle a yank and found, to her surprise, that it opened.

Horace whirled around with a look of horror. Jocasta saw him clasping something in his fist.

'Why didn't you knock?' he said. There was an uncharacter-istic edge to his voice.

'God, I'm sorry. I thought it was locked. I only came to say hallo.'

'They don't believe in locks,' said Horace, crossly.

'What are you doing?' Jocasta was worried that she was on the verge of an unpleasant revelation. One of Horace's hands was bunched into a fist, the other appeared to contain a tube of adhesive.

'Oh, fuck,' said Horace. 'I've glued the sodding thing to my hand.'

'Horace,' Jocasta's lip trembled, 'I think you owe it to me to tell me what's going on.'

Horace followed Jocasta into the library, standing far enough behind her to make it impossible for anyone to try and shake his hand.

'Horace is feeling a bit unwell,' said Jocasta. 'It was nice to meet you all.'

Horace waved feebly from the doorway with his good left hand.

'I suppose I'll have to drive,' said Jocasta, as they passed the creaking weathervane on the Boothbys' front lawn.

'Ha, ha,' said Horace glumly.

Like many people unfamiliar with extra-strength adhesives, Horace had overestimated the amount of glue needed to make a good seal. Then, in his panic, he had gripped the carving so tightly that it had bonded to his palm, while his fingers had become stuck to each other around it. The instructions on the tube recommended using soap and water to break down the adhesive. But when that failed, they had to go to the accident and emergency department to have the netsuke removed.

'I feel such a fool,' said Horace, as Jocasta drove him to the hospital, his hand a tightly sealed flesh-egg, with its tiny bone embryo trapped inside it.

'Don't worry,' said Jocasta. 'They see much worse than this.'

On a Friday night, the overworked staff of the accident and emergency department of St George's, Tooting, had much more life-threatening predicaments to attend to than Horace's. It was almost five in the morning and Horace was partially deaf from lack of sleep when he was finally seen by a nurse. To his relief the nurse didn't blame or mock, but simply dealt practically with his dilemma. 'That's well and truly glued, isn't it? Don't worry. We'll have that off in no time. We see a lot of these. Put your hand in this.' She wheeled a large plastic tub of liquid towards him.

'What is it?' said Horace.

'It's a solvent – basically nail-polish remover.'

'Will it damage ivory?'

'No, it shouldn't. It doesn't damage nails.'

Horace immersed his hand in the liquid and wiggled his fingers as the nurse had instructed. Jocasta held his other hand. 'It's coming loose!' He lifted his sticky fingers from the vat as the netsuke sank to the bottom.

'It's fizzing,' said Jocasta.

'That's highly unusual,' said the nurse.

Horace peered into the solvent. Sure enough, a trail of bubbles was streaming off the carving, which rocked and hopped across the bottom of the basin. Fragments of bone seemed to be spinning off with them, like sparks off a catherine wheel. The carving appeared to be shrinking as the gas bubbled off it.

Jocasta held her nose. 'It stinks!' she said.

It did. An awful eggy smell rose up from the vat. Now the carving was rising up too, hissing and spitting and emitting a strange blue smoke. It bobbed up to the surface, and began skidding as it did so, spinning this way and that, and shrivelling into a tiny crust of blackened snot, which, its transformation complete, sank back down to the bottom of the basin.

'Well,' said the nurse, 'I've never seen it do that before.'

Barnaby Colefax woke up before it was light. He was sure he had been having the same dream for weeks. He kept waking up at the same time with the same curious feeling of unease and no memory of what he had dreamt. He put it down to stress.

His wife lay asleep next to him, a lump in the bed, breathing regularly, with ears that sprouted yellow foam buds – the earplugs without which she couldn't sleep and which might have been her protest against marriage.

When he was sure he would not be able to sleep again he went downstairs to the kitchen, turned on the tap, ran the water over his hand till the stream turned cool and sighed in the pipes, then poured a glass of water. He went out into the garden to drink it, feeling the springy lawn under his toes.

The gate at the back of the garden opened with a creak and he stepped out into the private park. It was just possible, he supposed, that a tabloid photographer with a long lens on his camera was camped out in a tree somewhere, waiting to take a picture of him strolling around in his pyjamas. But the light was still dim.

The last week had been the busiest he could remember and no kind of scrutiny was out of the question. He had lectured his children on the absolute need for decorum in all public places from now on. Anything – picking a nostril, looks of boredom, yawning – might be used to denigrate him.

It had been a summer of intense and uncharacteristic heat that had persisted from the concert in July until September. The sun had seared the plants and grilled the unwatered lawns. Gigantism had broken out among the city's insects. He'd found a bird-eating spider hiding under the ruches of one of his wife's dresses the day before and flushed it down the toilet.

The fantasy of the photographer intruded again. Success was bringing with it an uncharacteristic caution. He decided to return to the house.

As he turned, he saw, trotting across the path ten feet away from him, a mangy dog fox. It was moulting. Its useless hot coat was coming away in tufts, but its brush was intact and the animal carried it erect like a plume. Colefax stood still in his candy-striped pyjamas and the fox put its pointed nose to the ground for a sniff, and then looked straight at his face. Its orange eyes held an unfathomable emotion.

It was strange that it should look him in the face, he thought, and strange that a human face should strike its fox-brain as bearing a resemblance to its own muzzle, and eyes, and pointed ears. Or did his face hold no more meaning for it than the bole of a tree or damp earth? Was he wrong to see in its eyes something more than simple hunger and curiosity – a premonition that made his skin crawl?

The fox paused for several seconds, looking at him, he thought, with intent. His bare toes felt pink and nervously edible. Then the small animal turned and trotted off.

His wife was in the kitchen, scratching the side of her leg through her night dress and shaking coffee into the jug from a packet she kept in the freezer. 'You'll never guess what I saw,' said Colefax. 'Just now, out in the park.' He tried to make the novelty of it displace his unease. 'A fox. First one I've seen.'

'Really.' Patricia Colefax took her coffee back up to bed. Then shouted down as an afterthought, 'The car's coming for us at eight, remember.'

Lakshmi's baby had been born three weeks premature. It was a tiny brown girl with a cross face and a loud voice. 'At least it was born with its eyes open,' Trevor had said, when Horace told him on the phone.

'You missed a good day yesterday,' said Trevor.

'Yeah?' Horace had had one eye on the newspaper in front of him, scanning the travel pages for cheap ferry crossings. He had finally received a cheque for damages from Brian Towton and was using it to pay for the holiday with Jocasta.

'Went down to Hastings for the day with the new woman.'

'The new woman?'

'Yeah. I met her a couple of weeks ago.'

'Who, what, when, where, how?' said Horace.

'She's a nurse. She's mad keen on foxes. Listen, I've got someone on the other line. Give us a call when you get back from your holiday. It's going to be mating season before long, you know. Whole thing starts all over again.'

'Did he say whether she was a psychiatric nurse?' said Jocasta, waving a car out of a junction and into the jam of oncoming cars. 'That would be perfect. Why the fuck is all this traffic about?'

'Diversions?' said Horace. 'The march?'

'Not this far south, surely. Is Trevor going, by the way?'

'No, he's boycotting it. He's boycotting Colefax, in fact. He's been ousted as chief sponsor of Fox Outreach.'

'Colefax must be absolutely gutted about that.'

'He'll get over it, I imagine.'

'How's the hand?' said Jocasta.

'Oh, that.' Horace looked at his unmarked palm. 'It's fine.' He gazed out of the car window with something like nostalgia. The thought of going away, even for a couple of weeks, gave a strange poignancy to the street scenes. He had spent less and less time round here since he'd moved. The Café de Paradise had reopened and its refurbished interior was unchanged from the old one. It even looked as if the same baked beans were congealing in the stainless-steel dish by the window.

'It's a one-way street. You have to go down the next,' said Horace.

Jocasta turned the car up Glenburne Road and parked about ten yards from the shop. They went inside. Darrell was serving at the counter. He gave them a sour smile. 'Don't get the wrong idea,' he said. 'He asked me to mind it while he went down to Croydon to pick up something.'

Horace examined the exploded diagram of the cot frame. It was printed on onion-skin paper with dots and symbols instead of words. It was as mysterious and tantalising as a treasure map.

'Look at that,' he said, pointing at part of the diagram. 'See. There must have been an Allen key with it.'

Mr Narayan, who had manhandled a cardboard box of

unforgiving weight and smoothness all the way from the Flat-Pak Centa in Croydon on the bus, was losing his patience. 'I am telling you, there is no Allen key!'

Darrell sorted quietly through the screws and washers that were laid out on a tea-towel on the grass. 'I can't see it.' He shook his head.

'You tell him, Darrell. He doesn't believe me.'

'All I said was, if you read the instructions –' Horace protested.

'Give me those instructions.' Mr Narayan snatched the piece of paper out of Horace's hand and pretended to study it while looking reproachfully at Jocasta and Lakshmi. They were sitting on the grass at the other end of the garden, drinking lemonade and chatting. Lola Shareen Mynott Narayan lay on a blanket beside her mother, gurgling happily at the trees, which were moving in the wind.

'I'll go and buy an Allen key, then,' said Horace. 'I think they sell them at one of the newsagents' round the corner.' Mr Narayan glared at him. Darrell tried not to laugh.

When Horace got back, he came through the lock-up shop and produced the Allen key with a flourish. 'I think you'll find this will do the trick,' he said.

'Sh,' said Jocasta, putting her finger to her lips and straining to listen to the portable radio that Mr Narayan had brought into the garden.

'*Violent clashes between police and quarantine protestors have marred the early stages of the march through central London. Initial reports suggest there have been no injuries. Meanwhile, the feral children found in a housing estate in Peckham have been reunited with their siblings.*'

'I wonder if it's worth calling Harvard,' said Horace.

'You're supposed to be on holiday,' said Jocasta.

'I know, but he might need some help.'

'It's not the Rambler's job.'

'I'm supposed to be doing more news now.'

'You see, Jocasta, you would never have thought it, but he is

268

*extremely* argumentative.' Mr Narayan had recovered from his bad mood and was posturing as a figure of peace and tolerance.

'You can talk, Dad,' said Lakshmi.

'All I said was –' Horace began.

'Well, it's up to you.' Jocasta turned away and started playing with the baby.

Darrell took the Allen key and began assembling the cot with the treasure map spread out on the grass in front of him. Mr Narayan put his big brown finger into the tiny palm of his granddaughter. 'See how she holds it. See. She is very clever. She will be a doctor or a scientist.'

Horace went inside to use the phone. 'That was a short holiday,' said Harvard, when Horace got through to him.

'I'm having lunch at my old landlord's place. We're not leaving until later. I heard on the radio that the march had turned nasty. I wondered if you needed a hand covering it.'

'Well, we've got someone down there. I don't know how nasty it's turned, really. It seems to have quietened down. But if you're *insisting*, I won't say no.'

Horace went back out to the garden. 'He says he could use some help. I'm just going to go up there and look around.'

'It's pointless, if you ask me.'

'You don't want to come, then.'

'I'm on holiday,' said Jocasta.

Mr Narayan held a pawn of each colour in his fists and offered them to Darrell, who tapped the hand containing the ivory one.

'White to the right,' said Mr Narayan, as he rotated the board through ninety degrees. 'Queen on her own colour. Bishops advise royalty. I bought these in Mombasa. They're very old.'

'It's hard to tell which is which,' said Darrell. The designer of the pieces had sacrificed strong variation between them for aesthetic effect. The minaret-shaped pawns differed only slightly in size from the bishops, which the king and queen also resembled, but with the addition of headpieces like the cap of a mushroom.

269

The two men played quickly through the opening. Each was testing the other's knowledge of the game: a quirky move might betray a poor grasp of principles, or be a novelty, designed to lure the other into hasty sacrifices. Both forced their way into the centre of the board, exchanged a pawn, castled, and then tested each other with feints and thrusts. The game slowed down. The calculation of moves and combinations produced the active silence of chess: the wordless enactment of an ancient story.

Mr Narayan's queen threatened to batter her way through the wall of pawns in front of Darrell's king. Darrell studied the board.

'We're going to have to leave after this, Dad,' said Lakshmi.

Darrell's hands began to sweat. He saw a chance, a hinge in the shapes in front of him. He anticipated the decisive thrill of checkmate and the false modesty that was the winner's prerogative ('Well, you were unlucky not to see that . . .'). The knowledge that Mr Narayan was as competitive at playing as he was bad at losing made the anticipation of winning all the more pleasant. As casually as he could, he uncorked the first of his moves.

Mr Narayan fidgeted slightly in his chair. Darrell watched his eyes for some clue to the direction of his thoughts. He wanted him to ignore his last move and concentrate on his own plans for checkmate: preferably fiddling around with his queen while the knight laid waste to the other side of the board.

Lola started to cry. Lakshmi was holding her and carrying her around the room. 'She needs changing. It's time to go.'

Darrell was about to say, 'It won't be much longer,' but stopped himself.

Mr Narayan said, 'Yes, yes,' and carried on staring at the pieces.

'I give up,' Lakshmi said, to no one in particular, and carried her baby out of the room.

Mr Narayan's hand hovered over the array of pawns surrounding his king and then, to Darrell's relief, adjusted the position of his bishop. Darrell made his second crucial move, as though it was a motion of less significance than hitching up a pair of trousers.

Mr Narayan scratched his face with an air of puzzlement, and then moved – quickly, impetuously, fatally. Darrell snapped the knight into place and said, nonchalantly, 'I think that might be mate,' as he wiped the sweat off his hands. A look at Mr Narayan's face confirmed it. 'You were unlucky not to see that,' said Darrell, as he got up to begin his farewell.

Police lined the route from Embankment station to Trafalgar Square, where the marchers were gathering. The few scuffles had taken place much earlier. Jumpy police officers had bundled two rowdy demonstrators into the back of a van and then added a couple of bystanders for good measure. But now, a sense of violence lingered over the gathering like a deceptive mist, transfiguring all gestures into threats.

Unmarked police vans waited in side-streets off the square. Police officers had taken up positions around the perimeter of the crowd, which milled around, not paying much attention as speakers took the podium one after another to upbraid the government through an echoing public-address system.

The officer in charge was standing in front of the National Gallery explaining to a television reporter, for the fifth time in an hour, that the number of arrests had been small, that the majority of the crowd had behaved irreproachably, and that he hoped that the good humour and the good weather would continue.

Derwent Boothby, for one, would have preferred the good weather to end immediately. He found the humidity intolerable. Standing by the podium at the foot of Nelson's Column, he could feel stored heat radiating from Landseer's bronze lions. Even the breeze brought no relief, just prickly little puffs of moist air, like the breath from a horse's nostrils. Young people without his sense of decorum had shed most of their clothes and were paddling in the fountains. The cascades had been turned off, but the stone basins were still knee-deep in cool London water.

The crowd contained the same heterogeneous assortment of people that Jocasta had identified at the concert two months earlier. Smartly dressed women in headscarves and men in tweed jackets stood next to radical animal-rights supporters dressed in military fatigues and tie-dyed T-shirts. One man had hair matted into big furry clumps like ewes' tails.

A ripple of polite applause greeted the next speaker. Boothby had been scheduled to address the crowd at two, but events were running about forty minutes late. Prettily flushed by the heat, Cassandra Thorfinnsdottir, one of Colefax's young helpers, made her way over to Boothby. She had a walkie-talkie clapped to her ear and was fanning her face with the edge of her clipboard. 'Mr Boothby, I've just been speaking to Barnaby – he asked, as we're running so late, if you could keep your speech to no more than a minute. I know it's a terrible pain, but we're asking everyone to do the same. Otherwise we'll be here all . . . Yes?' The radio in her hand squawked and she turned away to reply. 'What is it now?' The question was tinged with despair. 'I've already *explained* that to them.'

Boothby took the text of his speech out of his pocket, where it had become slightly damp, and smoothed it over his knee. One minute would barely cover his introductory remarks. He'd been told by Colefax he could speak for ten, and made a fairly generous estimate of the number of words that would allow him. He dabbed at his face with a handkerchief. His armpits felt sticky where sweat had dissolved the starch of his shirt.

'You must take your jacket off, dear.' Cilla Boothby was alarmed by her husband's obvious discomfort. She tugged at his sleeve.

'Don't fuss,' he snapped. 'Now, where's my pen?'

Horace and Jocasta had parked in a cul-de-sac off Haymarket. Throughout the drive in, Jocasta had been vocally sceptical about the wisdom of going.

'There won't *be* any trouble,' she insisted. 'The radio have puffed it up – it's one or two arrests. Someone's frightened a police horse and they've been carted off. They probably haven't even been charged. Honestly, baby, I know how these things work.'

Unmarked vans full of overheated police were parked along the side-streets around the National Gallery. Big wire visors had been lowered over their windscreens.

'I just want to have a look – we can leave straight afterwards.'

'It's one thing to be sent on a story, but this is absurd,' she said, as they emerged onto the square. 'Now, can we go?'

The central area of the square was two-thirds full of people. Some held placards, a few carried banners that flapped in the listless breeze. The crowd was concentrated at the base of the column, around the podium, where Derwent Boothby was rushing to make his speech ninety per cent shorter. Sweating, he scribbled some hasty revisions on the paper and stepped up to the microphone. 'For forty years,' he began, then stopped. 'For forty years.' He was having trouble reading his handwriting. The letters appeared to stretch and slide across the page. He blinked to clear his eyes and looked out into the crowd. His breathing was growing shallower and shallower. Boothby was conscious of one face in particular – a lady of roughly middle age, wearing dark glasses and a pale green headscarf, who first smiled encouragingly and then looked increasingly worried, as he clutched at the microphone and toppled backwards off the stage.

'That was your uncle Derwent,' said Jocasta, who was standing with Horace on the raised pavement on the north side of the square. 'What on earth happened?'

'Great-uncle,' said Horace. 'I'd better go and see if he's all right.' He disappeared down the flight of steps to his right, breaking into a run when he reached the bottom.

'Oh, Christ,' said Cassandra Thorfinnsdottir, as Boothby was helped away. 'Who's next?' She ruffled the sheets of paper on her clipboard.

'Can I just get the spelling of the name of the chap who keeled over?' asked a man with a notepad.

'Could you just wait a second? All right?' A note of hysteria had crept into Cassandra's voice. She turned her back on the reporter. 'Help, over,' she said into the walkie-talkie, which had gone stubbornly quiet. Colefax, she knew, had gone to get out of the heat for half an hour before he made the closing speech and led the march down Whitehall. She looked vainly at the faces around the podium.

'If you're looking for a stop-gap, I'll say a word or two,' said a pleasant-looking woman in a sensible frock. 'You go and get things sorted out.'

'Would you? I'd be so grateful. I'd better go and see if that man's all right.'

Horace was winding his way through the thickening crowd. He hadn't seen where Boothby had been taken. A woman's voice began speaking in mid-sentence over the public-address system.

'. . . better. Oops. There we go. Hello. Umm, I wasn't expecting to be asked to speak, actually. But I'm very honoured . . .'

After removing his tie and taking a couple of blasts from his inhaler, Derwent Boothby was recovering quickly. He was flushed and sweaty but breathing normally, and seemed pleased to see Horace hop over the barrier around the speakers' enclosure. 'Cilla says it's the shortest speech she's ever heard me give,' he said.

'Your voice sounds a bit hoarse.' Horace looked at his great-uncle with concern.

'I couldn't breathe. It was very odd. I think it must be the pollution. There's such a damn lot of it about.'

'Don't you think someone should take a look at you, in case it's something more serious?'

'Listen to Horace, love. That's what *I* said.' Cilla had been wearing a floppy white hat, which she was now trying to force onto her husband's head. 'It'll protect you from the heat.'

'Absolutely not,' said Boothby. 'I feel as right as rain.'

Horace could hear some agitation in the crowd. There were isolated boos and shouts of abuse. The speaker had started to remonstrate with an inaudible heckler. 'You're absolutely wrong,' she was saying. 'Hunters have more respect for the countryside than anybody else. We love foxes. We love all animals. And we know more about conservation and wildlife than any so-called animal liberationists.'

The booing was becoming louder, along with shouts of 'Let her speak!'

Colefax came running up. 'What's going on?' he demanded.

'Derwent's had a bit of a turn, but I think he's all right now.'

'Will you stop fussing, woman?' said Boothby.

'Christ Almighty,' said Colefax. 'Who on earth put *her* up there?'

Cassandra seemed to be on the verge of tears. 'She was just trying to be helpful.'

'Off, off, off!' chanted a section of the crowd.

A two-litre plastic bottle of extra-strength cider turned slowly in the air, spattering the heads beneath it, and then collided with the arm of the woman speaking. Fizzy liquid sprayed over the front of her frock. She rubbed the spot on her arm where she'd been hit. 'There's no excuse for that sort of behaviour,' she began to say, but two people had already ushered her off the stage for her own safety.

Half a dozen people standing close to where the bottle had been thrown had started brawling with one another. More bottles followed the first into the air. Colefax took the microphone and tried to appeal for calm.

'This is just the kind of spectacle that our opponents most want to see,' he said, doing a mad hopping rain-dance on the podium. A long stick that had been detached from a placard clattered beside him like a javelin. 'Someone's going to get hurt in a minute,' he predicted.

The fighting to the right of the stage had become more general. Little mêlées had detached themselves from the crowd. It wasn't clear at first who was fighting whom. Natural divisions in the audience had begun to assert themselves between Colefax's more radical supporters and those who had been incensed by the abuse directed at the hunter. In addition, the flight of the cider bottle had persuaded a large number of people that the afternoon would be better spent fighting than listening to boring speeches.

Horace and the Boothbys had dispersed with the majority of the crowd to the side of the square from where they were watching. Before the fighting could blow itself out, clumps of police with batons and riot shields had begun seizing individual rioters and taking them away.

Colefax and a handful of others had been trapped in the enclave between the two northernmost lions by a vicious scrimmage between police and about two dozen others.

A line of mounted police had taken up position at the southern end of the square and begun walking their horses forward. The line broke into two, which wheeled around the column, like the hands of a clock, and stopped, at five to one, with the remaining rioters stuck in the middle. At a signal, the horses moved forward. Determined to escape, the mob tried to flee over the podium to the base of the column, where the others who had been trapped by the fighting were sheltering. Snatch squads made sudden raids into the cornered men, and emerged with wriggling protestors. Colefax found himself behind a young man who was defending himself vigorously with part of one of the official placards.

'I'm not ashamed to say it,' said Jocasta. 'You were right, and I was wrong.' She had been on the phone to the newsdesk of the *Globe*, updating them on the violence.

'It's absolutely shocking.' Cilla Boothby was incensed.

'Does Harvard know you're here?' her husband asked Horace.

'Yeah. I told him.'

From the top of the steps they could see the cornered rioters, hemmed in on all sides by mounted police, being picked off by the snatch squads.

At that moment, Colefax was aware that he was equally in danger of having his eye poked out by the boy with the placard in front of him, as of getting dragged off, embarrassingly, by the police. He decided that the best course of action would be to offer himself up for capture. He began to slide around the fringe of the fighting.

The boy followed behind him. As Colefax approached one of the horses with his hands raised above his head, the boy flung the stick as hard as he could at the animal. The horse reared up. Colefax cowered underneath it, covering his head with his hands, and tried to move forward. The animal wheeled around, knocking the politician off balance with a flick of its enormous haunches. Colefax fell sideways, hit his head on the lion's pedestal, and lost consciousness.

'Time now for a look at early editions of tomorrow's papers,' said Brent Deal, ruffling a stack of them with his hand. The newsreader's voice echoed from a television set on the bar. 'All of them lead on the violence at the anti-quarantine bill rally. "Britain's Shame" is the headline of the *Daily Flag* . . .'

Horace had a copy of the same newspaper on the plastic table in front of him. Jocasta had been driving since London and had gone off to the toilet. They hadn't been able to leave until they'd finished writing their stories and Harvard had wanted to go out for a celebration after that.

The *Daily Flag*'s front page showed a picture of the boy with the stick scowling at the police while Colefax cowered behind him. On the inside pages, Britain's most provocative columnist, Raylena James, denounced the cack-handed organisation that allowed the demonstration to descend into a riot. 'Time's Up for Colefax' was the headline.

She'd evidently vetoed the photograph that had previously been used to illustrate the column. The new one showed her in horn-rimmed glasses, with the index and middle finger of her left hand making a thoughtful right angle on her cheek and chin.

'We're boarding in ten minutes,' said Jocasta, as she returned.

'I've got to go to the loo as well,' said Horace. 'I'll meet you by the car.'

Jocasta sank into one of the uncomfortable plastic seats and watched Brent Deal cross-examining a reporter about Barnaby Colefax's condition. The reporter was standing outside the Charing Cross Hospital in Hammersmith.

'Mr Colefax is out of danger, Brent,' said the reporter, 'but early indications are that he is suffering from a rare form of synaesthesic aphasia.'

'What's that when it's at home?' asked Brent Deal.

'Any severe head trauma can result in, if you like, crossed wires in the speech centres of the central nervous system.'

'Sounds nasty.' Brent Deal stretched across the cockpit of his desk.

'Well, Brent, doctors are keen to stress that there are forms of sign language that bypass the damaged speech centres in the brain. Neurologists know a lot more about this illness than they did, say, ten or twenty years ago. In that respect, the prognosis is good. They're looking on this as an important research opportunity.'

'So, a bad day for Colefax, a good day for neurologists?'

'I'd say that was about the size of it.'


Coming out of the toilet, Horace was surprised to hear a familiar voice behind him.

'Well, I'll be blowed,' said the voice. 'What are the chances of that happening?'

'Hello, Mr Tither,' said Horace. 'Hello, Betty.'

Betty Barmbrake smiled shyly and looked at her feet.

'We're off to France,' said Mr Tither. 'Keeping well?'

'Can't complain,' Horace said, and then found himself without anything further to say to them. His new life had taken him so far from Great Much he found it hard to believe it still existed.

'You look well,' said Mr Tither. 'I'd stay and chat but we'd best be off. Don't want to miss the train.' His wiry little hand shook Horace's with a surprising vigour. 'Perhaps we'll see you back at the village one of these days.'

278

'Perhaps,' said Horace, though he knew he meant *never*.

'Goodbye, then,' said Mr Tither.

'Goodbye,' said Horace.

'Goodbye,' said Betty Barmbrake, and gave his hand a slight squeeze.

As Horace was about to set off towards the car, Mr Tither added, as an afterthought, 'You want to watch those Frenchies, they're a sharp and unfriendly lot by all accounts.'

Jocasta was half asleep in the front seat of the car. 'Just bumped into an old girlfriend,' said Horace, with a trace of smugness as he got in.

'That's nice.' Jocasta didn't open her eyes.

Horace started the car and joined the queue of vehicles. Attendants in fluorescent jackets directed the drivers up the ramps.

Horace and Jocasta were both asleep by the time the train had moved off, out of the night air and into the permanent twilight of the tunnel.

The train swept on through the darkness, beneath miles of earth and water, before surfacing again into the same night air. Horace woke up with a transitory sense of bewilderment and looked out of the window. He nudged Jocasta.

'Wake up,' he said quietly, stroking her hair with his fingers. 'Wake up, we're there.'